THE PERFECT FAMILY

LORNA DOUNAEVA

INKUBATOR
BOOKS

Published by Inkubator Books
www.inkubatorbooks.com

Copyright © 2022 by Lorna Dounaeva

Lorna Dounaeva has asserted her right to be identified as the author of this work.

ISBN (eBook): 978-1-915275-40-0
ISBN (Paperback): 978-1-915275-41-7
ISBN (Hardback): 978-1-915275-42-4

PROLOGUE

The meeting had gone well, James thought. Shame it had overrun, though. He had really wanted to join his family for dinner. It was steak tonight, his favourite. Spurred on by thoughts of food, he pedalled furiously through the tunnel of trees and approached a junction known as The Dip. The bike's wheels squeaked as the road twisted and turned. He heard the purr of an engine up ahead and raised his arm to protect his eyes as he was caught in the glare of the car's headlights.

Too late, he realised the car wasn't going to stop in time. He lunged to the left but there was nowhere to go. The impact knocked the wind from his lungs, then he and the bike parted ways. His face smashed into the windscreen, then he somersaulted backwards through the air. He landed in the wooded area to the left of the road and felt his vertebrae crunch. His shoe landed right by his face. The lace tickled his nose.

Laughter bubbled up through the pain. He already knew what he'd tell his boy: "You should have seen me! I was incredible. I could have been James Bond's double!"

Pain throbbed at the back of his neck. He opened his mouth and tried to speak but his tongue felt thick in his mouth. He could feel the crack in his helmet, right down the middle.

He heard the sound of a car door opening and someone hopping out. Concerned eyes peered down at him. He caught a glimmer of recognition and stretched out a hand but the person retreated, getting back in the car.

999, he thought. *You need to call 999. For heaven's sake, don't move me.*

He waited a few agonised seconds. Then the car swerved around him, showering him with grit, and disappeared into the darkness.

1

VICTORIA

Flaxen pigtails bobbed up and down as the last child launched herself across the playground and through the classroom doors. There was a chorus of grumbles as the caretaker herded all the parents out of the gate.

"We're here for the play," Victoria objected, batting her lashes.

"You'll have to wait."

"But can't I just . . ."

The caretaker didn't pay her the slightest attention. He padlocked the gate and walked off across the playground. Victoria stuck out her chin and silently added him to her shit list.

The parents sorted themselves into their usual groups: the fashion-conscience mums with daggers for heels, the career mums who fretted about the value of Bitcoin, the sporty mums who jogged from the school to the gym, and the Reception mums who blocked the road with their buggies and parked wherever the hell they liked.

Her own clique were the PTA mums. They were the hardest group to penetrate and it had taken Victoria almost two years to claw her way in. It was a pain in the bum with all the meetings and fundraisers, but this was the group she wanted to be in. Her closest ally, Portia Arrowsmith, was the wife of a junior minister.

Victoria checked her phone. She had eighty-seven likes for the Instagram picture she'd put up of the children's bento boxes, packed with squares of chicken, avocado, and various salad items.

"Protein packed lunches to power them through the day!" she'd captioned.

"Avocados are bad for the environment," one of her followers had commented.

Dammit, she knew she should have used eggs.

"Anyone got the time?"

Victoria glanced at a woman with a big rip in her jeans and pretended not to have heard. She was one of the nobodies, who were not part of any of the established groups. Every so often, one of them would attempt to strike up a conversation, but it was invariably met with a wall of silence.

Victoria slid the phone back into her pocket and straightened her shoulders, flashing a calculated smile at Zara and Samantha who were both vying to stand next to Portia.

"I take it Joey's in this morning's performance?" Zara said.

"Of course, he bloody well is," Samantha said.

Victoria allowed herself to smile.

"Nice jacket," Portia commented, her hazel eyes flickering over Samantha's new purchase.

"Thanks!"

"What shade is that?" Zara asked, screwing up her eyes.

"Fawn," said Samantha.

"Really?" said Zara. "I'd have said it was beige."

"Definitely beige," Portia murmured in Victoria's ear. Victoria's lip curled.

"Hey, I saw your daughter in town yesterday," Portia said. "She's grown, hasn't she?"

Victoria nodded. "Yes, she's nearly a head taller than me."

"Pretty girl, isn't she?"

"Bright too," Victoria was quick to point out. "Did I tell you she's doing A-level Latin?"

"Isn't she a bit young to be doing A-levels?"

Victoria nodded proudly. "She's fourteen."

Portia leaned nonchalantly against the locked gates. "Did I tell you Ariadne has moved up another group at swimming? She's with the teenagers now."

"No!"

The head teacher strode across the playground and unlocked the school gates. She surveyed the waiting parents in much the same way she would her young charges.

"Morning, mums and dads. Everyone looking forward to the performance?"

The collective murmur of assent was worthy of a pantomime.

She beckoned them inside and they politely followed her up the steps to reception and through to the hall. The children were in their places, straight backed and cross-legged. Victoria had never seen such an obedient, tidy group of school children and her Joey, with his perfect blond curls and solemn little face, was the most angelic of them all.

Victoria settled back smugly in her chair as the head prattled on.

"And now for a word from Mrs Victoria Hill who has kindly agreed to be our parent Environmental Ambassador."

There was a smattering of applause as Victoria rose to her feet. She marched to the front and smiled down at the children. Such neat little children in their smart, royal blue uniforms. She thanked her lucky stars that she'd been able to send Joey here.

It hadn't been easy getting him in. As school places were decided by distance from home to school, she'd had to reject the place he'd originally been offered and held out for the better school. Joey had been number two on the waiting list, then a kid had moved away and he'd been number one. There had been a couple of long, tense months when she'd worried and fretted. Her husband, Kit, had said they should give in. Surely it was better for Joey to have any school place than none. Then she'd heard those mums talking in Waitrose, snickering at how one of them had given her mother-in-law's address. Victoria had abandoned a trolley full of shopping and trailed the woman back to Ockford Ridge, on the other side of town. There was no way this woman lived in the catchment area for St Bernard's. Victoria had reported her that very day, and the following week, the confirmation letter had come in the post. Even Kit had been impressed.

"You should have had more faith in me," she'd gloated.

"You couldn't have known it was all going to work out," he'd said.

But deep down, she had. Because she would do anything for her family. Always had, always would.

Now she stood on stage, beaming down at a sea of eager faces.

"Well, children, I'm delighted to announce that last week we planted our hundredth tree on the school grounds. Isn't that wonderful?" All the children nodded enthusiastically. "But it doesn't stop there. There's plenty more we can do to help our environment. If you haven't yet joined our Going Green campaign, the sign-up sheet is up on the wall behind you. We've got 118 children who've pledged to travel to school on foot, by bike or scooter, leaving those petrol guzzling cars at home! And finally, the closing date for the 'Recycle Me' poster competition is next Friday. The best poster wins a free box of organic fruit and veg so I'm sure your mums and dads will be very proud."

She looked at the head, who smiled her approval. There was a smattering of applause, started by the parents at the back, and Victoria beamed with pride.

"Thank you, Mrs Hill, and now without further ado, I give you today's performance: a summer celebration."

A dozen children rose gracefully from their seats and walked silently up to the stage. Victoria felt a familiar twinge of pride as Joey settled behind the grand piano. Two girls with cellos shuffled into place, one boy took up a saxophone and a really little one stood poised with a triangle.

The performance was well polished, and they all played in time. Then came Joey's piano solo and a great hush fell over the hall. The audience sat up straighter, even the children. They all leaned forward, listening intently as Joey built up to a breathtaking crescendo that made her want to punch the air.

For a moment, there was dead silence, then the hall filled with the clapping of hands and the drumming of feet. Several parents rose to their feet and she glowed with pride. She'd never seen a child receive a standing ovation before, but if anyone deserved one, it was her Joey.

"That was amazing!" said Samantha, as they filed out of the hall.

"Brilliant!" said Zara.

"He was good," Portia agreed. Praise indeed.

"Victoria?"

Victoria turned and found herself facing Belinda Solomon.

"Hi, I'm Belinda."

Victoria knew all too well who she was, even though they'd never spoken. Her throat felt a little dry and crackly and for a moment she considered ignoring her, pretending

she was in a hurry, but the throng around her made that
difficult.

"What an amazing performance. Your son is a very
talented young man."

"Thank you."

"I understand you give piano lessons?"

Victoria pressed her lips together. "Yes . . ." she said
through her teeth.

"I don't suppose you could teach my son, Ricky? His old
piano teacher retired earlier this year and I haven't got
around to arranging anything."

Victoria stole a breath. "I wish I could help, but I'm all
booked up right now."

Samantha grabbed her arm. "That's okay, he can have
Henry's slot."

Belinda blanched. "Oh, I don't want to steal anyone's
place!"

"No, really. Henry wants to change to electric guitar, so it's
fine."

Victoria stared at her in horror, fighting for the words to
make this right. "I really . . ."

"Well then," said Belinda. "When was Henry's slot,
Samantha?"

"Friday at four."

Belinda smiled at Victoria in a way that made her stagger
backwards into Portia.

"Watch it!" Portia snarled.

"Sorry!"

"Friday at four it is then," Belinda decided. "Got to dash
now, I was meant to be at work half an hour ago."

"I . . ."

Before Victoria could say another word, Belinda was
weaving her way through the crowd.

The sun beat down as Victoria made her way home.

Shoppers meandered in and out of Godalming's little boutiques or gathered at the little market outside the Pepper Pot. Victoria saw several of the mums from school there but scurried past, as fast as her heels would allow. She was almost breathless by the time she reached the waterside meadow.

She found a quiet bench where she was unlikely to be overheard and checked all around before dialling her husband's number.

"Kit!" she cried, when he picked up the phone. He'd be in the city now, working his magic on the trade floor. She could picture him leaning back, feet on the desk.

"Alright, Vic? Something wrong? I'm kind of busy here."

"It's Belinda Solomon." The words came out in a rush. "She's invited herself round for a piano lesson!"

There was silence on the other end of the phone. Then Kit said, "You'll have to cancel."

"How? I don't want to look rude."

"Just do it, Vic. Or we're completely screwed."

2

ANNA

"Shut the door!"

Obediently, Anna pushed the door shut just as Joey began his reign of terror, sweeping the ornaments off the mantelpiece, bits of debris flying to the ground.

"He's had a long day at school," her mother told her, as Joey shot into the bathroom. She heard the whoosh of water as he turned on all the taps and then he was in the utility room, pulling sheets and towels down off the shelves and screaming:

"Stupid bitch arseholes!"

Instead of making any attempt to calm him down, her mum ran through the house slamming all the windows shut because she lived in horror that anyone should overhear, despite the fact that their house was surrounded by an acre of grass and a wall of perfectly sculpted hedges. Even so, the dog in the house behind theirs must have heard something because he was barking up a storm.

Anna slipped out into the back garden and puffed on a cigarette until the sounds of destruction dissipated. Then came Victoria's gentle, coaxing voice and the sound of a hoover being switched on. She really should have waited. Joey hated the hoover. Just last week he'd kicked it down the stairs. Unfortunately for him, it lived on.

Once Victoria had finished hoovering, Anna headed inside and made for the fridge, looking for a snack.

"How was your day, darling?" Victoria was standing at the kettle, looking like a nineteen-fifties housewife wearing a neat little apron, her hair and make-up immaculate.

How did her mother do that? Ten minutes ago, the house had been a total disaster area and now it was like nothing had happened.

Victoria was making a pot of tea. Tea solved all problems, according to her. Anna accepted a cup.

"It was okay, I suppose. Maths was a bit tough. Do we have any of those caramel biscuits?"

Victoria pulled the packet out of the drawer. "Help yourself."

Anna went and found her school bag and pulled out her homework. She sat down at the kitchen table with it, keen to get it over with.

Victoria leaned over her shoulder, correcting her mistakes.

"Look, you've got the wrong angle there, darling. That's an obtuse angle, isn't it?"

"Oh, yeah."

Anna took another biscuit and crammed it into her mouth. She finished the last question as quickly as she could and scribbled a hurried answer.

Victoria squinted at the book. "I can barely read that. Don't you think you should write a bit more neatly?"

"Teachers are experts at deciphering writing. They're practically code-breakers."

"Even so."

She left her book out on the table, knowing full well that

her mum was going to re-do it. Victoria was obsessed with her schoolwork.

Joey was subdued by dinner. He came downstairs wearing nothing but headphones and a pair of boxer shorts. He sat down at the table, keeping the headphones on. Victoria didn't ask him to remove them. Anna had never been allowed headphones at the table, but she didn't say anything. Joey was calm, that was all that mattered. She focused on her dinner, a plate of chicken nuggets with oven chips and peas. Joey sniffed his food suspiciously before he ate it, as if he thought his chicken nuggets might be laced with vegetables.

Victoria's phone beeped. She checked it briefly and set it back down.

Anna finished chewing on a bland chicken nugget.

"Mum, why am I the only girl in my class who hasn't got a phone?"

Victoria stared at her. "What are you talking about? We've got a phone." She gestured to the landline, a shiny black replica of a much older model.

Anna tilted her chair back. "Oh, come on, Mum. Nobody uses a landline anymore."

"That's true," Victoria considered. "But you know, phones are expensive. I'll have to talk to your dad."

"Where is Dad?"

"Still at work."

"Just for a change."

Victoria reached across and patted her on the shoulder. It was slightly mechanical, that touch. Anna wondered if she repeated what she'd said, if her mother would reach out and do it again.

Joey finished his food abruptly and stood, picked up his plate and dumped it in the sink.

"You're welcome!" he called out as he clumped back up the stairs.

"Would you like some jelly?" Victoria called after him. But when Joey had his headphones on, the rest of the world ceased to exist.

Victoria looked at Anna again. "He was ever so good in assembly this morning."

"Cool." Anna slid down from the table and picked up her plate. "Mum, I think I'll go and work on my art project."

"Oh, do you want some help?"

"That's okay, I just need to sit quietly so I can concentrate."

In the sanctity of her bedroom, Anna opened the window. The house was so stuffy today, as if there wasn't enough air for them all to breathe. She pulled her burner phone from its charger under her bed. She'd missed a ton of WhatsApp messages during dinner. Her friends were talking about her birthday, planning it without her.

Bex: We could get pizza?

Harley: I'm so sick of pizza!

Bex: There's that new Greek place, Dionysus?

Anna: I think my family went there while I was on the French trip.

Bex: What was the food like?

Dina: Is it expensive?

Anna: Dunno. I'll find out. Laters.

She plodded back downstairs. She could hear her mother was on the phone: "Belinda? This is Victoria Hill. I'm afraid I won't be able to teach your son after all. It turns out my husband has already promised that slot to his boss's son. I'm sorry to disappoint you but I can give you the number for a lady in Shalford. I hear she's very capable . . ."

While she waited for her mum to ring off, Anna looked at the homework she'd left on the table. They were the diagrams she'd done for maths, except better. Her mum had rubbed out her smudged drawings and outlined them neatly in ink. She'd corrected the angles too, so they looked clearer, more precise.

Victoria finally ended her call. "God, I hate talking to answering phones!"

"Mum?"

"Yes?"

"You've been to that new Greek restaurant, haven't you? What's it like?"

Victoria smiled. "Lovely, darling. It was just lovely."

"But what was the food like?"

"Oh, you know, lots of Greek food. Little parcels wrapped in vine leaves and meat done on the grill."

"Was it expensive?"

"Not too bad."

"So like, what, a tenner for a main?"

Victoria scratched her neck. "I really don't recall. Why don't you take a look at their website?"

Anna nodded and plodded back up the stairs. Joey was sitting at the top, clutching his favourite chess piece, the bishop.

"We never went," he said, when she reached the top.

Anna narrowed her eyes. "You what?"

He cast a long look down the stairs, to check their mother wasn't listening. "That Greek place – we never went."

Anna tilted her head. "Then why did she say . . ."

Joey jumped to his feet and skipped back to his room, his mind now on other things.

Anna followed him. "Joey, are you sure?"

The computer beeped and Joey scurried back to his seat. "My turn!"

He focused his attention on his chess game, analysing his next move.

"Joey, why did Mum say you went, if you didn't?"

But Joey was deep in thought now.

"Joey?" she snapped, but he shoved her away. "Screw you!" she told him and headed back to her own room.

She pulled out her phone again and logged into Instagram, scrolling back through her mum's account, @SurreyMummy77. She looked at her mum's profile picture and rolled her eyes. It looked like a candid picture with her mum standing in the kitchen, wearing a pair of oven gloves. She had got in a professional photographer for that picture, Anna remembered. The same photographer had taken pictures of her and Joey larking about in the garden and one of Mum and Dad reclining on the swing seat, steaming hot cups of tea in their hands. There was nothing natural or candid about those pictures, just as there was nothing natural or candid about her mother. Everything was planned. Everything was staged. The picture she presented to the world was always one she had chosen.

It was ridiculous how many pictures Victoria posted. Pictures of the house. Selfies of herself and Joey. Anna didn't let her post pictures of her anymore. She didn't have any desire to have her life plastered all over the Internet. Last year, her mum had missed Anna's only line in the school play because she'd been so busy taking pictures.

Anna scrolled back, back, back. She recognised snaps of hot chocolate at the Natter Café, a plate of waffles at the park.

And there. There was a picture of the Greek Restaurant, taken from the outside.

#Openingnight, #GreekFood, #FamilyFun.

Joey must have got it wrong then. They must have gone. Maybe they hadn't taken him, but then, who would have looked after him? Her parents never left Joey with anyone. Her mum thought he was too precious. Her gifted golden boy. The funny thing was, if there was one thing Anna knew about Joey it was this:

Joey never lied.

3

JOEY'S DIARY

Deer Diary,

Miss H gave me this notebook and told me to write whatever
I like in it. I was going to use it as a chess strategy book but
she said no, it's more for thoughts and feelings and "thinking
through your day".

Well, what happened today was that I was outside at break,
watching the girls skipping, when the pointy-nosed one
suddenly cried: "He's staring! Joey's staring at me!"

Then one of the Dinner Nazis came over and said:

"What are you doing, Joseph?"

"Standing here," I said.

"Well," she said. "I suggest you go and stand somewhere
else."

So I moved six paces away.

Then she said: "I mean it. Hop it."

So I proceeded to hop on one foot.

The Dinner Nazi walked right up to me. I could smell fish
fingers on her breath. "Do you want me to report you to Miss
Henley?" she said.

"For what?"

"Don't give me your cheek."

I had no idea what to say to that. The girls were laughing and
I was confused. The Dinner Nazi pointed to the other end of
the playground.

"Go!"

I went gladly. I still don't get why she was so angry. She was
the one talking in riddles.

There was nothing much to do on the other side of the playground and I didn't want to stand too close to the football
goal in case I got hit by the ball, or worse still, someone might
ask me to play. Instead, I made my usual circuit of the playground but instead of completing the loop, I walked round to

the back of the building and ended up outside the teachers' toilets. There was no one around so I went inside.

I wanted to use the loo, but I was worried about the hand dryer. The brand the school uses is excessively loud, operating at 95 decibels. There was no way I was going to expose my ears to that so I climbed up into the sink to turn off the switch just in case someone came in while I was peeing. Then the door opened and Miss Henley was standing there with a funny look on her face. She blinked a few too many times. "Joey? Why are you in the sink?" she asked.

Something in her voice made the whole thing seem incredibly funny, me squatting there like a frog. I burst out laughing and then Miss H smiled too, even though she was trying not to. She didn't tell me off, but at home time she gave me this notebook and told me to use it as a diary. She said it was just for me and I didn't have to show anyone what I wrote in it. I wonder how she will mark it if she's not going to read it? Anyway, these are my thoughts for the day.

Evidence that Mum is losing her mind:

1. It's blue bin day. She put the grey one out.
2. She told Anna we went to the Greek restaurant when we didn't.
3. She forgot to give me my night vitamins.

4

VICTORIA

"Wake up!"

Kit moaned in his sleep but did not open his eyes. Victoria shook him hard but it had no effect. She padded into the bathroom and filled a glass with water. She perched on the bed and dipped her fingers in the water and sprinkled a few droplets on his face. Kit's eyes fluttered slightly, but he continued to sleep. She took the glass and trickled a little water over his face.

He sat up with a jerk. "Why are you waterboarding me?"

"You need to get up."

"For fuck's sake!" He reached with a groggy hand and grabbed his phone to confirm that she was telling the truth. He really did look tired. There were red spidery veins in his eyes and dark smudges underneath. "Can I at least have some coffee?"

"I've made you a flask for the train."

"You're a cruel woman, Vic."

She ignored him and pulled his work clothes from the wardrobe. Shirt, tie, trousers. She set them all on the bed.

"Come on, you've still got time for a shower if you hurry."

"Five more minutes!"

"You really don't have the time."

She reached for the glass of water again. His hand captured hers.

"Alright, alright. I'm up."

He grabbed his bottle of pills and swallowed a few, then climbed carefully out of bed.

"Don't forget your eye drops," she called as he walked stiffly to the bathroom.

She waited until she heard the shower come on, then she turned her attention to her own wardrobe and pulled out the frilliest undergarments she could find. Kit returned from the shower just as she was stepping into a pair of silk stockings. The eye drops had made him look less tired, but he couldn't hide his pain.

"Did you hear that?" she asked.

"What?"

She listened intently but all was still. "Nothing. I thought I heard a beep."

She pulled on her shirt and turned to face him.

"What are you getting dressed up like that for?" he complained. "I've got to go."

She smiled demurely and fastened his tie.

"You know, I could go in late, just this once?"

"No. You've got to earn your reward. Go on, get going. You've only got three more minutes."

"You're a bloody slave driver, you are."

"Someone has to be."

Victoria heard the kids clattering about in the kitchen, a cacophony of chairs scraping and spoons clinking. She followed Kit as he carefully navigated the stairs. He poked his head into the kitchen and waved to Joey and Anna.

"Have a good day at school!"

"Bye, Dad!"

"Hey, don't forget your coffee." Victoria slipped his flask into the pocket of his bag. She planted a kiss on his cheek, then closed the door behind him and turned her attention to the children.

"Joey, isn't it meant to be mufti day today?"

"Yes."

"You're wearing your uniform?"

"No, I'm wearing mufti. Look!"

She looked under the table. Joey had on black socks instead of grey. Anna burst out laughing.

"Don't forget you've got debate club at lunchtime," Victoria reminded her.

"But, Mum, have you seen what Joey's wearing?"

"He looks fine," she said sharply. "But, Joey, wouldn't you like to wear something else today?"

"Like what?"

"What about your *Star Wars* T-shirt?"

"Then what will I wear on Saturday?"

"I can wash it."

Joey stopped shovelling cereal into his mouth and stared at her like she'd said something crazy.

"Or what you're wearing is perfectly fine."

A large white van pulled up outside the house and Victoria rushed to the door. The driver walked up the path and consulted a handheld device.

"Is this right?" he scratched the back of his head. "Looks to me like they've sent you way too much Vicodin?"

Victoria forced out a laugh. "No, that's right. My husband has a lot of pain."

"What is he, a horse?" He chuckled at his own joke and walked back to the van, returning with more boxes.

"So, are the gummies for your husband too?"

"Oh no, they're for . . . me."

She grabbed Joey's melatonin, before the nosy man could

ask any more questions. She'd have to switch to another company for next month's delivery.

"I THOUGHT you were on a green crusade and we all had to walk?" Anna said, when her mum picked her up from Godalming Grammar after school that afternoon. Joey was already in the back seat, his head bent over a chess strategy book.

"We're going aspiration shopping," Victoria announced, as she clipped on her seat belt.

Anna yawned widely. "You mean we're going to look at houses we have no intention of buying."

"One house," Victoria said. "And it doesn't hurt to see what's on the market."

She pulled a comb from the glove compartment and handed it to her daughter.

"Run that through Joey's hair, will you? It's important we look the part."

"Get away from me!" Joey yelled.

"Okay, you do it," Anna said, thrusting the comb in his face.

A few minutes later, they stopped at the traffic light and Victoria looked with disdain at the teens loitering outside the community college. They were all puffing on cigarettes, hands stuffed in the pockets of their oversized jeans. The lights turned green and Victoria gladly drove on. The address she'd been given was a few miles out in the countryside off a road she'd never driven down before.

"What is it, a farm?" Anna asked.

"I shouldn't think so," Victoria said, turning into the estate. She could see Fernsworth House now: a magnificent manor house set in stunning landscaped gardens. She beamed with pleasure. One day, they too would live in a house like this.

She took a picture of the house and uploaded it to Instagram.

#Fernsworth_House, #SurreyMansions #Livingthedream

This open house was by far the grandest they'd attended. The house had at least twelve bedrooms, and there were half a dozen cars parked out the front, including a couple of Porsches. Victoria suspected they weren't the only ones who'd come along for a nose.

Joey looked up from his book. "We're not moving, are we?"

Anna burst out laughing. "As if. This is just another of Mum's fantasies."

"Come on, kids, out the car."

Victoria hopped out and opened Joey's door to help him out. She kept the child lock on on his side because he had a habit of fiddling with the door latch while she drove. For an intelligent boy, he could be very silly at times.

She took Joey's hand and approached the woman in charge of the viewing, who handed her a brochure.

"Look," she said to Anna, showing her the glossy pages.

"Gross, Mum, you're practically salivating!"

"Don't speak to me like that!" Victoria glanced around, but it didn't appear that anyone had heard. She flipped the page and they all looked at the picture of the garden. "We could put a hot tub in next to the pool," she mused.

Anna gave her a look.

The agent invited them to explore the grounds. Joey and Anna enjoyed trampling through the landscaped gardens. There was a little maze and Anna challenged Joey to go inside. He was out again within minutes.

"How did you know which way to go?" she asked.

Joey shrugged. "It's really quite logical. You just follow the left hand . . ."

"Oh, that's no fun!"

"Come on, we don't want to miss the talk," Victoria said. They headed for the courtyard, where everyone had gathered.

"Note the plentiful windows," the estate agent was saying. Anna let out a titter. Victoria shot her a look.

"Is that a Jacobean chimney?" she asked.

"It is indeed." The estate agent smiled. "Well spotted."

Victoria glowed with the praise.

"It looks like Downton Abbey," the woman next to them ventured.

"Wrong era," the estate agent said, and the enjoyment sagged from the woman's cheeks.

"And now I have the great privilege of showing you the house," the agent said.

———

THEY FOUND THEMSELVES IN A LARGE, breezy hallway. Glass chandeliers hung from the ceiling and portraits of plump aristocrats adorned the walls, all lacy collars and pink cheeks. The estate agent pointed out the sweeping staircase.

Victoria tried to enjoy the tour, but there was a heavy, unsettled feeling in her stomach. She couldn't get Belinda out of her mind. She hadn't run into her since she'd cancelled Ricky's lesson. She wished the woman would phone her back to confirm she'd got the message. Perhaps she should send her a follow-up text, just to check?

"And here we have the drawing room and the smoking room. Or perhaps it would be considered a vaping room nowadays."

The group laughed politely and continued to explore the

stairs that curved around the building. All the little nooks and crannies had the estate agent circling back on herself.

"I believe the exit was this way," she said uncertainly.

"No, it was to the right," Joey said.

"How would you know?" Anna muttered, but Joey was right. The exit was just where he'd said it was.

"So, what did you think?" Victoria asked as they made their way back to the car.

"That estate agent really couldn't be arsed, could she?" Anna said.

"I meant, what did you think of the house?"

"It was like a palace," Joey said.

Victoria nodded, satisfied. "Just think, if you work hard, you could live in a place like that one day."

"Yeah, right," Anna said.

"You can have anything you want, if you want it badly enough. The universe will provide."

Anna folded her arms. "Oh, come on!"

Victoria turned and looked at her daughter. "You may think it's silly, but it's important to set your sights high. You know, growing up, our family never had any money . . ."

"I know, I know," Anna finished for her. "Your dad lost his job and your mum was a cleaner and you think that made you a loser or something."

Victoria swallowed. It was hard to convey quite how painful it had been. "My mum worked at my school, for pity's sake. She scrubbed the loos. Can you imagine the flack I took from my classmates?"

But Anna didn't get it. Why would she? She and Joey didn't want for anything. They'd never had to eat cold baked beans for dinner or wear their coats to bed because there wasn't enough money for the meter.

"I want better for you kids. Your dad does too. We've both worked so hard to get everything we have. We have to aim high, Anna. It's not just about money. It's important that people respect you. You have to work hard to get anywhere in this life, don't ever forget that."

She caught her daughter's eye, but she could tell she still didn't get it.

"Alright, Mum. Can we please go home now? I have a ton of homework to do."

5

VICTORIA

Victoria spotted Belinda amongst the crowd of parents on Friday morning, but by the time she'd shoehorned Joey into his classroom, she was gone.

"Are you alright?" Portia asked, as she stomped back across the playground.

"Yeah, fine," Victoria said, but she wasn't. Belinda had not yet replied to either her phone message or her text. It was the height of bad manners as far as Victoria was concerned and it left her feeling on edge.

She tried to catch Belinda again at the end of the school day too, but she was nowhere to be seen. Someone else must have come to collect Ricky. Had Belinda got her message? She could only hope so.

When they arrived home, Joey and Anna raided the kitchen cupboards, tearing into biscuits and packets of crisps like they hadn't eaten all day. In Joey's case, he probably hadn't. The beautiful lunches she packed him invariably arrived home fully intact, with little more than a few breadsticks or chicken pieces eaten.

Victoria left Belinda one last voice message, just to be

sure she didn't turn up, then turned off the downstairs lights and headed up to her bedroom with a glass of wine. She couldn't relax though. She had a nagging feeling that if Belinda had got her messages, she would have replied.

When the doorbell chimed, Victoria's first instinct was to duck under the bed. She sank down to her knees, making sure she wasn't visible from the window. Perhaps, if she remained very still, Belinda and Ricky would go away. Perhaps the silent house would convince them there was no one home. Perhaps Belinda would look at her phone and finally see all the messages she'd missed.

She braced herself and waited. The doorbell did not sound again. Gradually, she came out of hiding and brushed the dust off her skirt. She would have to have a good hoover under there. She headed cautiously down the stairs and walked through the lounge, towards the kitchen, intent on getting another glass of wine. She needed it after . . .

Ricky was sitting at the piano.

"Hello!" he said in his slightly squeaky voice.

Victoria swung round and saw Anna emerge from the kitchen. She was carrying a pot of tea which she set down on the table.

"Here's my mum now," she said and Belinda stepped out too, an unreadable expression on her face.

Victoria gripped the table. Her legs trembled beneath her.

"You're here! I . . . I sent you a couple of messages . . ."

"I'm afraid I had my phone stolen," Belinda said in her low, dulcet tones. "Bit of a crap week, but at least I remembered our appointment."

She picked up the cup of tea Anna had made and took a careful sip. Poor Anna probably thought Victoria wanted to impress this woman. She was such a good girl, going to all this trouble. If only she knew . . .

Victoria's mind whirled. What now? She could hardly pretend she was teaching another student when there was no one else in the room. She clenched and unclenched her fists.

"What a lovely place you have here," Belinda said, admiring the soft grey upholstery and pale wooden furniture.

"Thank you." Victoria walked over to the piano. "Perhaps, Ricky, you could play something for me. What's your favourite piece?"

Ricky gladly obliged with a stumbling rendition of "Clair de Lune". He followed that up with "Ode to Joy". His playing improved as he loosened up. His face lit up and he played with all his heart.

Victoria forced herself to breathe. She could do this. Ricky was just another student and Belinda seemed perfectly . . . not that she really knew Belinda. She knew of her, everybody did. But they'd never really talked before.

"You're welcome to leave him and come back in an hour," she told Belinda, but the other woman didn't pick up on the hint. Then she saw Joey standing in the doorway. She watched him, curiously.

Joey walked past her and reached for the chessboard he'd left on the table.

"You like chess?" Belinda said.

Joey looked at her. "Do you play?"

"A little."

Joey waved at the seat opposite. "Sit."

Victoria looked at Belinda, embarrassed. "You don't have to . . ."

"I'd love to," Belinda said. She pulled out a chair and sat down, so Victoria had little choice but to continue with Ricky's lesson.

"I'd like you to try this," she said, placing some music in front of Ricky.

He played in a stilted yet practised manner. His foot was

heavy on the peddle and he made a number of errors, but he didn't let it get to him.

"Very nice," she said, casting another glance at Belinda.

Joey won the game in a few moves and they started over. She hoped Belinda would give up once he'd beaten her a couple of times but they kept on playing.

She caught Belinda watching her. Of course, Belinda was assessing her, noting how she taught her son. It was nothing personal, nothing Victoria wouldn't do herself, and yet she'd never felt so watched. She tried to concentrate on the lesson. She just had to get through this so she could get these people out of her house.

She finished up with a more challenging piece that was probably a little too sophisticated for Ricky. He tried several times but could not get past the first movement.

She was about to wrap things up when Joey rose to his feet and walked over to the piano. It was as if he'd only just noticed Ricky. He stood and watched as the other boy stumbled over the music. Ricky noticed him looking and met his eyes.

"Perhaps you'd like to demonstrate, Joey," Victoria said.

Ricky moved aside and Joey slid into his place at the piano. His fingers found the keys and the room filled with music. There was always magic when Joey played. He didn't even have to work at it, it just came naturally, that gift. Even Victoria, who'd been playing all her life, would never be able to play like that.

When he'd finished playing, their guests broke out in applause.

"Play something else," Ricky said.

Victoria bit her lip. Usually, she could listen to Joey play all day, but now was not the time.

"What do I owe you?" Belinda asked, reaching for her purse.

"Oh, no. The first lesson is free," Victoria said, swallowing bile. She could not accept money from this woman. It was impossible.

"Are you sure?" Belinda said. "I must say, that's most generous!" She nodded at the boys. "They seem to have hit it off."

They had moved away from the piano now and were looking at Joey's collection of Star Wars Lego buildings, discussing their favourite characters.

Victoria allowed herself a smile. Brilliant as he was, Joey struggled to make conversation with kids his own age. It helped that Ricky was slightly older and more mature despite his squeaky voice.

"So, same time next week?" Belinda asked.

Victoria's smile froze. Her mind raced for a valid excuse. There was a ripple of laughter from the boys, and the next thing she knew they were thundering up the stairs to Joey's bedroom.

No! She wanted to run after them. *Get back down here! Stop that right now!*

She needed Belinda to leave now. She wanted to shove her out the door. But she could hardly do that, could she? She had to wait until Belinda had finished her tea, and until Ricky emerged from Joey's room.

Anna came in to get her homework.

Belinda looked at the book in her hand. "Crikey, is that Latin?"

"Anna's taking Latin A-level." The words sprang automatically from Victoria's lips. "She's the youngest in the class."

Belinda looked suitably impressed. "Brains must run in the family."

There was a click as Kit turned his key in the door. Victoria's heart faltered. She didn't want him to have to deal with this. This was her mess. She should have . . .

She sprang forward. Belinda followed.

"Kit, this is Belinda," she said urgently. "I've just been giving her son a lesson."

Kit's jaw dropped and she had the urge to kick him, anything to get him to behave normally.

"Joey!" she yelled up the stairs. "It's time for Ricky to go home now." She glanced nervously at Belinda. Did that sound rude? Kit hadn't moved from the doormat.

"Why don't you go upstairs and get changed?" she urged.

He darted a startled look at Belinda and then seemed to come back to life. Belinda's eyes trailed him as he shuffled past her and walked stiffly up the stairs.

There was an awkward silence as they waited for Ricky to come back down. Eventually, Belinda went up to coax him out of Joey's room. The boys were having too much fun.

"Joey, come and see Ricky to the door," Victoria called, as Ricky pulled his shoes on.

Joey appeared at the top of the stairs.

"Why?"

"Because that's what we do."

Joey did as he was told for once, chatting to Ricky as he got ready. They stood on the doorstep and watched as Belinda and Ricky walked back down the drive. Victoria exhaled as she locked the door behind them. She picked up a cushion from the sofa and hugged it to her chest.

"I like Ricky," Joey announced.

"That's great." Victoria headed for the kitchen and poured herself a large glass of wine.

"Can I have some?" Anna asked.

"You're too young."

She poured a glass for Kit and headed up the stairs, where she found him sprawled out on the bed.

"You okay?" she asked, setting down the wine.

"No, I'm broken. Completely fucking broken." He took a

couple more pills from his nightstand and washed them down with the wine. "What was that woman doing in our house?"

"I cancelled but she came anyway."

"Did you tell her not to come again?"

"I couldn't. Ricky and Joey got along so well. You should have seen them."

He gave her a long, hard look. "Can't he find some other kid to play with?"

Victoria took a gulp of her wine. "Apparently not."

She picked up the remote and put on a programme he liked. Then she sat down beside him on the bed. Kit lay his head on her shoulder and closed his eyes.

"Did you hear that?" Victoria asked.

"What?"

"That beeping sound."

"Can't hear a thing."

Victoria shifted position. "There it is again."

"Still don't hear anything."

She levered herself up off the bed and padded out into the hallway. She took a broom and poked at the smoke alarm. Maybe it was the other one, the carbon monoxide detector. She listened intently, but all had gone quiet now. She opened the window just in case.

6

VICTORIA

Victoria's heels clacked on the polished floor as she walked into the school hall on Monday evening. She spotted Portia, and quickly slid into the empty space beside her. The hall hummed with the voices of their fellow parents as everyone waited for the chance to talk with their children's teachers. The recent round of budget cuts meant that the school hadn't bothered to lay on refreshments, and Victoria was parched.

"Look at the state of her," Portia murmured. Victoria glanced across the room at a rosy-faced woman wearing grey jogging bottoms and a matching hoodie. "Do you reckon she sleeps in that outfit?" Portia went on. "Or are those her best clothes, the ones she wears to impress?"

Victoria stifled a laugh and turned it into a cough.

"What's so funny?" asked Samantha, plonking herself down beside Victoria.

"Nothing," Victoria said quickly. "Hey, did Henry get an invitation to Eloise's birthday party?"

"No, I don't think so." Samantha looked a little crestfallen, as if she was the one missing out, and not her son.

"Ariadne did," Portia said, "but we can't make it. She's got a swimming gala that day."

"Oh, shame."

She became aware of Belinda on the periphery of her vision. Belinda didn't sit down like the other mums. She preferred to stand by the window, silent and aloft. People barely noticed her. Apart from Victoria.

"Did you hear the latest about Paul Schooner?" a woman sitting next to Samantha said.

Samantha regarded her with interest. Paul Schooner was fairly new to the town. He lived in the large house behind Victoria's and had once been a professional footballer.

"What about him?"

"He's been at it again, playing away with a girl who works at All Bar One."

"No!"

Portia glanced at the woman with mild interest. "Wouldn't put it past him. He came on to me in the Waitrose car park once."

The woman's eyes widened. "Are you serious?"

Portia stretched out her long slim legs and regarded her perfectly manicured fingernails. Victoria waited for a moment, but it seemed she'd grown bored of the topic.

"I'm surprised his wife hasn't left him," Samantha said.

"She spent last night at her mother's, apparently. But she was back home this afternoon, so she must have forgiven him."

The door opened and Kit came rushing in. Victoria rose to her feet and walked over to him.

"Sorry I'm late," he murmured.

She discreetly straightened his collar.

"Luckily for you they're running late."

"Mr and Mrs Hill?" The receptionist smiled at Victoria. "Miss Henley is ready for you now."

Kit and Victoria strode past a display of children's artwork. Joey's pencil drawing of the Tower of London was by far the most realistic of all the drawings. They turned the corner and she spotted a display case containing the trophy he had won at the regional chess championships. She pointed it out to Kit and he grinned broadly.

"That's our boy!"

Victoria had always enjoyed Joey's parents' evenings. She loved it when his teachers marvelled at how quickly he could solve maths problems and how little help he required to do so. Often, he didn't even need an explanation. He just seemed to know instinctively. Of course, he was a little ropier on some of the more wishy-washy subjects, but who cared if he listened attentively during RE, or if he had any interest in Shakespeare's sonnets? The boy could play the piano like a professional, and could draw even better than Anna, who took a weekly fine art class online. He was a wonder.

Joey's classroom was an assault on the senses. Brightly coloured displays covered every wall and there were paper chains and lanterns made by the children. Miss Henley sat behind a wooden desk piled high with children's workbooks. She was fairly new to the school, having taken over from Joey's old teacher who was on maternity leave. She appeared to be in her thirties, but she dressed like a woman twice her age, in frumpy dresses and long baggy cardigans she no doubt knitted herself. Victoria forced herself to smile pleasantly but Miss Henley's forehead creased as she looked from Kit to Victoria.

"Please, take a seat."

Victoria sat down and waited while Kit lowered himself into the chair beside her.

"Are you alright?" Miss Henley asked, seeing him wince.

"Never better!" Kit treated her to his megawatt smile, but Miss Henley broke eye contact, glancing down at her notes.

"Right, so Joey is an exceptional pupil. He's clearly very gifted in maths, art and music."

Victoria nodded proudly. She knew all this already, but she could never hear it enough.

"However." The teacher steepled her fingers together, and Victoria glanced at Kit. What was wrong with the woman? Why had she stopped singing their son's praises? "However, I'm concerned about Joey's progress . . . socially. Tell me, what's he like outside of school?"

"He's very busy with his hobbies," Victoria said. "He plays the piano and chess."

"He does a lot of drawing too," Kit chipped in.

"Has he got any friends?"

Victoria glanced at Kit. "Of course," she lied smoothly. "In fact, he was playing with Ricky Solomon just last week."

Miss Henley gave a tight smile. "Really? I have to tell you that at school, I've never seen Joey play with anyone. I mean, he might have the odd conversation with the other children, but he quickly loses their interest if he persists too long on one topic."

"He's too clever for them," Victoria concluded.

"There is that," Miss Henley agreed. "But did you know, he still hasn't learnt the names of all the children in his class?"

Kit looked startled. "That can't be . . ."

"It also occurs to me that Joey is very set in his routines. He doesn't cope well if there is a change to our usual schedule."

"Don't all children like routines?" Victoria said.

"And he seems to prefer the company of adults to children."

"Well . . . that's because he's gifted. The other children can't keep up with him."

Miss Henley leaned forward. "Tell me, has it ever occurred to you that Joey might be autistic?"

"The . . ." Victoria felt her throat close. She tried to speak, but no words would come out.

She turned and looked at Kit. *Say something! Defend our child!*

Miss Henley pushed a leaflet across the table. "Please, have a read of this, both of you, and let me know what you think. There's a checklist there, see if you think Joey meets the criteria. I know he's gifted, but I have dealt with gifted children before and I see something different in Joey. I think he's struggling."

Kit picked up the leaflet and flipped through it, deep in thought. Victoria kicked him under the table, and he looked up sharply.

"If Joey was autistic, wouldn't it have come up before now?" he asked. "He's nine years old!"

Miss Henley crossed her arms. "I believe Joey has the ability to mask his differences very well. Have you seen any signs of stress?"

"No," Victoria said firmly. She got to her feet. "Well, thank you for your time, Miss Henley, but I think you're mistaken. If Joey is struggling at school, it's because he's not being sufficiently challenged."

Miss Henley's frown grew deeper. Two parallel lines appeared on the bridge of her nose and Victoria yearned to straighten them out.

It's fine. He's fine.

Kit scrambled to his feet. She took his hand to drag him out of there, but he stopped and looked at the teacher.

"If Joey is autistic, what would our next move be?"

"With your permission, I would like to call in an educational psychologist to assess Joey in the classroom."

Victoria's stomach clenched like a fist.

"Let's not get ahead of ourselves. Leave this with us. We'll have a look at the leaflet."

They walked out to the car and Kit sat quietly in the passenger seat.

"There might be something in this," he said, holding out the leaflet.

Victoria refused to take it. "No. I know my boy."

"But what about the way he goes on and on about stuff and doesn't care if anybody's listening?"

"He's gifted."

"You have to admit, he is socially awkward."

Victoria clenched her jaw. "What we need to do is to get him out of this school. Joey should be in a private school, where he'll get the best education. This school can't handle his brilliance. That's the real problem, not him."

7

JOEY'S DIARY

Today I asked Miss H how to be normal. She said:
"My dear boy, normality is not something we should
aspire to."
But I know Mum wants me to be more normal. She said so
the other day when I couldn't tie my laces, and again this
morning when I went out in the rain to watch the bin men
empty the bins.
I haven't said anything to Mum, but I've done a whole week
without my night vitamins! She thinks I'm still taking them
but I just hide them in my drawer. I feel just fine without
them. Mum worries when I don't sleep but I kind of like it. I
like having that extra time.
Last night I hid under the covers until Mum went to bed. I
heard Dad come in just after midnight. They had a conversation in loud whispers. I'm not sure, but I think it might have
been about me. Dad must have fallen asleep after that
because when he sleeps, the whole house trembles, and I
heard Mum laughing in the darkness. Or perhaps she was
crying. It's hard to tell.

"Will you be alright by yourself for a couple of hours?" her mum asked on Tuesday after school.

Anna nodded. "Actually, can you drop me off in town? I've got a study group tonight."

"Whereabouts?"

"We're meeting at the library, but we'll probably go for coffee after."

"Okay. Does Maddie need a lift too?"

"No, she's not in this study group."

"Why not? I thought you two always worked together?"

"I know but we were put into different groups for this project. Where are you off to anyway?"

"I'm taking Joey to a party."

Anna's eyes flicked to her brother, who was currently upside down on the sofa, staring into space. "Does Joey actually want to go to a party?"

"Of course, he does. It's a party! He was lucky to get an invite."

"Why *did* he get an invite?"

Victoria lowered her voice. "I don't know. Maybe because I'm on the PTA now. Anyway, it would be rude not to go."

Imelda Daniels had a very nice house. Victoria knew this because Portia had been there once.

"Put it this way," Portia had said. "My entire house would fit into her kitchen."

Portia had not exaggerated. Imelda's house was almost as big as the Fernsworth estate. Victoria smiled to herself as she parked the car and turned to look at her son.

"Joey, we've arrived."

Joey didn't raise his head from his book.

"Joey!" she said with frustration. She didn't want to be late. It was better to arrive early for these things, easier to mingle.

"Joey!"

Joey looked up from his book. "What?"

"We're here."

He glanced out the window. "Oh."

She got him out of the car and straightened his collar. She had chosen his outfit with care: a navy blue polo shirt with soft cut jeans and brand new trainers. Joey didn't care what he wore as long as it was comfortable. She was sure that would change as he got older but for now she enjoyed dressing him in beautiful outfits. He was the little Ken doll her parents would never buy her.

She handed him the present.

"What is it?" he asked, looking at the large gift box, tied at the top with purple ribbon.

"It's a glitter tattoo kit."

It had been bloody expensive. She really hoped Eloise appreciated it. Nine was such an awkward age for girls. They weren't babies anymore, but not quite pre-teens either.

They walked towards the door, and Victoria practised her smile while she rang the bell.

Eloise opened the door.

"Hello?" she said, blankly, looking past them as if expecting someone else.

"Happy birthday, Eloise. Joey, give her the present."

Joey held it out. "It's a glitter tattoo kit."

"Joey, you're not meant to tell her!"

"That's cool," Eloise said. She turned her back and Victoria was half afraid she'd close the door on them.

"Is your mum about?" she called after her.

"Somewhere."

Victoria edged forward, peering into the grand hallway. There was music, she just had to find where it was coming from. She took Joey's hand and pulled him inside.

Imelda was in her newly remodelled kitchen. Victoria took in the large Belfast sink, the double ovens, the kitchen island and the massive pantry. Imelda looked busy, laying out platters of olives, sun-dried tomatoes and ciabattas.

"Hello?" she said, with an affected laugh. "And you are?"

Victoria swallowed her annoyance. She bet she knew perfectly well who she was. They saw each other at the school gates every morning, and just last week, Imelda had engaged in some witty repartee with Portia, while Victoria stood right beside her.

"Victoria Hill," she said smoothly. "And this is my son, Joey."

She looked at Joey, who was staring up at the light fittings.

"Are these smart light bulbs?" he asked.

Imelda inclined her head. "Yes. Yes they are."

"Paul Schooner has those lights."

Imelda raised an eyebrow. "You've been to Paul's house?"

"His lights have speakers in them so you can stream music through the bulbs."

"Oh, well ours can change colour."

"His do that too."

Joey looked like he was going to ask something else, but the doorbell interrupted him.

"I'd better get that," Imelda said, seeming to remember her manners. "Help yourselves to snacks."

Imelda returned with two little girls bearing obscenely large gifts. They were greeted with shrieks of delight from Eloise.

Imelda glanced distractedly at Victoria. "You don't have to stay," she said. "Why don't you take a little time for yourself? I'll take care of Jonny."

"Joey," Victoria corrected her.

Joey was still looking at the light fittings.

"Do these have built in wi-fi radios?"

Imelda laughed. "I have no idea." She went to the fridge and pulled out a tray of glasses with ice on the rims.

"I think I'll hang around if that's okay," Victoria said, because there was no way she was going to leave Joey to fend for himself. "Looks like you've got lots to do. I could lend you a hand?"

Imelda blinked. "Okay. Why don't you get the champagne out and start filling the glasses?"

The doorbell rang again, and the house filled with people. Dozens of children, and a handful of parents, all dressed to the nines.

Imelda had set up a soft drinks station for the children, but half the kids couldn't work it, so Victoria helped them, while Joey sat beside her.

"Why don't you go and join in with the party games?" Victoria asked him.

"That's alright, I'd rather be here with you."

"That's really sweet, Joey, but this is a party. You're meant to be enjoying yourself."

She recalled Miss Henley's words, and suddenly it was

really important to her that Joey did enjoy himself, if only to prove her wrong.

"How are you, Victoria?" a tall brunette asked her, as she grabbed a glass of champagne.

"Fine thanks," Victoria said. "The weather's looking good for the weekend, isn't it? I was thinking of . . ."

Before she could finish the sentence, the woman raised her hand in greeting to a friend who had just walked in and sashayed off across the room.

"Rude cow," Victoria muttered under her breath.

"Moo," Joey said, a bit too loudly. The woman didn't appear to hear.

There were squeals of excitement as the bouncy castle was inflated. Victoria walked out to the patio and watched as the children threw themselves on it with wild abandon. Kids bounced up and down, expending endless energy. They shrieked and tagged one another. Looked to be having the time of their lives.

"Don't you want a go?" she asked Joey.

"Do you?"

She took a long swig of her drink.

They wandered back inside, and Joey stood next to a group of boys who were playing with Eloise's train set. The trains were battery operated, and the tracks were set up in a sophisticated pattern that looped up and down, rising above bridges and down through tunnels, past model houses and round again for another circuit. It was really something.

Joey watched in fascination. His eyes kept darting to the control panel and Victoria knew he was itching to play with the switch. He inched closer and she grabbed his hand just in time.

"You mustn't touch, understand?"

"Why?"

"Because the other children will be annoyed."

"Why?"

"Victoria Hill?" She turned and found herself looking at a short blonde woman she knew well from the PTA.

"Hi! How are you?"

"Great. I didn't know you were friends with Imelda?"

Victoria swallowed. "I'm . . ."

Out of the corner of her eye she saw Joey darting towards the switch again. She caught him just in time.

"Have you tried the bruschetta?" she asked, changing the subject. "They look really good."

The blonde woman smirked. "Have you actually tasted them?"

Victoria held Joey with her legs whilst trying to look casual. "Not yet."

She leaned in a little closer. "I suspect Imelda mixed the salt up with the sugar."

"No!"

"Go on, try one."

Victoria took Joey by the hand and yanked him over to the kitchen.

"What did I tell you?" she hissed in his ear.

"Ow, stop it. You're hurting me."

"Just behave."

She released him and reached over to grab a bruschetta. She brought it to her lips and took a bite. Then she locked eyes with the blonde and nodded slowly.

Over the next few minutes, more of the mums came over to sample the bruschetta, laughing and nudging each other as they tasted the sweetness. Victoria felt a pang of sympathy for her host.

Presently, Imelda returned. Victoria watched as she opened her gargantuan fridge and pulled out trays of delicate little sandwiches with the crusts cut off.

"Would you like me to help bring those outside?" Victoria asked.

"That would be great, thanks."

Imelda skipped off, leaving Victoria to do all the work.

She picked up one of the trays and carried it carefully towards the door. Joey picked up another and followed her out.

"Isn't he the charmer?" one of the mums said, as he offered her a sandwich.

Victoria smiled.

They set the trays down on the outside tables. Most of the children were still killing it on the bouncy castle, or else chasing one another around the lawn. A few little girls sat one in front of the other, styling each other's hair the way Victoria had seen girls do when she was young. Never her though, the other girls used to say she had lice.

Victoria and Joey returned to the kitchen to collect more trays of food. They came in and out about five times in all, carrying all Imelda's fancy party food. By the time they brought out the last two trays, most of the children were already sitting around the table.

"Quick, Joey, go and sit down," Victoria told him.

"Where do I sit?"

"It doesn't matter, sit anywhere."

Joey looked from one end of the table to the other. He must have known some of those children but no one called out to him to come and sit with them, and he didn't seem to have any idea where he should put himself.

"Just go and sit on the end there," Victoria said, desperately.

She placed a hand on his shoulder and steered him over to what was by now the only remaining seat. Reluctantly, Joey sat down.

Victoria spotted a tired looking woman sitting alone and sauntered over.

"Hi," she said. "Which one's yours?"

The woman looked at her a little oddly. "Ryan," she said shortly. "He's in the same class as Joey."

Victoria darted a glance at the table. Ryan was in fact sitting right next to Joey.

"They've been in the same class since reception."

Victoria forced out a little laugh. "Yes, yes of course. Hasn't he grown?"

The children went through the food like locusts. It was remarkable the way they honed in on the crisps and biscuits but most of the sandwiches remained untouched. Victoria's stomach rumbled, reminding her that she'd barely eaten anything all day. She waited until the children ran back to the bouncy castle, then grabbed a sandwich from the tray.

Imelda was walking towards her. She put a hand to her mouth to cover the fact that she was eating.

"Are you hungry, Victoria?"

"Oh no, I was just admiring the napkins. Are they satin?"

"They're pure silk."

"Nice," Victoria spoke through a mouthful of goat's cheese. "Much better than the paper ones. Better for the environment."

"Oh, that's right, you're the school environmental thingamy, aren't you?"

"Yes, well I like to get involved. It's important to support the school. That's why I joined the PTA."

Imelda tilted her head. "You're on the PTA?"

"Yes, I joined in January."

She couldn't believe Imelda didn't know this. There had been a lot of competition for her position. In the end it had been down to her and one of the Year Four mums. Kit had been astounded.

"Isn't it a voluntary post?" he'd said. "I mean, it doesn't pay anything, does it? You'd be helping them out."

"That's right."

"Then why don't they take you both? I'd have thought it would be the more the merrier?"

How naïve he could be.

Someone turned up the music. It was too loud for Victoria's liking, the beat made her head pound. She wanted to get up and turn it down but Imelda was looking at her.

"Hey, I've just realised. Your son is the boy who played the piano in assembly!"

"Yes, that's right."

A light went on in Imelda's eyes. "He's amazing, isn't he? I wish Eloise could play like that."

"I could teach her if you like."

Imelda was nodding. She reached for her phone. "Mondays is out, we have swimming. Tuesday is tennis, Wednesday is gymnastics, Thursday is horse riding. We can do Fridays?"

"Fridays?" she swallowed. Could she possibly cancel Belinda? What reason could she give?

The music changed and Victoria realised with horror that it was The Song. She turned and looked at Joey and he looked at her. His face was stricken.

"Excuse me," she said to Imelda. "I think my son needs me."

Joey sprang up from the table. She ran towards him just in time to stop him from flipping it over altogether.

She threw her arms around him and marched him as quickly as she could out of the house.

"Hold it," she begged him. "Hold it in!"

Joey could not hold it in. By the time they reached the car, he was shrieking and howling into her chest. Victoria pulled him inside and shut the doors. Then she soothed him as best she could by playing Mozart on her phone. Joey's cries subsided, but every so often he'd let out an extra loud wail.

She glanced nervously back at the house. She'd left her handbag behind. She'd have to go back but what the hell was she going to tell Imelda? She waited until Joey wore himself out. His body went from tight and tense to floppy and relaxed. He curled up on the back seat, his thumb finding his mouth the way it had when he was little. It had taken Victoria years to wean him off that habit, and here he was doing it all over again. Still, at least he was quiet.

"You stay here," she told him softly. "I'll just go and thank Imelda for the party."

Joey did not speak but his eyes grew large and fearful.

"I'll just be a minute," she said, stroking his warm pink cheek.

She jogged back to the house. The door was locked, so she walked around to the back, where Eloise was giving out the party bags.

Imelda cornered her. "Is Jonny okay?"

Eloise marched over, flanked by two other girls. "Tell me the truth. Is he a werewolf?"

Victoria drew a breath. "He got a bad earache. They come on very suddenly. I need to take him home to bed."

"Oh dear! What a shame," Imelda said.

Victoria glanced at her closely. It was hard to tell when she was being sincere.

"Here." Eloise thrust a party bag into Victoria's hand. "For Joey."

"I ... thank you."

She looked at Imelda again, wondering if she should explain herself better but she didn't quite know how.

"Thank you for the lovely party. It really was ... lovely."

Why the hell did she keep saying lovely? Was there no other word?

The blonde woman came up to Imelda. "Yes, we've got to get going too," she said. "But thank you. I particularly enjoyed the bruschetta. Perhaps you could give me the recipe?"

"Oh yes," another mum said. "Why don't you share it on the WhatsApp group for the class?"

She flashed a smile at Victoria, who backed away, almost forgetting her handbag in her rush.

Back home, Victoria set the keys down on the counter and flicked on the kettle. While she was waiting for it to boil, she drifted into the lounge, where she sat at the big bay window. She focused on a spot in the distance, her eyes seemingly unable to budge. There was nothing wrong with Joey. Nothing at all. Miss Henley didn't know what she was talking about.

Anna loomed in front of her.

"Mum? I asked what's for dinner? I'm starving."

Victoria looked up sharply. She glanced over at the table, where Joey was hunched over a notebook, headphones clamped to his ears. He held a pencil in his hand, and he was sketching frantically, the pencil making a scratching sound as he worked. She took in what he was drawing, and her eyes flickered in surprise.

"What's that Joey?" Anna asked.

Victoria could see damned well what it was: A life-like drawing of a deer. Except its antlers were twisted and mangled and where its eyes should have been, there were lasers. Joey caught her looking and tore the page out in a fury and tossed it into the fireplace. Then he turned to a new page in his notebook and started all over again.

Anna sat on the sofa, idly watching a cooking programme on TV. Every so often she would flip a page of her book, so that her mum would think that she was revising for her Latin test.

"Mum?"

Her mum didn't answer. She was attacking invisible dust with a feather duster. Anna sometimes wondered if she actually preferred doing the housework to chilling out.

"Mum!" she said louder. "Can I have a lift into town?"

Victoria stopped dusting.

"Why?"

Anna doodled on the carpet with her left leg. "I need some art supplies for my homework."

Victoria sighed. "I'd like to help, darling, but Dad's using the car to pick his boss up from the station."

Anna stopped doodling. "Why don't you use the other car?"

"Anna, I'm the school Environmental Ambassador. We can't be seen to be running two cars."

Anna stifled a laugh. "Are you serious? As if anyone gives

a shit."

Victoria threw her a look.

"Alright, fine. I'll get the bus."

She grabbed her coat and bag and headed for the door.

"How long are you going to be?" her mother called after her.

Anna hesitated. "I don't know. Probably a few hours. I'm going to meet up with Maddie after and we'll probably get a snack or something."

"Will there be anywhere open at that time?"

Anna watched her mum's face carefully. "Maybe that Greek place. I hear the coffee's good?"

"Oh, it is! Quite strong though. Don't drink too much or you won't be able to sleep."

"I can always take one of Joey's gummies."

"I hardly think that's necessary."

Anna reached for her backpack. "Alright, Mum. Laters."

She left the house under her mother's watchful eye. She swung left, walking towards the bus stop, then crossed the street and headed back the other way. Bex was waiting for her outside the train station. A cigarette dangled from her lips. Bex didn't especially like smoking. It was just part of her look, like the stud that protruded from her nose and the beat-up leather jacket she wore whatever the weather.

Bex put out her hand and they bumped fists, then she stubbed out her cigarette and they walked onto the platform.

"Uh-oh," said Anna.

"What?"

"I've just seen one of my mum's friends."

"Has she seen you?"

"I don't think so."

"Let's walk right up to the other end," suggested Bex. "And keep your back turned. You'll be fine."

"I hope so."

The last thing Anna needed was to have her mother's spies reporting that she'd been seen heading off to Guildford when she was supposed to be in Godalming.

"Honestly, you can't fart in this town without someone knowing about it," she complained.

They stood by the bike rack, and Anna tapped her foot, impatient for the train to arrive. Bex opened her bag and rifled through it.

"Here, I did your laundry."

She handed Anna a carrier bag.

"Thanks."

"I can't believe your mum still doesn't know. Why don't you just tell her?"

Anna gripped the bag. "You don't know my mum."

The signal lights changed from red to green and Anna glanced back to check on Portia, but she was busy flirting with the man who sold the coffee. They boarded the train and Anna sank gratefully into her seat. She pulled the red shirt from her bag and slipped it on over her T-shirt. She'd put the baseball cap on when they got there.

It was dark by the time Anna returned home and her feet ached like mad. She saw a black Lexus parked outside the house and remembered that her parents had people over. She groaned inwardly. Her parents' dinner parties were always excruciating. She walked round the back, hoping to slip in quietly through the kitchen, but her mum was there, emptying plastic trays of food onto plates.

"Good, you're home. Quick, help me."

Obediently, Anna picked up a tray. She knew the drill by now. Her mother always had these parties catered, no shame in that but for some reason she felt she had to hide all the evidence and serve up the food as if she'd cooked it herself. It was a bit ridiculous, Anna thought. After all, Victoria was a working mother, not a fifties housewife but she seemed to think that if anyone found out she hadn't cooked everything herself, they would think less of her or something.

"Mum, I'm not really hungry. Can I just go up to my room? I still have homework to do."

"Your dad's boss is here. I need you to come and sit nicely. You don't have to say anything, he does most of the talking. Just smile and nod your head."

"Do I have to?"

"Just for a little while, then you can excuse yourself."

It was the last thing Anna wanted to do, but she took her seat at the table and smiled at Eddie's terrible jokes. He really was a pig, she thought in disgust. She couldn't believe her dad worked for this man. How did he stand it? And there was her mum, falling over herself to top up his glass.

"Can I have a bit of wine?" she asked Victoria. It was about the only thing that would make this dinner bearable.

"You're much too young," her mother said, dismissively.

"Not even a little bit?"

Victoria pretended she hadn't heard.

Eddie had brought a woman along. Anna couldn't remember if she was his wife or girlfriend. There had been a number of them over the years. Some he married, some he didn't. She'd been to at least two of his weddings.

Joey was noticeably absent from the dinner table. He'd been allowed to eat upstairs in his room, the lucky boy. Probably because Victoria didn't want the guests to see him eat chicken nuggets. There was no way he was going to touch any of this fancy stuff.

After they'd eaten the main course, Victoria summoned Joey downstairs to dazzle everyone with his piano playing. He played brilliantly as always, but Anna thought he seemed a little distracted, as though his mind was somewhere else. Once he'd finished playing, the guests erupted in enthusiastic applause. Joey didn't like the noise and clapped his hands over his ears.

Kit turned to Eddie. "Did I tell you I got us a meeting with Adam Walters?"

Anna had no idea who that was but apparently this was a good thing because Eddie slapped her father on the back.

"Nice one!"

Kit shuddered, but quickly recovered his composure. Eddie turned his attention to Joey, who was scuttling past the table, intent on getting back to his room.

"Joey, my man! How's tricks?"

Joey squinted at him, unable to decipher his language.

"Joey just won a major chess tournament," Victoria said.

"Nice one, son!" Eddie leaned forward and gave Joey a slap on the back.

Joey smacked him back, right across the face.

Everyone froze. Anna sucked in her breath. For a moment, she couldn't breathe.

Then Eddie burst out laughing, loud, raucous laughter that had them all laughing too.

The grown-ups moved on to dessert and Anna affected a big yawn and rose from the table.

"I think I'm about ready for bed."

"You can help your mother clear the table first, please," Kit said.

She looked at her dad curiously. He looked tired this evening, leaning heavily against the wall. He maintained a neutral, pleasant expression and he appeared to listen intently to everything that was being said. He kept saying, "That's hysterical!" and his eyes were glazed, as if held open by invisible pins. It surprised her, because she'd always thought her parents loved these dinner parties but to see him now, she could see he was every bit as bored as she was. Her dad was such a workaholic. He had no hobbies that she could think of. What was it all for, if he didn't even like it?

Anna herself was far from enthralled by the conversation. Still, the party would keep her parents occupied all evening. At least, she hoped so, because she had a party of her own to get to. But first, she needed to pick up some alcohol.

Since she had first started drinking, around six months ago, Anna had discovered that it was fairly easy to nick the odd bottle without her parents noticing. The first time she'd done it, she hadn't actually drunk the wine. She'd just hidden it in her room for a couple of weeks to see if anybody said anything, and when they didn't she took it to the park where she, Bex and Dina had had the best night of their lives.

She headed into the kitchen and stood in front of the wine fridge. Her parents had already served quite a few wines tonight, but the bottom row was still intact. There were lots of red bottles left, but Anna didn't like red. She wanted white.

***

Victoria walked in, carrying a pile of dishes and Anna retreated. "Going up to bed," she told her mother.

"Make sure you finish your homework," Victoria said with a nod. "You can leave it out for me to check if you want."

Why was her mum so obsessed with her homework? Bex's mum didn't give a stuff about hers.

She walked out to the hallway, pausing briefly in front of the coats. She would have to get going soon, if she was going to get to the party, but she couldn't go empty handed. She had money. Perhaps she could ask some older kids to buy her a bottle? But then she ran the risk that they might just steal her money. It had happened to Dina once and it had totally sucked.

Then she remembered the garage. Didn't her parents have a wine rack in there? She darted a glance towards the lounge. Her parents were still busy with their guests. Quickly, she retrieved the keys from the drawer and snuck outside, pulling the door closed behind her.

The garage was a small brick building positioned to one side of the house. You could see it from the lounge window if you happened to be looking that way. Hopefully nobody was. She heard a fresh burst of laughter, as Eddie told one of his outrageous jokes. That man really did need a kick in the balls.

She slid the key into the lock. A huge cobweb hung like a washing line across the doors. In a silly, paranoid corner of her mind she thought perhaps her parents had put it there, as a booby trap so they'd know if she nicked their wine.

It was a double garage, large enough for her parents to park both their cars but at some point, her dad had decided he couldn't be bothered with all the opening and closing of the doors so now he parked his car out on the street.

Darting one last glance back at the house, Anna unlocked the garage. There was a clink, clank, clunk as the rusted spring coils rubbed together. She was afraid the doors would get stuck but slowly they opened and she peered inside.

The light flickered like a bad horror film, illuminating the dark, damp space. She kept an eye out for the spider that had spun the web. She could see the wine rack. It was well stocked with bottles, though she couldn't make out which were white and which were red. She took a step towards it.

Then her eye fell on her mother's Volvo. The glass on the front windshield was fractured in an intricate vein-like pattern and there was a massive dent on the bumper, as if someone had taken a bowling ball and dropped it from a great height. Anna swallowed a gasp and backed away. She had a horrible feeling that she wasn't meant to have seen this.

10

JOEY'S DIARY

1.36 AM
I heard someone creeping about downstairs. I'm going to take
my cricket bat and investigate. I'll use stealth mode so they
don't hear me.

1.49 AM
It was just Dad. He was walking up and down the lounge, like
a broken robot who needed his batteries taken out. He asked
me what I was doing up so I asked him what he was doing up.
He smiled and said, "Fair point." Then he went into the
kitchen and took some vitamins. His ones are different to
mine. He said they taste like stinky blue cheese whereas mine
are quite nice because they're gummies. I didn't tell him I've
stopped taking them. I don't want him to tell Mum. She still
thinks I'm a little kid but I'm not. I'm getting quite big now.
I asked Dad if he wanted to play chess but he waved his hand
at me and told me to go back to bed. He didn't come upstairs
though. I think he must have gone to sleep in the lounge
because the house has started to rumble again. I wonder if he
thinks about the deer too.

11

ANNA

Anna woke up in a fog. She reached for the glass of water on her bedside table and downed it. Her phone beeped and she grabbed it from the charger under her bed. She giggled as she saw a text from Bex. There were pictures from the party: Harley and Bex making faces at the camera, Dina snogging that boy, Anna chugging beer from a funnel. She slipped the phone into her pocket and headed to the bathroom. Her mum would have kittens if she knew.

Downstairs, she found Victoria cooking sausages. The smell turned her stomach. She pushed past Joey to get to the toaster.

"Come on, Joey," Victoria cooed. "You need to eat up."

"My cereal tastes weird," he complained. He pushed his bowl away as if the sight of it repulsed him.

"Joey, it's the exact same cereal you always have."

"It tastes all wrong."

"The sausages are ready." Victoria plonked them on a plate.

"I want cereal."

"Joey, I don't care if you have cereal, toast or sausages. Just have something."

"The sausages are too hot."

"Then blow on them."

Anna's toast popped and she pulled it out of the toaster, slathering it with butter and jam. She ate hurriedly, standing by the sink.

"I wish you'd sit down," Victoria said.

"No time." Anna glanced at Joey and his sausages. He still wasn't eating.

"Why don't you go and get ready while they cool down?" Victoria suggested.

To Anna's surprise, Joey actually did as he was told. She suspected he just wanted to get back to his computer, but she was glad he was gone. It was too weird, the way he sat there watching the spirals of steam. Victoria moved on to preparing their lunches.

"Mum?"

"Yes?"

"What happened to your car? I saw it when I was looking for . . . the turpentine."

Victoria stopped chopping the chicken. She released an odd little laugh that sounded as though she'd just swallowed gas. "It's a bit embarrassing really . . ."

"What is?"

"I hit a deer. I couldn't stop in time. It came out of nowhere."

"Oh no! Was it hurt?"

"The deer was fine. It's my car that took a beating."

"Yeah, it's a wreck."

"I know. Do you know how much one of those things weighs? Anyway, don't tell anyone, will you?"

Anna met her mother's eyes. "Why not?"

"It's a bit embarrassing. I don't want people making jokes about it. My reputation is at stake."

"If you say so," Anna said slowly. "I really don't see why—"

"Hey, did you finish your Latin?"

"I'll do it later. I have time before class."

"Alright but don't go leaving it till the last minute."

"Are you okay?" Maddie asked in biology, as Anna laid her head down on the desk.

"Fine," Anna answered. She wondered how Maddie would react if she told her she was actually hung-over. Maddie wouldn't dream of drinking alcohol or sneaking out to a party that didn't finish until after midnight.

"Today, we'll be looking at levels of organisation within an ecosystem," the teacher announced. Anna's eyelids felt heavy. She could hear Maddie scribbling notes in her exercise book.

". . . for example, the male deer compete for mates by locking antlers and pushing one another . . ."

Deer, Anna thought and her mind catapulted back to her mother's confession. What a state her car was in. She couldn't understand why her parents hadn't got it fixed. It was so weird that her drama queen mum had kept quiet about it. Victoria didn't get a ladder in her stockings without throwing a wobbler. It seemed bizarre that this big, scary thing had happened to her and she hadn't breathed a word. She watched as an image of a deer appeared on the screen at the front of the class. The teacher zoomed in a little too close, so that the deer appeared to be staring at them. An amused murmur rose from her classmates but the longer Anna looked at it, the more unsettled she felt.

"Anna! Anna, wake up. The lesson's over!"

Anna opened her eyes. All around her, the students were gathering their books and legging it out the door.

"Are you coming to the canteen?" Maddie asked.

Anna shook her head. "Sorry, I told my mum I'd come home for lunch."

Maddie's face drooped and Anna felt momentarily bad. She knew Maddie didn't have any other friends to eat lunch with, but she really needed to find out why her mum was bullshitting her.

Come to think of it, why hadn't her dad said anything? Even if her mum was embarrassed, Dad usually saw the funny side. Perhaps that's why the car was still sitting in the garage. Perhaps he didn't know.

"Hello? Mum?"

Anna rang the doorbell. She was beginning to regret her impulsive decision to come home. Her mum was usually home during the day but occasionally she'd be off somewhere running errands or teaching and Anna hadn't thought to bring her key.

She leaned on the door, then to her relief she heard footsteps on the stairs. She looked through the glass panelling and caught her mother checking her appearance in the hall mirror.

"Mum, it's just me!" she called out with impatience. "You don't have to fluff your bloody hair."

Victoria opened the door. "I do wish you wouldn't talk like that. What's wrong, have you forgotten something?"

Anna shook her head. "No, I just thought it would be nice to come home for lunch. Unless you don't want to have lunch with me?"

"No. No of course I do, don't be silly. Come on, let's eat."

Anna watched as her mother dished up salmon quiche on willow patterned plates with a sprinkling of salad on the side. Victoria paused to take a photo. It was second nature to her, the photography, as natural as adding a dash of milk to her tea.

"How are you getting on with your Latin?" she asked.

Anna felt a stab of irritation. Couldn't she talk about anything else? She tasted the quiche. It was delicious. She wolfed it down in three bites and her mother automatically served her more. She'd barely touched her own.

Anna noted the dark rings under her mother's eyes.

"Joey told me about the car," she said, seized by inspiration, because she had a feeling that whatever had gone on, Joey knew about it.

Victoria's jaw went slack. "Joey doesn't know what he's talking about."

Anna didn't take her eyes off her mum. Her mind whirled. When Victoria had dropped her off for the French trip, she'd been driving her own car, but when she'd picked her up, she'd been in her dad's car. She'd thought it a bit strange at the time, but she'd been tired and keen to get home. Victoria hadn't driven her own car since, so whatever had happened, it had been while she was away. She tried again.

"Joey told me you didn't go to the Greek restaurant. Why did you say you did?"

Victoria looked at her quiche like it was a quivering pile of slugs.

"How did the car get so dented?"

"I told you, I hit a deer."

"Try again."

Victoria's shoulders slumped. "If you must know, I hit a tree to avoid the deer."

"So what damaged the car? The tree or the deer?"

"A bit of both I should think."

Anna tilted back her chair. "Why are you making stuff up, Mum? Why don't you just tell me what's going on?"

Victoria gave her an anguished look. Her face looked so pinched Anna was worried. She laid her hand on top of her mother's.

"Come on. You can tell me."

Her mother let out a deep sigh and leaned closer, conspiratorial now. "You're a bright girl, Anna. I should have known I couldn't hide it from you."

"Hide what?"

"It was while you were on the French trip. We were on our way to the Greek restaurant for their opening night."

Anna nodded, in what she hoped was an encouraging manner.

"Just as we were leaving the house, I noticed someone had moved into that big house behind ours."

Anna sat up. "That's where that footballer lives, isn't it?"

Victoria nodded and Anna remembered how excited her mother had been when she'd discovered they'd have a celebrity in their midst. Paul Schooner had retired years ago, but he was still well known.

"I saw the gates to his house were open, so on impulse, I turned into his drive."

"You didn't!"

"Well, why not? I thought it would be nice to welcome him to the neighbourhood. It seemed like the neighbourly thing to do."

Anna's eyes widened. "Did you meet him?"

"We did. He was ever so nice. He was pleased to meet Joey. Apparently, he has two daughters around the same age. I was hoping they'd be going to St Bernard's but he's got them in at Orchard Fields, you know, the private school."

Anna nodded.

"Anyway, we stopped and chatted for a while and then we headed off for the Greek restaurant. We hadn't gone more than a mile or so up the road when something shot out in front of me. I thought it was a deer but . . ."

Victoria looked down at her nails. She seemed to struggle for words.

"What was it?" Anna asked, gently.

Victoria lowered her eyes. "It was a cyclist."

"What?"

"I didn't realise it at the time, but it was James Solomon, Belinda's husband."

Anna dropped her mother's hand. "The man who . . . died?"

All at once, her ribs felt too tight. She tasted acid in her mouth and an invisible flame scorched her throat.

"Oh, Anna. You don't know what a relief it is, finally being able to talk to someone about it! It was his own silly fault, of course, riding down those narrow country lanes in the dark. I didn't see him until it was too late. And then . . . what could I do?"

"What did you do, Mum?"

"I drove back home as fast as I could, and we hid the car in the garage. It was just awful. I didn't sleep a wink."

"Didn't you help him?"

"What could we do? When we got home, your father took the other car and drove to a pay phone to call for an ambulance. He never gave his name of course. He just said there had been an accident."

"What about Joey? Was he in the car with you?"

Victoria pressed her lips tightly together. "We told him . . . we told him we'd hit a deer."

"I see."

They both sat very still. Then Anna forced herself to her feet.

"Mum, I've just noticed the time. I have to run."

She picked up her bag and hurried from the house on trembling legs. She waited until she was halfway down the road, then she pulled out her phone. Her fingers shook badly as she texted Bex.

Anna: I think my mum is a murderer.

Halfway down the road, Anna changed her mind. She couldn't face school. She didn't feel right. Her palms were sweaty, and she was very aware of her heart pumping in her chest, almost as if it were trying to beat out a message. She turned abruptly and walked back towards the bus stop. The 46 would be along in ten minutes. She sat down on the bench, letting her hair hang over her face. She didn't want any of her mum's nosy friends to stop and ask what she was doing.

She texted Maddie and asked her to cover for her. Maddie would freak, of course but she'd do it.

No one paid Anna the slightest bit of notice as she walked into the town library and logged on to one of the computers. She thought for a minute, then typed in "James Solomon, hit and run," which led her instantly to the local paper. Her hand was slippery as she reached for the mouse:

Father of one critical after road collision

Anna's scalp prickled. She read on:

*Cyclist, James Solomon, 39, is fighting for his life in the
Royal Surrey Hospital, following a serious road collision.
The father of one was found in a back road near Loseley
Park on Friday, 9 February. Sources say the next 24 hours
will be critical. Police believe the driver of the car that hit
him fled the scene without assisting the injured man.*

*Detective Lisa Rendall said: "Our investigation is ongoing
and we are keen to hear from anyone who was in the area
at the time, especially any motorists with dashcam as this
could assist us with building a clear picture of the moments
leading up to the crash. This was a very serious incident
which has left a man fighting for his life."*

Beneath the article was a picture of James's mangled bike.
It was in two pieces and one of the wheels had snapped in
half. A wave of revulsion ripped through her, but she clicked
on the next article.

Local man dies after hit and run.

*Police have confirmed that a cyclist found in a critical
condition in a country road near Godalming was James
Solomon, a senior executive officer with Wirral and Sons.
James was killed in a hit and run collision with an
unknown vehicle. James, who is an experienced cyclist,
was travelling home from work at the time. It is believed
that the accident happened around 6pm on 9 February.*

*One local resident described the incident as shocking and
said that James's family deserved answers.
"It's always been a tricky junction, very poorly lit. You can
see how it could happen. But to just drive off like that –
that's shocking."*

*James's best friend described him as a "lovely, lovely man",
and his family are said to be devastated at the news. James
is survived by his wife, Belinda, and ten-year-old son,
Richard.*

*Police are examining CCTV footage and speaking to
witnesses in the area. Anyone with information should
contact the police or speak confidentially to Crimestoppers.*

*Road closures remain in place whilst road collision recon-
struction officers investigate.*

Anna clicked away from the article and blew the air out
slowly through her mouth.

"You okay?" a passing librarian asked.

"Yes, fine."

Anna cleared the browser history and packed up her
belongings, then hurried out of the library, taking the footpath that led down to the park. She found a large stone and
hurled it into the river, startling the geese. An old woman
shot her a disapproving look but she kept on walking, faster
and faster until her walk turned into a run. Her backpack
jiggled up and down. She jogged to the other end of the park
and started back again, puffing and panting. Eventually she
slowed down and leaned against a tree. How could her mum
live like this, day in, day out, knowing what she had done? It
had only been a couple of hours and already Anna felt like
she was losing her mind.

On her way back home, Anna stopped at the florists and
bought a bunch of lilies. She didn't know the first thing about
flowers, but lilies were for dead people, weren't they? And
they looked kind of nice. Maybe she could lay them on
James's grave.

She pulled out her phone and searched for the location.

According to Google, James Solomon had a memorial stone in the crematorium. She knew where that was. They often drove past it in the car. She clutched the flowers and began to walk.

As she approached the crematorium, Anna's confidence waned. She looked at the lush green grass and the simple stones. It was too quiet. The whole place was . . . dead. She couldn't see anyone about, but there was a building. Surely someone would know where to find James? She wanted to go and ask, but what if they asked her why? She wasn't a relative. She hadn't even known him. And she was meant to be at school. She took a few faltering steps, but she found the silence a little eerie and she had the strangest feeling she was being watched. It was an odd sensation, like a trickle down her back. Then she heard the sound of a car approaching and almost jumped out of her skin. She darted quickly out of the way and scurried back towards the gate. She kept on walking, clutching the bunch of lilies in her fist.

Victoria was listening to music when Anna got home, something classical and upbeat, like a waltz. Anna stood in the doorway, watching as her mother floated around the kitchen like a great weight had been lifted from her shoulders. She clenched her lilies tightly and forced herself to step inside.

"Mum?"

When her mum saw Anna, she smiled broadly and tried to twirl her around. It was all too much for Anna. Her mother's music sliced right through her skull.

Victoria patted a stool and beckoned Anna to come and sit with her. Anna sat down heavily and laid the flowers on the table.

"Oh, you bought lilies! How lovely!" Victoria swept them up and plopped them into an empty vase.

"No, Mum, I . . ."

Victoria wasn't listening. Now she was rattling around in the kitchen. Anna heard the clinking of spoons and the sound of the cupboard opening and closing. Her mother returned with the teapot and two cups. Without asking, her mother poured her a cup of tea. She didn't particularly want it, but she took a sip anyway. Sometimes it was easier not to argue.

"Where's Joey?"

Her mother's smile dropped. "Joey's feeling a little . . . sensitive."

"He's having a tantrum, you mean?"

"He didn't like the crisps I bought so he emptied the bookshelf all over the floor and stomped up to his room."

Anna couldn't understand for the life of her why Joey was allowed to get away with behaving like that, but Victoria seemed ready to excuse anything he did because he was "gifted". Anna wasn't convinced Joey was gifted. He just had very particular interests. If she did nothing but play chess or piano for hours on end, she'd probably be good too.

"It was so nice to talk earlier," Victoria said, her eyes bright. "It's been such a struggle all these months. Of course, I had your dad, but he's always at work, you know, and he's been in so much pain . . ."

Anna stared at her. "That's how he hurt his back, isn't it? In the accident?"

Victoria shifted uncomfortably. "Well yes, but you know what men are like. The slightest whiff of pain and they're pathetic. Us women just get on with it, don't we? Well, we bloody well have to." She took a thoughtful sip of her tea and looked at Anna a little more closely.

"You look a little pale, darling. Are you worried about your coursework?"

"No, Mum . . ."

"I remember what it was like. So much work to do and so

little time, but don't worry I can help you. You drink your tea and then we'll get started, shall we? We still have an hour before Latin."

Anna rubbed her temples as Victoria fussed about fetching biscuits and textbooks. Did she not care that she had killed a man? How could she just carry on like this, as if nothing had happened?

"Now, this is actually quite fun," Victoria said. "We've got to choose a family motto."

Anna looked down the long list in her book. "I like this one. *Non ducor, duco.*"

"I am not led, I lead," Victoria translated.

"Or what about this: *Qui totum vult totum perdit* – He who wants everything, loses everything."

Victoria shook her head. "No, this is perfect. Look. *Familia supra omnia.*"

"What does that mean?"

"Family over everything."

Anna shrugged and her mother wrote it down.

Latin was taught as an evening class in Guildford. The rest of the students were adults and they'd only let Anna join because her mum was on the course, a fact Victoria failed to mention when she told everyone Anna was doing A-level Latin. So far, they had worked together on all the coursework. Anna wondered what they were going to do when it was time to take the exams. Was Victoria going to sit behind her and whisper the answers?

Victoria worked through the rest of the homework with barely any involvement from Anna.

"Right," she said, as she finished the last exercise. "That's that done. Why don't you go and change? Pop into the bathroom while you're at it and splash some water on your face. You really could use a little colour."

"Mum, I'm not sure if I'm up to going to class tonight. I've got a bit of a headache."

Victoria frowned. "I thought you looked a little pale. Wait there, I can give you something for that."

She walked into the kitchen and returned with a pill and a glass of water.

"What is this?"

"It's just like aspirin, only a little stronger."

"Should I be taking this?"

"Honestly, it's fine. That headache will be gone in no time."

Anna looked at the pill doubtfully. It looked like one of the ones her dad took for his back pain. Weren't they meant to be really strong?

"Trust me," Victoria said. "It'll work."

Anna felt a knot in her stomach. "Why don't you go to the class without me? I can look at your notes."

Victoria's lips twitched. "I think you should make the effort. Take the pill, Anna. I promise you, you'll feel much better."

Anna popped the pill in her mouth then she headed up to her room where she spat it into the bin.

As she was coming back downstairs, she saw Victoria talking to someone at the door. Her body language looked stiff and unwelcoming. She shut the door firmly and folded her arms.

"Who was that?" Anna asked.

"Some girl, asking for you. I told her we were about to leave for Latin."

"For me? Why didn't you let me speak to her myself?"

"I didn't even recognise her," Victoria said, reaching for her handbag.

"What did she look like?"

"She had a disgusting piercing in her nose."

Bex! Anna kept her face neutral. "Doesn't sound like anyone I know."

Victoria looked at her closely. "She asked for you by name."

Anna kept her voice level. "I can't imagine who she was. They don't allow piercings at my school."

"That's what I thought."

Anna ventured to the door, but Bex was nowhere to be seen.

"I just need to pop to the loo," Anna said, setting down her books.

"Oh, Anna. I thought you'd already done all that! Well, go on then, hurry up, we don't want to be late."

Anna ducked into the bathroom and closed the door. She pulled the phone from her pocket.

Anna: Soz about Mum. We're going out now but I can meet after?

Bex: R you going 2B OK with her? I'm really worried about U.

Anna: I'll B OK. Laters.

Anna immediately felt guilty. This was her mum they were talking about. Of course she would be safe with her.

She heard her dad in the hallway and she walked out to greet him.

"Hi, Anna, have a good time at Latin!"

"We will," Victoria sang.

Anna waved goodbye and followed her mum out to the car. She swallowed hard as she fastened her seat belt. She watched Victoria turn on the engine. How could she do that so calmly, knowing she had killed someone? If it was Anna, she would never drive again.

She sucked in her breath as her mother drove round the corner. They headed across the main road and Anna almost gasped. Surely her mother wasn't going to take the country road? But she was. They were on the very road where the accident had taken place, heading towards The Dip.

The council had cut back the foliage so it was easier to see the road ahead. A wilted bunch of flowers was tied to a tree with a bright red ribbon to mark the spot where the accident had happened and there was a wine-coloured stain on the ground. Anna's stomach lurched. Was that his blood?

Her mum must have noticed as they drove past, but she kept up a constant flow of chatter. Anna gazed out the window, wondering how her dad could be complicit. She could just about believe that her mum had done this terrible thing, but her dad? It seemed unbelievable.

———

CHEESE AND GARLIC wafted through the house on their return. It was Kit's night to cook, which meant he'd ordered a take-away pizza. She found Joey picking all the cheese off his slice.

"I thought you liked cheese," Anna queried as she poured herself a drink.

"Not this kind of cheese," he said, looking disgruntled.

Kit shrugged and handed her a napkin. Anna ate her food fast then excused herself from the table. Bex was waiting for her in the garden. She stood quite blatantly in front of the garage, smoking a roll-up.

It was her turn to clear-up but she was hoping her mum would do it for her. She'd been all nicey-nicey this evening, like she thought they were friends, rather than mother and daughter.

Anna still had the garage keys in her coat pocket. She unlocked the door and waited. Clink, clank, clunk. Finally, the doors opened and on came the lights.

"Just look at it," she said, pointing Bex towards the damaged car.

"That's quite a wreck!"

"Wait till I tell you how it happened."

Bex's eyes went to the wine rack. "Do you think your parents would miss one of those?"

"Don't really care if they do."

Anna grabbed a bottle and twisted the lid off. Then she proceeded to tell Bex the whole story.

"Someone set up a fundraising page for him and there was a picture of him in the ICU. He had his eyes closed and there was a big tube coming out of his mouth, but they were really fighting for him, all those doctors and nurses. They operated and everything but in the end they just couldn't save him."

She gripped the bottle tightly as fresh anger flooded her veins.

"And do you know what my mum did? She went on Instagram and posted lies about going to the opening of the Greek restaurant. That's psychotic, isn't it? She should have stayed with him and given him first aid, but all she could think about was covering her arse."

She swallowed hard, hating the way the acid crept back up her throat. "All this time, my mum's just carrying on like nothing happened."

"Evil bitch," Bex said, without smiling. She looked at Anna. "We should do something. We should go and see James's wife and tell her what we know."

"I'm not sure about that," Anna said. "I need to think it through."

Bex gave her a hard look. "What is there to think about? A

man died, Anna. We can't just let her get away with this. One way or another, she needs to be punished."

Anna nodded slowly. "You know what? Mrs Solomon is coming over to my house tomorrow. My mum's giving her son piano lessons."

"How charitable of her."

"Not charitable at all. She's paying good money."

Bex's nostrils flared. "You have to say something."

"I don't know . . ." Anna said. "If I tell her my mum will go to prison."

"Your mum should go to prison."

"I know, but she's my mum?"

"You asked me what you should do."

"No, I told you what happened. She's my mum. I really need to think this through."

"Seems pretty simple to me."

They eyed one another grimly, then Bex took the bottle and drank in angry silence.

13

Victoria was teaching an elderly lady called Louisa the following morning. While most of her students came to her, she made an exception for Louisa, driving out to her house at the top of Farncombe Hill. Louisa had a beautiful old Eberhardt piano, and she played it with great care, like she was stroking the hands of a loved one.

"Come in, come in," Louisa said, when Victoria arrived at her house.

Her hands were stiff and shaky, but she could still get a tune out of the piano nonetheless. Victoria settled beside her and listened as she began to play. She winced as Louisa hit a bum note.

"Can I start again?" Louisa asked.

"By all means."

The music flowed more easily the second time and Victoria's mind drifted. She wasn't seeing Louisa anymore. She saw a dark, narrow lane, lined with trees that leaned inward in a great green arch.

"Do you think he liked us?" she was asking Kit. "Do you think we made a good impression?"

"Of course, he liked us," Kit said with so much confidence that Victoria burst out laughing.

"What's so funny?" demanded Joey from the back.

"I am," said Kit, his smile a little broader. He reached across and squeezed Victoria's knee and she glanced at him, just for a moment.

They had been so happy, so in love.

"So, what did you think, dear?"

"Deer?"

Victoria blinked. Then she remembered where she was. Louisa was looking at her, waiting patiently for her to deliver her verdict.

"I think," she said, after some consideration, "that I'd like to hear it again, but this time a little faster."

If Louisa was surprised, she didn't show it. Victoria closed her eyes and tried to concentrate on the music this time.

"YOU DON'T HAVE TO STAY," Victoria told Belinda on Friday afternoon. "It's perfectly okay if you'd like to have a bit of time for yourself whilst Ricky has his lesson."

"No, that's fine," Belinda said, striding into the lounge. "I don't have anywhere I need to be."

Anna skipped down the stairs. She stopped abruptly when she saw Belinda. Stopped and stared. *Snap out of it!* Victoria scolded her silently. Anna looked like she was in a trance.

"Why don't you put the kettle on?" Victoria said through her teeth.

"Right!" Anna appeared to come unstuck. She drifted off to the kitchen.

Belinda raised an eyebrow. "You've got her well trained."

"Oh yes, she's such a good girl and I thought the teenage years were meant to be the worst!"

"That gives me some hope," Belinda said. She settled in the same chair as she had last time and her eyes scanned the walls. Why did she do that? What was she looking for?

Victoria had told Joey to stay in his room, so as not to disrupt the lesson but here he was charging down the stairs. He and Ricky grinned at one another.

"You can begin when you're ready," she told Ricky, setting the music in front of him.

"Why don't we play chess?" Belinda said to Joey.

"Okay, if you don't mind losing."

Anna came in with the tea and set it down next to Belinda. Victoria wanted her to leave, but instead she loitered by the bookcase until Victoria caught her eye, then she folded herself into a chair and watched the lesson.

Ricky was a little less enthusiastic this week. He played well but seemed keen to skip to the end. Victoria saw that he was getting bored and placed a new piece in front of him, one that she thought he might enjoy. Belinda seemed more relaxed this time. She didn't watch as closely as Victoria instructed her son but Victoria felt her presence all the same. She tried to act normal, but her shoulders stiffened whenever Belinda was around and she could never quite make her arms hang naturally.

"Very good, Ricky. I think that will do for today."

She had expressly forbidden Joey from taking Ricky up to his room, but no sooner had she closed the piano book than the two boys were hurling themselves up the stairs like they were taking part in a steeple chase.

She turned to Belinda. She'd always prided herself on her ability to talk to anyone but now, looking at this woman, she couldn't think of a single thing to say.

"More tea?" Anna asked from her chair.

"No, thank you," Belinda said. "We really ought to get going. How much do I owe you, Victoria?"

"Oh, it's twenty pounds per lesson," Victoria said. "But most of my students pay at the end of term."

"So you'll invoice me?"

"Er, yes. If you like."

Victoria picked up the tea things and carried them out to the kitchen. She took her time rinsing out the teapot and washing the cups, even though she had a perfectly good dishwasher.

"They're getting on well, aren't they?"

The hairs on the back of her neck prickled. Belinda was standing in the doorway. Victoria felt like she'd invaded her inner sanctum, stepping into her kitchen like this.

"Joey clearly enjoys his company," she acknowledged. She wanted to pretend Joey had other friends, but perhaps Belinda had noticed how solitary he was. Perhaps she'd asked her son to play with him.

Belinda's gaze drifted from the lavender curtains to the copper saucepans hanging above the stove. She studied every inch of the walls as if she was taking inventory.

"How do you think Ricky's doing?"

"I think he plays very well," Victoria said. "If he continues to practise, he could be very good indeed." She wrung out the dish towel and turned to hang it on the hook.

"He'll never be as good as your Joey."

"I'll never be as good as Joey either."

"You're very accomplished though. I heard you play in assembly once. You were very good."

"Thank you."

She found it almost impossible to look the other woman in the eye. She had such sad eyes: they were a pale misty grey, as if all the colour had leaked out of them.

Belinda looked at her watch.

"Time to go, Ricky!" she called up the stairs. "Ricky James Solomon!"

Victoria shuddered at the very mention of his name.

Moments later, Ricky padded down the stairs.

"Same time next week?" she said to Belinda, and immediately wanted to smack herself. She was still searching for a reason to stop the lessons and here she was, inviting them back.

"Yes, see you next week," Belinda said. She looked at Anna, who sat quietly in the armchair, curled up like a cat. "Thank you for the tea."

Victoria closed the door behind them, feeling instantly drained. Anna jumped up and walked into the kitchen, opening and shutting the freezer, pulling out ready meals.

"What are you doing?" Victoria asked.

"What does it look like? Making dinner."

"I was going to make lamb."

"I want to eat now, not in three bloody hours."

Anna slammed the microwave shut with such force that the copper pans rattled.

"Is something wrong?"

Anna shot her a dark look. "Why would anything be wrong?"

Victoria laid a hand on her shoulder. "Come on now . . ."

"That was so awkward!" she burst out. "Tiptoeing around that woman as if—" She stopped talking abruptly and bit her tongue. "Anyway. I've got homework to do."

"I can help you if you like."

"No, thank you. You can watch the microwave. Check the food doesn't burn."

Victoria watched as Anna stomped up the stairs to her room. It was most disconcerting. She knew her daughter was under a lot of pressure but it wasn't like her to snap. Could it be the accident that was concerning her? Perhaps she was worried about Victoria getting into trouble? But no, Belinda hadn't said anything. They were fine, just as long as they all kept their mouths shut. More likely, Anna was worried about her coursework. Studying didn't come naturally to her like it did Joey. Perhaps she needed some help. Some kind of pills to help her concentrate. She'd have a look online.

Anna seemed calmer when she came down for dinner. Kit wasn't home yet so Victoria put his plate in the oven. Joey brought his chess strategy book to the table and barely looked up for the whole meal but she didn't attempt to stop him. She was dog-tired and it was Friday night. All she wanted to do was put her feet up and enjoy a glass of wine.

"You know, I haven't seen Maddie for a while. Why don't you invite her over? Perhaps you'd like a sleepover?"

A harried look crossed Anna's face. Victoria didn't get it. Sleepovers had been Anna's favourite thing not so long ago. The mere suggestion of one would have had her dancing around the room. Now, she seemed too cool to care.

Later, she went up to her daughter's room to check on her. Anna's glare surprised her.

"Don't you ever knock?"

Victoria swallowed. "Sorry, darling. I just wanted to say goodnight." She straightened Anna's duvet so that it sat neatly on the bed. "You should be getting to bed soon."

"It's Friday night!"

"I know, but you still need your beauty sleep. Have you made a start on your Latin yet?"

Anna turned and looked at her. Her left cheek trembled slightly, as if she was having a muscle spasm.

"I don't even want to do bloody Latin, Mum! In fact, what I really want to do is drop it. I'm not going anymore. I'm sick of it. No one else has to go."

Victoria's mouth fell open. "I know it's hard, darling, but it will look so good on your university application forms. It will give you an edge."

"I don't have to worry about that yet. I've got three years, Mum!"

"It will go faster than you think."

"Stop trying to run my life! I'm sick of it!"

Victoria took a step back. Why was she being so vile? She had always been such a bubbly, energetic child, but right now she didn't recognise her at all.

"Everything I do, I do it for you," she said quietly.

"Well, I'm dropping Latin."

Victoria opened and closed her mouth. "You can't!"

"Can't I?"

Victoria's hand flew to her chest. She'd never heard such defiance before, not from Anna.

Anna tilted her head back, her chin raised. She stared at her mother, right between the eyes.

Victoria backed out of the room. There was no point arguing about this now, not when Anna had got herself worked up into such a state. She would talk to the girl in the morning, once she'd had a good night's sleep. She had to make her see sense, because even with all her help, Anna's marks were not going to cut it. Her exam grades always let her down. That was why she needed something extra. Something to impress.

She said good night to Joey and plodded downstairs. Kit was late, but there had been no text to say when he'd be home. She flopped down in front of the TV, flicking through the channels until she found something to watch. She had an unsettled feeling in her stomach, like everything was about to unravel.

She lay half asleep on the sofa, waiting for Kit to come home. Her programme finished, but she left the TV on for company. She could never sleep properly until she knew everyone was home. Her eyes were closed, her breath coming in a slow, easy rhythm, when she heard a tapping at the window. She opened her eyes. There it was again, three distinct taps, then silence.

She pulled her cardigan around her. If that was Kit, she needed to let him in. But what if it wasn't? It seemed strange that he would be tapping on the window like that. If he'd forgotten his key, why not knock on the door? She froze with indecision. She was alone with the children, and their house was separated from the next one by high hedges and long lawns on either side. If an intruder was out there, she could be in trouble.

A bang at the door had her leaping back behind the sofa. There was a click and then another bang. It sounded like someone was kicking the door in. With trembling hands, she grabbed her phone from the table.

"Vic?"

It was just Kit! She ran to let him in. The moment she opened the door, he slumped heavily against her. The smell of whisky was unmistakable on his breath. She helped him to steady himself and steered him over to the sofa, where he dropped like a dead weight.

"Kit!"

She tried to shake him awake, but it was useless. He was wasted. His shirt was soaked in sweat and his breathing was slow and noisy. She ran a hand through his thick, unruly hair and returned to the door to bolt it, still not entirely over her fright. Then she covered Kit with a blanket and left him to sleep it off.

In the morning, Victoria headed straight downstairs to check on him. As it was a Saturday, neither of the children had left their rooms yet. Anna was comatose and she'd heard Joey playing chess on his computer. All the same, she didn't want them seeing their father like this.

"Kit!" she whispered. "Come upstairs. It's morning."

Kit opened one bleary eye. "I'm broken," he groaned.

"You're telling me."

His eyes widened and he gripped her wrist. "I mean it, Vic. My back is killing me, and I had to entertain clients last night. Between the pills and the drink, my liver is shot."

She rubbed his shoulder gently. "Are you hungry? I kept you some dinner..."

"I don't need food. I need a doctor. A proper one."

Victoria swallowed. "Are you sure? I mean, we don't want the doctor asking how you hurt your back?"

Kit rubbed his eyes. "It's been four months, Vic. Four bloody months."

"I know, I know ..." She glanced at the door, concerned that Joey might hear.

Kit lowered his voice. "Serves me right, doesn't it?"

"What?"

"Because I didn't do anything. I mean, I could have made you go back that night, but I didn't, did I? So perhaps this is my penance."

"Now you're being ridiculous. It was an accident."

He heaved a sigh. "I'm still going to have to go to the doctor. I can't carry on like this, I really can't."

Victoria searched for a reason to talk him out of it but she knew she was being paranoid. There was no reason why the doctor would link his injury to the accident, and yet, it felt as though more and more of her secret was slipping away.

14

JOEY'S DIARY

Things I like about Ricky's mum:

1. She plays chess, even though she's rubbish.
2. She listens.
3. She always tells the truth.

15

"This way, ladies and gents."

Victoria trotted along in her heels, struggling to keep up with Kit's boss. She suspected Eddie did this on purpose, taking lengthy strides with his long legs, forcing everyone else to chase him.

Joey didn't even attempt to keep up. If Kit didn't have him firmly by the hand, he'd still be standing in the car park, gazing at his shoes. Eddie led them to a "VIP" entrance and in they went.

The sun was shining brightly. Even the clouds appeared to have been arranged neatly in the sky so that they were plumped and fluffy and evenly displayed. Victoria felt a wave of pleasure as she gazed around. She noted the women in their splendid dresses and the men in their top hats. Ascot was a bit pompous for Kit's taste, but Eddie insisted it was the perfect venue to entertain clients and Victoria could see why.

Eddie's girlfriend, a different one from the woman he'd brought to dinner, told her that the queen would be here today. Victoria felt as though her body was flowing with electricity, crackling and sparking with excitement.

Kit had barely said a word. He seemed put out that they had to do this on Father's Day, when he would have preferred a quiet day at home with the kids. He'd had another rough night, the pills not doing their job, and was still set on going to the doctor first thing on Monday. He looked so run-down that she'd had to dab some concealer under his eyes before they set off.

Eddie stopped talking abruptly.

"What do you think, Kit?"

Kit blinked at him. Victoria could tell that he hadn't been listening.

"It will be fun to go and look at the horses, don't you think?" she prompted.

Kit looked at her vaguely. "Er, yeah."

Eddie studied him with concern. "You alright, mate? You look a bit peaky."

"I'm right as rain," Kit said, forcing a smile. "Just overdid it a bit last night."

Eddie grinned. "Ah, better get the drinks in then. Hair of the dog is what you need."

Kit's smile waned. Great. More alcohol. Eddie took off again, striding towards the bar and they all hurried along behind him.

"I can already feel my liver bleeding," Kit complained to Victoria.

They collected their drinks and walked closer to the rails so they could watch the horses thunder past.

"I feel ridiculous," Anna said, adjusting her fascinator.

Victoria turned and looked at her daughter. "Nonsense, darling. You look beautiful."

It was nice to see Anna in a pretty dress for a change. She had chosen an elegant yellow lace that covered her shoulders and fell just below her knees. She was the height of sophistication, unlike Eddie's lady friend, who had opted for a black slip with spaghetti straps in direct contravention of the dress code. Still, it wasn't Victoria's place to say.

Kit worked hard, entertaining the clients. It was his gift of the gab that had got him his job in the first place. He'd always been a charmer, even at school. But lately he'd been so run-down, Victoria was lucky if she got a complete sentence out of him.

She turned and saw Joey tugging at his shirt. He'd been complaining he found the material itchy and she was nervous he was going to take it off.

"I'm hungry," he complained.

"Don't worry, we're going to have afternoon tea in a bit."

"I don't like tea."

"Oh, Joey! It won't just be tea."

She was right. There were dainty little finger sandwiches with smoked salmon and cream cheese and a selection of freshly baked scones with strawberries and clotted cream. It all looked absolutely delicious but Joey looked dismayed.

"Here," she pressed a ten-pound note into his palm. "Go and buy yourself a hot dog at that stand over there. Just make sure you come straight back."

She reached for a scone and ate it delicately, careful not to get any jam on her clothes while the woman next to her droned on about the horses. At first, Victoria listened politely, but the sun was in her eyes and she was worried about Joey. He was easily distracted, she wouldn't put it past him to wander off in the wrong direction.

"Excuse me," she said to the woman. "I need to go and check on my son."

The woman smiled tightly and reached for another sandwich.

Anna set her plate down and followed. "You can't leave me with those people," she said in Victoria's ear. "I just had the most boring conversation of my life."

Victoria couldn't help but smile. "Me too."

As they walked towards the hot dog stand, Victoria kept an eye out for the royal family. She wasn't sure if the queen would be willing to pose for a selfie, but it couldn't hurt to ask.

Joey was stuck in a long queue. Victoria swallowed. Joey didn't tolerate queues well. He was too impatient. She hoped to god he wasn't going to just plant himself on the floor, the way he sometimes did. Oh Lord, he was. People were looking at him as he shuffled along on his bum. The little girl behind him seemed to think this was a great idea and she sat down too. Victoria winced at the sight of her white dress on the grass.

She heard a loud laugh and glanced to the left. She saw a familiar oval face, with small blue eyes and a distinctive scar on the chin.

"That's Paul Schooner!" she hissed.

Anna followed her gaze. "How weird! We've come all the way to Ascot just to bump into our neighbour!"

"We're not going to 'bump' into him," Victoria said. "I've been avoiding him for months."

"Why?"

She leaned closer. "I don't understand why he didn't go to the police when he heard about the accident. He saw us drive off, minutes before it happened."

"Maybe he didn't hear about it."

"He must have! It was all over the news."

"So maybe he did go to the police?"

Victoria shook her head. "If he had gone to the police, they would have come round and asked to see the car."

"I suppose they would."

Victoria caught her breath. Paul hadn't noticed her. All she had to do was keep on walking. They were almost at the hot dog stand now. She just needed to get Joey up off the floor and . . .

Anna streaked ahead of her.

"Anna?"

"I'll just be a minute, Mum."

She thought at first Anna was rushing over to Joey. She was such a good big sister. But no, Anna was walking right past Joey and the mega long queue.

Victoria licked her lips, nervously. What was she doing?

Her worst fears were confirmed as Anna marched up to Paul. He smiled slowly, clearly liking what he saw. Dressed in her mother's heels and her elegant dress, Anna looked older, more sophisticated.

Don't look at her like that. She's fourteen! she wanted to call out. But she didn't dare. She didn't want to remind him of her existence.

Anna flipped back her hair. She appeared to be laughing. Bloody hell, when did she get so self-assured? Paul was looking at her like she was the most fascinating creature he'd ever encountered. It took every ounce of Victoria's willpower to stop herself from marching over there and yanking her daughter away. What the hell had got into the girl? Then, to Victoria's horror, Anna turned and pointed right at her. Paul turned too and Victoria felt her blood run cold. The look in his eyes was unmistakable. He recognised her. Of course, he did. She was hardly the sort of person people forgot.

Anna beckoned to her, but Victoria could not move a step. She shook her head from side to side. Her vision tunnelled, and she wondered if she was going to pass out. She concentrated on her daughter. Anna's gaze was like a bullet between the eyes and it was at that moment Victoria realised she might not be on her side. She gasped for air, heat creeping up her neck as Anna and Paul moved towards her.

"Who's this, Paul?"

Paul's wife had materialised at his side. She placed a proprietary hand on his arm, eyeing Anna with amusement. She made a little shooing motion and Anna stepped away.

Paul turned to his wife, laughing and giving her his full attention, but Victoria caught the glance he shot back at her, and she knew that he remembered.

16

Anna curled herself into a ball and pressed her head against the window as soon as she got into the car. With any luck, she'd be able to get some sleep, and if not, she could at least evade her mother's probing questions.

"Will you stop pissing about with your seat?" she heard Victoria snap. "It's very distracting."

"I'm sorry but my back is killing me," Kit said. He adjusted his seat further back so it was digging into Anna's legs. Anna knew he couldn't help it. He was in pain.

"Why are we going this way?" he asked a moment later.

"I want to drive past Windsor Castle."

"Oh my God, are you still trying to meet the queen?"

Her dad was laughing but Victoria wasn't. "It's a beautiful castle. You know, it's open to the public . . ."

"Not today, Vic. Please. I literally cannot move."

"You'd like to see it, wouldn't you, Joey?"

Joey grunted. Anna felt her mother's gaze on her so she stayed still. If her mother insisted on dragging them to Windsor Castle, she was going to stay in the car.

"How about we come back another time and see the castle?" Kit said. "We could bring a picnic. Make a day of it?"

"A picnic?"

"Alright, we could go out for lunch? Oh look, isn't that our neighbour in the car in front?"

"Paul Schooner," Victoria said. "Don't look at him."

"Why not?"

Her mother murmured something inaudible.

"Oh, yeah right! Er, so, Joey, what did you think of the racecourse?"

"They had Airblade hand dryers. They're 80 decibels which is way too loud but they do dry your hands in ten seconds which is quite efficient if you don't mind the noise."

"Right."

Anna did manage to sleep for most of the way home. She woke up just as they were passing the Schooner's house. There was no sign of Paul, but his wife was outside, ushering the children into the house. She glanced up as they drove by, but Victoria pretended not to see.

Anna's eyes narrowed. Paul Schooner was as bad as her mum. He knew her family had been in the area at the time of the accident and he hadn't told the police. Perhaps it was like when the boy who sat behind her in maths turned the clock forward quarter of an hour so they could all get out early? It had worked a treat, but the next day, the whole class got a detention because no one would own up. Snitchers were worse than criminals, that's what everybody said.

Joey bounded upstairs while Anna and her parents headed straight for the kitchen. The dainty bites they'd eaten at the racecourse had not sustained them for very long.

"We've got nothing in the fridge," Kit said.

"Why don't we try that Greek place?" Victoria asked. "They should give us a discount, after the stonking review I left them. Might as well check if they live up to it."

Her dad's mouth fell open. He looked at Anna.

"It's alright, she knows," her mother said.

Kit blanched. Was that shame she saw in his eyes, or was he just tired?

"I'm not sure I want to go there now," he said quietly.

Victoria scowled. "Well, we can't go to the Indian. Joey won't eat anything with spice in it."

"Why don't we just order pizza?" Kit said. "At least then we know he'll eat it."

"I'm meeting my geography project group at four," Anna said. "Can you give me a lift into town?"

"Isn't the library closed on a Sunday?" Victoria said.

"Yes, I know. We're meeting at the coffee shop."

"Which one?"

• "The Grill."

"I wouldn't call that a coffee shop."

"Well, whatever. I need to get going or they'll lumber me with all the crap stuff."

Her mum watched her for a moment and Anna stared back, careful not to look away.

"I'll give you a lift," her dad said.

Victoria's head whipped round. "I thought you said your back hurt?"

"It does. All the same, I don't want Anna waiting around for ages. You know what the buses are like on a Sunday."

"Thanks, Dad."

Anna darted upstairs and texted Bex to let her know she'd meet her there. Honestly, she couldn't wait to get out of the house. She couldn't bear to be under the same roof as her mother. The woman was toxic.

Her dad was unusually talkative on the short drive to town. He went on and on about the football. Anna listened and nodded, but she couldn't help wondering if he was trying to keep her occupied, so she wouldn't ask him about the accident. Because he'd been part of it too, hadn't he? Her mother had driven the car, but he'd been there, and he'd kept her secret.

The town centre was quiet when he dropped her off. Most of the shops were shut by now and there were only a few people milling around.

"Are you sure you're okay for a lift back?"

Anna nodded.

"Okay, I'll see you later then. You've got my number if you need it."

Anna gave him a wave and hopped out of the car. She walked quickly up the deserted high street. Bex was waiting outside the burger shop, openly smoking a cigarette. She didn't give a damn who saw.

"Can I have one?" Anna asked as she approached.

"I thought you'd given up?"

Anna shrugged. "I can't right now. Too much stress."

Bex handed her the pack. "Have you decided what you're going to do about your mum yet? Because I've got a cousin who works for the *Gazette*. I bet he'd love to get a scoop."

Anna shook her head. "No, don't do that. She's my mum. I want to deal with her myself."

Bex blew a smoke ring in her face. "Just as long as you do."

17

"Kit, wake up."

"Leave me alone."

"Kit! It's Monday morning. You need to get ready for work."

Kit sat up slowly, wincing as he changed position. "No."

"What do you mean, no? Are you ill?"

He looked at her in wonder. "Haven't I been telling you for the last four months? My back is broken, Vic. It's bloody killing me."

Victoria took a deep breath.

"You can call in sick this once," she calculated. "Tell Eddie you've injured your back, as if you've just done it, and I'll make you an appointment with the doctor."

"Don't do me any favours!"

"Don't be like that, I'm trying to help you. Give me your phone. I'll text Eddie. Then you can go back to sleep. I'll wake you when it's time for the appointment."

She rubbed his shoulder gently, but Kit already had his eyes closed.

She heard the door bang and ran to the window just in

time to see Anna walking up the path. Why the hell was she leaving so early? She occasionally met up with Maddie before school, but that was usually when they were working on a presentation. She knew of no such thing today. She watched as her daughter disappeared from view, her school bag swinging behind her. Not such a little girl anymore. She felt as though she was slipping from her grasp.

Joey, on the other hand, was in slow motion all morning. She tried not to snap when he stopped to investigate every twig he found in the street, and she managed not to swear when she got mud on the heel of her new wedges. She smiled pleasantly as other people overtook them and her cheeks ached with the effort. Thanks to Joey's dawdling, all the other parents were coming out as they were going in and by the time they finally reached Joey's classroom, she had to restrain herself from shoving the boy inside.

"Have a nice day, Joey!"

Even then, Joey seemed not to care that everyone else was in a rush as he stopped to tie his shoelaces in the doorway. Miss Henley caught her eye and Victoria felt all her fortitude slip away.

"Mrs Hill? Can I have a quick word?"

Victoria shook with rage as she remembered parents' evening. How dare she say those things about Joey? She looked coldly at Miss Henley, arms folded as she waited to hear what she had to say.

"We have a wonderful new SENCO joining the school next week. I think it might be good for you to meet her. She'll be having a coffee morning for parents on Tuesday so I can . . ."

"I'm working Tuesday," Victoria said abruptly. This was like some kind of nightmare. She did not want to meet the special needs coordinator. She didn't want Joey to be singled out.

"Oh, I see. Never mind, I'm sure she can set up another time to see you then. If you wait a moment, I can give you her number."

Victoria dug her nails into her thigh. Why couldn't she just leave it alone? She waited politely whilst Miss Henley ducked into the classroom and produced a notelet from the mess on her desk. Her handwriting was so appalling, Victoria could barely read it. Not that she needed to.

"Thanks," she muttered, shoving it into her pocket. She walked off abruptly, not wanting to take the conversation any further. If she had to listen to that woman for one more minute . . .

"Victoria?" Portia caught up to her near the gate. "Goodness, you're on a mission today!"

"Got to get back to my baking!"

Portia looked at her closely. "Something wrong?"

Victoria forced out a laugh. "No, not at all! Just busy, busy! Those cakes aren't going to bake themselves."

For a moment, she wished Portia was the sort of friend she could confide in, but she knew that anything she said to her was liable to be passed on to Zara and Samantha. The only way to safeguard a secret was to keep it to herself.

"Oh yeah, the cake sale," Portia said without enthusiasm. "What are we raising money for this time?"

"Godalming donkey sanctuary."

Portia's eyes flickered. "Personally I couldn't give a monkey's about a bunch of old nags. Why don't they just grind up their bones for jelly?"

Victoria snorted. "I don't particularly care about them either," she admitted. "But Orchard Fields are having a fundraiser too. We can't have that snotty little school doing better than us."

Portia nodded. "I'll get my housekeeper to whip up a tray of flapjacks."

Victoria forced her lips into a smile. One day, she too would have a housekeeper. It was the next thing on her list, once they'd got Joey into a private school.

She waved goodbye to Portia and walked briskly home, stopping to pick up some plain sponge cakes on the way. She'd do the icing herself, just to make them look authentic.

Kit was still asleep when she got home. She woke him with a cup of tea and a crumpet. Eddie had responded to her text with a voicemail. They listened to it together:

"Kit, you'd better get your butt back here tomorrow, mate. We're slammed without you. I've got to leave the new lad in charge when I go to the management meeting and he doesn't know his arse from his elbow."

He said it all in a jokey manner, but she felt the sting in his words. Eddie was the sort of bloke who would pat you on the back one minute and shove you under the train the next. She needed to get Kit up and mobile again as soon as possible.

"Tell the doctor you need the strongest painkillers," she said, as she drove him to his appointment.

Kit looked down at his lap. "How? I can hardly say I've been taking black market Vicodin."

"Just tell him you've been on strong pills in the past and they didn't have much effect. I doubt he'll bother looking back at your medical history."

His brows lowered. "I'm sick of lying, Vic."

"It's not a big lie. You really do need something stronger. Do you want me to come in with you? Because I'd be more than happy . . ."

"No," he said shortly. "I do not need you to hold my hand. Besides, there are never any spaces in the car park. You'll probably have to drive round and round."

He was wrong about that. After a few minutes of circling, Victoria did find a space, a very good one. She locked the car and dashed into the surgery, but it was too late. Kit had already gone through. She walked up to the counter. The receptionist had her head down, reading something.

Victoria tapped on the glass.

"Can you tell me which room my husband went into?"

The receptionist looked up. "I beg your pardon?"

"My husband . . . his name is Kit Hill. He just went in for his appointment. I need to know which room?"

"I'm sorry, but I cannot divulge that information."

"But I'm his wife!"

"I'm sorry . . ."

"Oh, for fuck's sake."

The receptionist looked startled at her outburst. She felt a little startled herself.

"Sorry." Contrite now, she shuffled back out the door, keeping her head bowed until she reached the car. She got in, sat behind the wheel and screamed into her fist.

She thought of what a state Kit had been in. The pain was getting to him, that's what it was. She should never have let him go to the doctor on his own. What if he said something stupid? What if he confessed?

"Well?" she asked, when Kit eased himself back into the car. "Did you get the pills?"

Kit nodded. "He gave me a small supply, but I'll have to go back in a fortnight. He's referred me for a scan at the hospital and he reckons I'm going to need a lot of physio. I'll probably have to go private or I'll be waiting for ages. For the time being, I'm supposed to take it easy so he's signing me off work."

Victoria burst out laughing.

"What?"

"You can't take time off work. Your career will be over."

"Yes, I know."

Back home, Victoria went straight to the kitchen to ice the

cakes. She laid both sponges on the table and covered them with pink and blue icing, then she sprinkled handfuls of Smarties over the top. Kids loved sugar. You could always win them round with sweets. At least, you could when they were little. A bit more tricky once they reached their teens.

She was just covering up her creations when Kit shuffled into the kitchen. He sat down at the table and looked at her keenly.

"It's got me thinking, Vic. We could cut down our living expenses. I mean we don't really need this big house, do we? If we sell up and move somewhere smaller, perhaps we could even get Joey into a private school like you wanted. There are some nice little flats down by the station. We could afford . . ."

Victoria's ears burned. "Sell our house? You must be crazy! After everything we've been through? After all our hard work!"

"Vic!"

She closed her eyes and opened them again. "You can't stop work, Kit. We can't afford anything on my income. We . . . we'd be . . . broke."

Kit swallowed. "There has to be some middle ground, hasn't there? Perhaps I could work part time, like you."

She leaned across the table. "I do not work part time," she said through clenched teeth. "Yes, my piano lessons are part time, but I work just as hard the rest of the week . . ."

"Sorry, that's not what I meant . . ."

"Kit, I know you need a break, but this isn't the way."

"Then find us a better way." He slapped his hand down on the table and hobbled slowly, painfully up the stairs.

Victoria drove to the school that afternoon. Environmental Ambassador or not, she could not transport the cakes on foot. She arrived just as the gates opened and headed inside. There was a magnificent cake already on display. She knew without asking that this one was Samantha's. The icing was intricate and beautiful. It looked like the ice castle from *Frozen* and it made her pathetic efforts look so amateur she wanted to throw them in the bin. She placed her cakes on the table and walked out quickly, hoping no one would know they were hers.

Miss Henley was running late, so all the Year Five parents were gathered outside the classroom, gossiping amongst themselves. She spotted Imelda Daniels and gave her a little wave. She was aware of Belinda, waiting outside Ricky's classroom. She stood alone as always. She didn't like the way Belinda looked at her, as if she could tell from a glance what she was thinking. She avoided her gaze and huddled between Zara and Samantha.

"How's Kit?" Zara asked, as the children filed out.

Joey was heading towards her, carrying a twig in his hand.

"He's fine."

Zara raised an eyebrow. "I saw him at the doctor's this morning."

"Oh!" Without meaning to, she cast a glance at Belinda. Was she being paranoid, or had she inched closer?

"What's wrong with him?" Samantha wanted to know.

Victoria shrugged. "He's just had a touch of man flu."

"No, he hasn't," Joey piped up.

Victoria stared him down. "Yes, he has. It started this morning."

She took her son by the arm and hurried him across the playground.

"Ow, you're hurting me!"

She loosened her grip. "Sorry, but we really need to get going."

"Why?"

"Because I'm tired and I want to get home."

"What about the cake sale?"

"I just want to get home."

"But I want a cake!"

Joey was alarmingly loud when he got going.

"I'll get you one from the baker's."

"I want a cake sale cake."

"Oh, for f— I don't have any cash on me."

"I want a cake!"

Victoria closed her eyes and opened them again.

"Right." She took Joey by the hand and rushed him into the hall. The cake sale was teaming with children and parents. Three long tables had been crammed with home-baked cakes of every variety. There were a couple of volunteers manning the tables, but they were no match for the swarm of children and their sticky outstretched fingers. A donation box had been left out and people could contribute as much or as little as they liked and her fellow mums were using it to empty the shrapnel from their purses. She spotted a couple of buttons in there, along with a chewy toffee and a pom-pom.

"Right, get a cake and we'll go," she told Joey.

Joey walked on tiptoes, inspecting every item on offer before selecting one of the cakes she'd made herself. It was the crappiest one. All the sweets had fallen off, leaving a boring blue square of sponge.

"That one? Really?"

He nodded. She turned to go.

"Wait!" he cried.

"What?"

"You have to pay."

"I'll have to bring the money in tomorrow."

"But you have to pay now!"

"I know, Joey."

"Here."

She turned and saw Belinda pop a fifty pence piece into the box.

"My treat, Joey. Enjoy."

Victoria shot her a grateful glance. "Oh, you don't have to do that."

"Not a problem," Belinda said. Her eyes were deep and searching.

It was probably all the sugar, but Victoria was starting to feel nauseous. Joey and Ricky had found each other. They were jumping about like frogs.

"Come on," Victoria said to Joey. "You've got your cake. Let's go."

If she spent another minute in that room, there was a strong possibility she'd be sick.

When she and Joey arrived home, Kit was there to greet them. Joey looked at him uncertainly.

"You're meant to be at work."

Kit smiled and ruffled his hair. "Hello to you too."

Joey pulled away from him and walked through the hall, discarding clothes as he went until he was down to his underpants.

"Aren't you going to pick that lot up?" Kit called after him.

Joey turned and glared at him. "You're meant to be at work!"

Kit's jaw dropped. "You come back here and pick up your—"

Before he could finish his sentence, Joey pulled a picture from the wall and hurled it at his father. Kit leapt back just as the glass hit the floor and shattered into tiny fragments.

"Stay back!" Victoria yelled. She hurried to the cupboard to get the dustpan and broom.

Joey galloped up the stairs to his room whilst Kit stood frozen on the spot.

"Are you alright?" Victoria asked.

"I'm ... what the hell just happened?"

"I think he's just tired," she said, sweeping all the bits into the pan.

Kit shook his head. "Victoria, we can't let him behave like that. It's not normal."

"I know," she said, nodding her head.

She had just finished cleaning the mess when Anna came home.

"Dad!" she cried with delight and she threw herself around his neck.

"Careful, I've got a bad back."

"Oh, poor Dad! Is that why you're off work?"

Victoria smiled at her daughter. "Hi, Anna, how was your day?"

Anna shrugged, not meeting her mother's eyes. "It was fine."

She followed her dad into the lounge where she fussed over him, bringing him pillows and cups of tea.

"Your poor back, Dad. There, is that any better?"

Victoria felt herself tense. It wasn't that she objected to Anna showing Kit sympathy, but she needed to get him back to work tomorrow. The last thing she needed was Anna taking Kit's side, convincing him that he should put his health first. He could put his health first in a few years. She didn't plan on him working forever, she just needed to know her children were set up for life, then maybe, she could take her foot off the pedal.

She watched her daughter carefully as she set the table for dinner. Anna was still adamant she was dropping Latin. Victoria could keep going for her of course and make excuses. She could even do the coursework for her, but Anna herself would have to sit the exams, there was no way round that. Perhaps Kit could have a word with her, make her see sense.

Joey had gone quiet now. She'd give him a few more

minutes, then she'd go and see if he'd calmed down. He was usually filled with remorse after one of his little outbursts. Often, he wanted a hug. Victoria enjoyed these moments. She liked holding him close and kissing the top of his head as she had when he was a baby.

She flapped around the kitchen getting dinner started, chucking pasta in the pan, throwing Joey's nuggets and chips in the oven. All was still quiet as she headed for the stairs.

"Vic," Kit called from the lounge.

"Yes?" she looked in on him, expecting him to ask for more tea.

"What the hell was that with Joey? What came over him?"

"What do you mean? He was just . . ."

She bit her lip. Of course, Kit was normally at work when Joey came home from school. By the time he got home of an evening, she had tidied everything up and got Joey settled. He was never here to see the worst of Joey's aggression. Perhaps he had no idea.

"He's a bit tired," she reiterated but Kit's brow furrowed further.

"Victoria, Joey needs to see someone. He needs help."

"No, he doesn't! He's fine."

She couldn't have this conversation. She hurried from the room, rushed up the stairs and peered tentatively into Joey's room. Anna was there and Joey had his arms wrapped around her. It should have been a pleasing sight, Anna was such a good sister, but when Anna looked up at her, she had a terrible glint in her eye.

This is your fault, that look seemed to say. *You caused this. You need to make him better.*

Victoria backed away, not knowing what to do with herself. She'd thought telling Anna her secret would make her life easier, instead Anna seemed to be using every opportunity to make things worse. Teenagers could be so selfish.

Did she really think her mother deserved to go to jail for one innocent mistake? The accident had been that, after all. An accident. She'd never intended to harm James Solomon. She wished with all her heart the man had lived.

She headed into her own room and flopped down on the bed. Downstairs, the food was probably burning but she couldn't think about that now. Her skin felt too tight and she had a crushing realisation that telling Anna her secret had been a very, very bad idea.

She had to do something, anything to get things back on track. Her eyes fell on her planner, lying on top of her night-stand. She reached for it with eager hands, a light bulb going off in her head. Anna's birthday was fast approaching, and she was going to make it extra special. She was going to win her daughter back.

18

JOEY'S DIARY

I saw Ricky in the playground at break time. He was standing by the goalposts so I walked up and talked to him. I knew he had lost his dad and I tried really hard not to mention it but it was all I could think about until I just blurted it out:
"What do you do on Father's Day if you haven't got a dad?"
I looked at Ricky, expecting him to reply, but he just walked off very quickly like he'd forgotten something.
I waited and waited but he never came back.

"Oh my God, it's an iPhone!"

Anna's eyes shone with excitement as she tore into the wrapping paper. She hadn't even opened it yet, but she knew what it was just by the weight and feel of the box.

Her dad smiled. "Sometimes I wonder if you have X-ray vision."

"Do you like it?" her mum asked.

They must have gone to a bit of trouble choosing it. It was her favourite colour – rose gold. Anna was surprised her parents had picked up on that. Of course, she already had a rose-gold pencil case, and her calculator cover was the same colour so you wouldn't have to be a genius to work it out but, all the same, they didn't usually get it so right.

She marvelled at the shiny new phone, shocked that her mum had finally backed down. She'd been asking for a phone since she was twelve, but Victoria had been adamant she couldn't have one. Last year, her dad had relented and given her a cheap pay-as-you-go.

"Just between you and me," he'd said. But it wasn't a

pretty phone like this one and it didn't have all the essentials like TikTok.

"What's wrong? Don't you like it?" Victoria asked.

Anna held it tightly. "Of course I do."

"Then what's wrong?""

"It's just . . . I wasn't expecting to get a phone."

Victoria looked hurt. "It's your birthday, for heaven's sake. If I can't spoil my daughter on her birthday, then when can I?"

Anna squinted at her, unable to read her expression.

"Come here!"

Anna felt her mother's arms around her. It had been a long time since they'd had a proper hug. She breathed in her mother's jasmine perfume. It felt safe and familiar. Her mother released her a little abruptly.

"Now come on, let's see what else you got."

Anna sat back down on the floor and reached for the next parcel.

When she'd finished opening her gifts, Victoria brought out doughnuts for breakfast. Hers had rose gold icing on. She couldn't believe it!

"Thanks, Mum!" she said, a little awkwardly.

"Are you doing anything special with your friends?" Victoria asked.

Her mum was still disappointed Anna hadn't wanted a party. She'd fed her some sob story about how she'd longed for a party when she was her age, but her family never had enough money. Anna wasn't even sure if it was true. Surely parties didn't cost that much? All you needed was a bit of food and some music.

"I've got a study session after school. We've got to finish our group presentation for biology."

"Well maybe Maddie would like to come for tea afterwards?" Victoria suggested.

"Not tonight, she's got choir."

"Can't she miss it, just this once?"

Anna placed her new phone back in its box. "Seriously, Mum. It doesn't matter. It's just a birthday."

She turned and saw her dad slipping on his shoes.

"I've got to get to work now," he said, "but have a lovely birthday, darling."

Anna looked at him anxiously. "Are you sure you're up to working, Dad?"

"He's fine," Victoria said quickly before Kit had a chance to speak.

"I was asking Dad," Anna said, pointedly.

Kit kissed her on the cheek. "You have an amazing day."

Eight hours later, Anna sat at the end of a long table at the Golden Grill. She was surrounded by her fellow students, all of them hunched over a large sheet of paper. Really, they were all taking this presentation far too seriously. She leaned heavily on her elbows and let her hair fall across her face. Perhaps she should have let her mum throw her a party after all. Anything would be better than this.

Maddie was in her element, droning on and on about blood types. She could do the whole project by herself if they'd just leave her to it. She'd done enough research for all of them, but one of the boys felt the need to interrupt her every few minutes. He didn't have anything important to contribute. He just liked the sound of his own voice.

Anna sank further into her chair, wondering if the session would ever end.

"Anna, it's your mum!"

Maddie had clearly intended to whisper, but her voice was so loud, everyone turned and stared.

"Don't mind me," Victoria said with a self-conscious laugh. "I just popped in to see the birthday girl."

"Oh, is it your birthday?" one of the girls said. She knew full well it was.

Anna rose from her chair and gathered up her pens.

"Are you leaving?" Maddie's eyes grew wide and watery.

"Birthday plans," Anna said.

"I can wait till you finish your meeting," Victoria said.

"No," said Anna. "We'll be late . . . for that thing." She gave an apologetic wave to the group. "Sorry, guys. Can't be helped. I'm sure you can manage without me."

She was met with a sea of blank stares.

"Happy birthday," Maddie called after her.

Anna fled before anyone could object.

"So, what are you doing here?" Anna asked as they stepped outside.

"I wanted to surprise you. I thought we might go out for dessert. Would you like that?"

Anna shrugged. "We can if you want."

They walked round the corner to the sweet shop. It was old style, with jars of dolly mixtures and lemon sherbets. They found a seat by the window and ordered lattes and strawberry tarts. Anna couldn't remember the last time they'd done something like this, just the two of them.

"Where's Joey?" she asked as the waitress brought their desserts.

"Dad took him to Homebase to get light bulbs."

"Exciting! How is Dad?"

"He's fine. He's just got a bad back. It's not like he's ill."

"He looked kind of grey this morning."

"Yes, well men aren't good at dealing with pain, whereas us women just get on with it."

"That's not what you said when you twisted your ankle. Didn't the doctor have to sedate you?"

"It was a very bad sprain."

Anna's phone beeped.

Her mother looked at her expectantly. "Aren't you going to get that?"

"It'll just be birthday messages," Anna said, scooping strawberry tart into her mouth.

"Oh. That's nice. So, what do you want to do after this? I thought we might go to the cinema?"

"Actually, Mum, I'm going to spend the evening with my friends."

Victoria exhaled. She was glad Anna had plans, but also a little put out she hadn't told her.

"Where are you meeting them? Back at the Grill?"

"No, I'll ask them to meet me here, then we'll probably go bowling or something."

They both finished eating and hugged their coffee cups. They were so similar in some ways. Their looks, their mannerisms, the way they stood. But the similarity ended there, because Anna was determined she was going to be nothing like her mother.

Victoria finished her coffee. "What time are your friends getting here? I can wait with you till they come."

"If it's all the same to you, Mum. I'd rather you didn't. I am fifteen . . ."

"Right, well I'll just . . . Do you need some money?"

"Yes, please."

Victoria looked through her wallet and plucked out a few notes. "This is all I've got."

"Thanks, Mum."

Anna couldn't quite meet her eye.

Victoria leaned over like she was going to kiss her, the way she did with Joey. Anna rose from her chair, muttering something about needing the loo. She patted her pockets to check she still had both phones.

Victoria's smile grew stiff. "Okay, well happy birthday, darling. Don't stay out too late."

Anna didn't make any promises. She waited until her mum retreated down the road then she set off up the High Street, scurrying past the Grill, where the boffins were still hard at work.

Bex lived in a neat little house on the outskirts of town, just round the corner from Sainsbury's. Her place wasn't as new as Anna's but it was homely and inviting and it was nice to kick back without her mum poking her nose in every five minutes.

"What time do you have to be home?" Bex asked, as they munched toast and chose outfits from Bex's wardrobe.

Anna shrugged. "Who cares? I do what I like."

Bex raised an eyebrow and reached behind her nightstand for a bottle of vodka. "Right, well I think it's time we celebrated your birthday in style."

She poured two shots and they drank them, shuddering with pleasure as the alcohol warmed their insides.

"So what are you going to do about your mum?" Bex asked.

"I don't know. I don't want to be too hard on her, she did just buy me an iPhone."

Bex eyed her with suspicion. "Yeah, funny that. Do you think she's trying to buy you off?"

Anna chewed her lip. "Is that what you think?"

"Seriously, Anna? She was dead against you having a phone, and all of a sudden, she's changed her mind."

"She had to give in some time. I can't stay a child for ever."

"I wouldn't be surprised if she's put a tracker on that thing. She probably wants to know what you're up to."

Anna frowned. "She can't do that, can she?"

"You'd be surprised. I still reckon you should go to the police," Bex said. "What your mum did is bad, Anna. That man died. She can't just get away with it, like he didn't matter. If we keep quiet, that's really disrespectful to the dead."

Anna nodded unhappily. "I know. It's just . . . I don't want my whole family turned upside down. She's the guilty one. It's her who should be punished but Joey would suffer too if they sent her away."

Bex was silent for a moment. "Don't worry about it tonight. It's your birthday. We're going to go out and get pissed." She leaned over and poured more shots.

Anna took hers and tried to relax. Bex was right. It was her birthday, she shouldn't have to worry about such heavy stuff tonight.

They didn't get into the first nightclub they tried, even though they wore a lot of make-up and Bex changed her trainers for pumps. The doorman took one look at them and told them to come back in a couple of years. Bex got insulted and started mouthing off. Anna and Dina had to haul her away before she got them all into trouble.

They didn't have any luck at the next place either, even though Harley's brother worked there. After the third attempt they gave up and bought some cider. Then they went to the park, sat on the climbing frame and drank directly from their bottles.

"I can't wait to finish school," Bex said. "I'm going to art college."

"I'm going to do childcare," Dina said. "I want to start making money straight away."

Harley shook her head. "I'm outta here. I want to see the world." She looked at Anna. "What about you, birthday girl? What do you want to do?"

"I'm going to uni," Anna said automatically. And then she stopped. "At least, my mum wants me to."

"And you don't?"

"I don't know. I've never thought about it. I don't really know what I want."

"Imagine if we'd never met," Dina said. She was always really morose when she was drunk.

"That would be so heartbreaking," Bex said. "I can't imagine my life without you guys. You're my rocks."

"I'm not sure I want to be a rock," Harley said.

"You're my crew," Bex amended.

"Better."

"You're like family."

"Better than family," Anna said.

"Better than your family," Bex agreed. "Your mum is Cruella!" she whispered into Anna's ear. Only, she whispered it loudly enough for everyone to hear.

"Why does she keep saying that?" Dina asked.

"Don't listen to her," Anna said. "Her brain is poisoned with alcohol."

Bex leaned back against the slide. "My brain is just fine."

After a while, Dina was in the mood for a few bops. She played some songs on her phone and they sang along. The neighbourhood dogs joined in, howling like a pack of wolves. Anna probably should have felt guilty about this, but she didn't. She was having the time of her life.

Her dad was still up when she staggered into the house. She'd forgotten her key, but the door was unlocked. She tiptoed into the hall and had a quick glance in the mirror. Her hair was all frizzy and her eyes looked a bit wild. She saw the light on in the lounge and poked her head in.

"Hi, Dad!" she said, hanging on to the sofa. The whole room was tipping her this way and that and she felt like she was on an ocean liner.

Kit set down the book he was reading. "Come on, let's get you some coffee."

"I'm totally fine," she protested, pulling off her shoes. She felt really short now she'd taken off her heels.

"You are not fine, but I'll let it pass because it's your birthday. Or at least, it was your birthday . . ." he checked the clock and Anna saw that it was past one.

"You're lucky your mum's gone to sleep. She'd be having kittens if she saw the state of you."

"Let her have kittens." She stumbled heavily and her dad caught her.

"Sit down. I'll get you that coffee."

While she was waiting, Anna took out her phone. Bex had made her a playlist, containing a bunch of her favourite songs. She pressed play and smiled as a funny dance number came on, then The Song came on, the one Joey hated. He'd hated it since he was tiny. She remembered one time it had come on the radio and he had started banging his head against the side of his cot. She was the one who'd pointed it out to her mum, who couldn't understand for the life of her what had upset him. She glanced up at the ceiling, but all was quiet upstairs.

Her dad stood in the doorway, holding a steaming cup of coffee. "Turn it off!"

"Why? He's supposed to be asleep."

"All the same, I wouldn't risk it."

Anna shrugged. She didn't feel like listening to music now anyway. She put her phone away and took a sip of the coffee he'd made. "How was work today?"

"Not too terrible."

She looked at him closely. "You don't like it, do you?"

"It's work. What can I say?"

"I don't get it. Why don't you take time off if you're in pain?"

"Because if I do that, I might not have a job to go back to."

"That's so unfair!"

Her father sighed. He looked exhausted. "Life is unfair, sweetie."

"Why don't you just tell them to shove their job?"

"Because my job pays for this house."

Anna looked around at the pastel walls and tasteful cream carpets. "Sod the house. We could live somewhere else."

He gave a tired laugh. "Your mum would hate that."

"I wouldn't mind." She reached out and touched her father's hand, suddenly intent on making her point. "I mean it, Dad. I know I'm pissed, but I'm being serious. I'd rather you had a job you liked. The house doesn't matter. You do. What is it Mum always says? Family comes first."

She thought she saw a glimmer of a tear in his eye but all he said was, "Drink up, Anna. We should both be getting to bed."

"Dad, I want to know about the accident. What happened? Why didn't you help that man?"

Kit changed positions slowly, straightening himself up inch by inch. "I was in so much pain I couldn't think clearly," he said. "We never saw James coming. I don't think he saw us either. When we hit him, it was such a shock. It wasn't like real life. I felt like we were just actors in a film. That kind of thing isn't supposed to happen to real people."

"But it did happen, Dad," she insisted. "Why didn't you help him?"

His Adam's apple bobbed up and down. "Your mum was horrified at what she'd done. She was beside herself. And we had Joey in the back to think of. He didn't really understand what had happened, and we didn't want him to know. He's just a kid. We wanted him to go on being a kid, you know? Your mum needed a minute to get herself together, so I said I'd take a look. I opened the car door and stepped out into the road. I could see him, lying all mangled beside a tree. His arm stuck out at an unnatural angle and his eyes looked glazed. I thought he was dead."

"Didn't you check if he was breathing or take his pulse?"

"I couldn't. I'd done my back in in the crash. Even getting out of the car was agony. There was no way I could get down on the ground."

"But Mum could have."

"Yeah, I suppose neither of us were thinking straight. We hit him so hard, his bike was in two pieces . . . I'm sorry, Anna but I really don't like talking about this. It was really harrowing. I know I'll never forget . . ."

"Just tell me one more thing, Dad."

He looked at her blankly.

"Whose decision was it to drive off, yours or Mum's?"

His eyes flicked left to right. "You have to understand, we were both in shock. We never even talked about what we were going to do, she just put her foot on the pedal and went. And that was it, decision made."

"You didn't argue with her?"

He let out a puff of air. "You can't reason with your mum, you know that."

Anna nodded sadly. She still loved her dad fiercely, but it was hard to respect him, knowing what he'd done. If her mum was a psycho then her dad was a weasel.

Happy birthday to me, she thought.

Victoria paused to snap a picture of Joey with his bike. He looked gorgeous standing beside the disused railway, with the wooded trail ahead of him. She posted it to Instagram.

#active #outdoors #bikeride

She'd chosen neighbouring Bramley so no one from school would see them. Joey needed to practise riding his bike without stabilisers. He really ought to have mastered it ages ago. The problem was, he was too easily distracted. He would be cycling along, perfectly fine when he'd hear a rustle in the bushes and bam, he'd dive off into a hedge. He was so bright in some ways but . . .

"Hello! Vicky, isn't it?"

She twirled around and saw an owl-faced woman with round glasses that were totally wrong for her face. She looked like she'd put on the first clothes she'd grabbed off her washing line. Her outfit was too bright, too garish.

"It's Victoria," she said automatically. She had no desire to talk to this woman, and yet she couldn't think of a suitable excuse to avoid her.

"Kayla," the other woman said. "And this is George."

Victoria saw a snotty-nosed boy behind her.

Kayla honed in on Joey, who had tipped his bike upside down, and was now spinning the front wheel, staring in fascination as it whizzed round and round.

"And you're Joey. I've heard your brilliant piano playing."

Joey did not respond. He seemed mesmerised by the motion of the wheel.

"How is Joey finding Year Five?" Kayla asked.

Victoria forced a smile. "Joey finds the work a little too easy. He's very advanced for his age."

"George is very bright too," Kayla said.

Victoria regarded her son sceptically. The boy was champing his jaw like a horse.

"Really?"

"Oh yes, he was reading before he was three."

Victoria's eyes widened. Joey hadn't shown the least bit of interest in reading until he started school. She remembered the hours she'd spent, trying to get him to sound out his words. It had been painful. He'd had no interest in the stories she read him. He only seemed to like non-fiction. She'd had to scour the library for books about electricity and transport. Half the time, he wouldn't even look at the book. Then, overnight he seemed to get it. After that, he'd quickly advanced to reading on his own. What a relief that had been.

"Right, well . . . We'd better get going," she took a couple of steps forward, hoping Joey would follow.

"George has just been diagnosed with autism," Kayla told her back.

Victoria stopped and looked at her. She needed to shut this down but the words wouldn't come.

"It took ages to get an assessment. We had to go private in the end, but it was worth it."

"In what way?" she asked, against her own will.

"For one thing, he's going to have a teaching assistant fifteen hours a week. They're just recruiting now."

Victoria glanced at George. "Why does he need a teaching assistant?"

"It's hard for him to concentrate. The classroom is such a busy environment, there's so much noise. George finds it all a bit overwhelming, so he needs help to stay on track. And he's working at a higher level than most of the other children, so if he gets stuck, he can't just turn to a friend and ask for help."

Kayla was looking at her so intently, that Victoria had a sudden suspicion that Miss Henley had put her up to this. Had she asked Kayla to talk to her? Worse still, had she told her about Joey? How dare she? It was none of her business.

"Luckily for us, Joey doesn't need any special treatment," she said.

Kayla watched the way Joey spun the wheel, clearly drawing her own conclusions.

Victoria took hold of Joey's bike and tipped it the right way up. "Come on, Joey, let's go for a ride."

"Hey, Vicky? How about we swap numbers? It might be nice to meet some time for a coffee and the boys can have a play date."

Victoria couldn't think of anything more vile, but she reeled off her number for Kayla.

Kayla grinned and Victoria forced her own mouth into a smile. She helped Joey up onto his bike and led him down to the disused railway line where they'd planned to ride.

She was glad none of her friends had seen her talking to that woman. Portia would find it hilarious, of course. Kayla had sounded so desperate to take Victoria's number, like she wanted to stalk her or something. She shuddered and concentrated on her son.

"Come on, Joey. We need to get you riding. You've got cycle training next week."

VICTORIA SCRUBBED at the coffee table. She had dusted and polished every bit of wood in the house and still she couldn't relax. Belinda and Ricky would be here any time and her stomach was making weird gurgling noises, probably due to the copious amounts of tea she'd drunk.

When the doorbell rang, Victoria marched straight to the door and opened it. No messing around this week. She wanted to get Ricky's lesson over with. She did not pause to chit-chat but led the boy directly to the piano and asked him to begin. Belinda was still removing her coat as the first notes filled the air.

Ricky had clearly done his homework this week and Victoria was pleased with the progress he was making. He wasn't half bad, and if he kept working at it, she thought she could make a decent pianist out of him. If only he wasn't James Solomon's son.

As always, Joey sat at the table, the chessboard set out ready, but he didn't say anything as Belinda took her chair. He looked a bit down in the dumps, or possibly just tired, she couldn't be sure. She thought she'd caught a few terse looks between the boys.

Anna seemed to have noticed too. She set Belinda's tea down on the table and looked from Ricky to Joey with a quizzical expression on her face. Victoria wished Anna would make herself scarce. It wasn't helping her nerves, having her hang around. She was always so weird around Belinda – ultra-polite one minute and openly staring the next.

Victoria rubbed the back of her head. Perhaps she should

fake a migraine after the lesson, so she could send Ricky and Belinda on their way.

In the event, she didn't need to make an excuse. Joey barely looked up as she concluded the lesson, and Belinda told Ricky to put his shoes on. Victoria smiled to herself as she picked up the sheet music and tidied it away.

"Hey, Ricky, do you want to see Joey's Millennium Falcon?" Anna asked. "He's set it up in his room."

Victoria bit down hard on her tongue. *What was she doing?*

Ricky looked mildly interested.

"Come on," Anna said to Joey. "Show him how you built it."

Victoria watched as the three of them disappeared upstairs.

"I take it they've had a falling out," Belinda said, in hushed tones.

"Oh," was all Victoria could say. Joey hadn't said anything to her. What had they fallen out about? Had he said something?

She stood awkwardly by the piano, making a great show of shutting the lid and replacing the music on the stand. All quite unnecessary really, but she felt the need to keep her hands busy. If only it were anyone else but Belinda occupying space in her living room. But every moment Belinda and Ricky were in her house caused further strain on her heart. She felt as though she was carrying around a great weight that she could only set down once Belinda left.

There was an outburst of laughter from upstairs, then Joey appeared on the landing, grinning from ear to ear. Ricky was there with him, also grinning.

"Looks like they've made up," Belinda said.

"Yes," Victoria agreed. She suspected her daughter had

played peacemaker. Maybe there was a role for her at the United Nations.

"Mum!" Joey was looking at her, dancing about on the top stair.

"Careful!" she called. "You don't want to fall."

"Mum, can Ricky stay for tea?

For goodness' sake!

Victoria searched her mind for a suitable objection, but nothing came. Joey had never asked to have a friend to tea before. She had invited various children over the years, but he took little interest, and there was never an invite back. How could she deny him a real chance at friendship?

"Of course, Ricky can stay," she said. She looked at Belinda, hoping for a lifeline. "Unless it's too last minute?"

"No, that would be lovely," Belinda said. "If you don't mind, I've got to pop to the shops now. How about I collect him around six?"

She was going. That was something.

Victoria nodded mutely and showed Belinda the door.

"He doesn't have any allergies?" she checked.

She had a sudden vision of James lying prone in the road. The spinning wheel of his bike . . .

She thought Belinda had said no, but she'd have to check again with Ricky. Better safe than sorry.

Victoria shut the door and staggered into the kitchen. She could hear the boys upstairs, leaping about and laughing. She went to the freezer and rummaged inside. Right at the back, she found a pizza. She'd do some chips too. Everyone liked chips. As she straightened up, she noticed that Belinda was still outside. She stood directly in front of the garage, phone pressed to her ear. Victoria's knees felt weak. Why would Belinda be looking at her garage like that? Did she suspect something?

Fingers shaking, she dialled Kit and whispered her predicament down the phone.

"Hold your nerve," he told her. "If she knew, she'd have gone to the police already."

Yes, he was right. Perhaps Belinda's phone had rung just as she was walking past the garage. She said goodbye to Kit and switched on the oven. When she turned back, Belinda had finally got in her car and driven away.

21

"Hi, Vicky!"

Victoria kept moving, striding across the playground like she was taking part in a race. She knew without looking that Kayla was trying to get her attention, but she also knew that talking to that woman would mean social suicide.

"Portia, save me," she muttered in Portia's ear.

Portia got that gleam in her eye. There was nothing she liked better than a bit of bitchiness.

"She's trying to latch onto me," Victoria muttered. "She got hold of my phone number and she's been texting me all bloody week."

Portia glanced back at Kayla, a mischievous look in her eye. "Oh, I don't know. Why don't you be friends with her? I'm sure we could both use some style tips."

She burst into a fit of giggles. Victoria smiled but it wasn't really funny. She needed to shake that woman off. Fast. They reached Portia's car, a gleaming new mini convertible. Victoria pictured herself in the driving seat, whizzing down the Hog's Back with the top down, her hair streaming behind her.

"You need a lift?"

"Oh no, I've got a few minutes to kill. I'm helping out with the bike safety programme."

"Rather you than me!" Portia adjusted her sunglasses and gave her a little wave.

Victoria watched her drive off. Portia didn't work. All she had to worry about was getting to her masseuse on time, and then she'd be having lunch with friends, followed by an afternoon siesta before picking her kids up at three. Portia hadn't earned that lifestyle. She had married into it. Her kids only went to a state school because her husband had left-wing leanings. She could pluck them out at the first sign of trouble, and she could afford all the tutors and additional classes her children required. On days like this, Victoria envied her more than she liked her.

She walked slowly back towards the school. The crowds were thinning out now, and just a few stragglers remained.

"Hello, Victoria, glad you could make it," the receptionist said when she walked inside.

Victoria supposed she ought to know her name by now, but she couldn't remember it, so she just smiled.

"I assume you know our other parent volunteer, Belinda?" The receptionist gestured towards the chairs.

Belinda lowered the book she was reading: *Keeping Our Roads Safe.*

Victoria felt the urge to punch the wall. Belinda patted the seat next to her and Victoria had no choice but to sit down.

"I think they just need us for the numbers," Belinda confided. "It's all about ratios, these days. They need one adult to eight students, or something like that."

"Are we going to be going out on the roads?"

"They're just going to be practising on the playground today, I think. Cycling around cones and practising hand signals."

"Okay. I think I can handle that."

Belinda returned to her book and Victoria concentrated on her breathing. She tried not to think about James Solomon. Tried not to hear the screech of brakes or the squeal of tires. She straightened the kink in her neck, bit her knuckle, then realised what she was doing and sat on her hand.

A teacher stepped out of the staff room.

"Belinda? Victoria? So glad you could make it. A couple of parent helpers have dropped out so I'm so glad you both showed up or we might have had to cancel the training. Wouldn't that be a pity?"

"Absolutely!" Victoria's voice came out too loud.

She coughed and touched her throat, wishing her cheeks weren't so hot. She wiped her forehead and found her fingers damp. Never mind, they'd be going outside soon. She'd be cool enough out there.

"Mrs Hill?" She turned and saw Miss Henley. "Hello, I thought it was you! Have you got a minute?"

Victoria bit back an excuse and nodded.

"I've arranged for an educational psychologist to come in and see Joey. Normally it would take weeks but she's had a cancellation, so she'll be able to come in next week."

"No!" Victoria said.

Miss Henley looked at her oddly.

"I mean, I've already arranged for a private ed psych," she said quickly. "He comes highly recommended. I'd rather he evaluates my son."

Miss Henley frowned. "If you're sure. I mean we have already got one booked in. It wouldn't cost you a penny . . ."

Victoria shook her head vehemently. "My ed psych is very experienced. I'd really rather he evaluated Joey."

Miss Henley nodded solemnly. "If that's what you'd like."

She went to the receptionist and picked up the file she'd evidently come for, then walked out the door, shooting Victoria one last puzzled glance. Belinda and the teacher waited for her politely.

"We'll go and join the children now. They're just finishing the safety talk."

Victoria nodded and they stepped into the hall.

The children had evidently been watching a video. The teacher in charge had paused the screen and was now facilitating a discussion.

"Any other hazards you should look out for on the road?"

Joey raised his hand.

"Yes, Joey?"

"You have to look out for deer."

A ripple of laughter broke out among the children. Joey looked around, startled. He clearly didn't think he'd said anything funny.

"Yes, wildlife can be a hazard. Not just deer. A dog could run into the street. A horse could get loose. There are instances of sheep and cows blocking roads."

Victoria's eye roamed to the back row, where Ricky sat with his chin resting on his knees, a bleak expression in his eyes. She looked away quickly. The teacher had just instructed the children to go and collect their bikes. The front row clambered to their feet.

"Mrs Hill and Mrs Solomon, please can you check everyone has their helmet fitted correctly?"

Victoria was glad to have something to do at last. She and Belinda filed out of the hall and walked across the playground to the bike rack.

Most of the children didn't need any help at all but Joey

had his helmet on backwards. She switched it round for him
quickly. Luckily, no one had noticed. She turned and saw
Belinda walking between the children, checking the tightness
of their helmets. She spoke in a jovial manner, but the smile
did not reach her eyes. Of course, all this must be very hard
for her. A whopping great reminder of James's accident.
Victoria couldn't help but wonder why she had signed up for
this. Perhaps she felt she had a duty to prevent such an accident from happening again.

The teacher clapped her hands and all the children gathered around.

"Okay, children, I'd like you to cycle round the playground practising your arm signals."

The children did as they were told, cycling in one long
line. Joey did well, she thought. All that practise had paid off.

For the second part of the training, the teacher put out
cones for the children to cycle around. They were divided
into three groups for this activity. Victoria grabbed Joey to
make sure he was with her. Ricky Solomon ended up in her
group too. She could have done without that, but she could
hardly complain.

Ricky took the course a little too fast. He seemed eager to
get it over with, finishing with a big skid. A couple of the
other boys did wheelies, until the teacher looked over and
told them to pack it in. The girls all cycled nicely, one after
the other. By the time it came to Joey's turn, most of the other
children had been allowed out onto the upper playground for
their break.

"I'm going to be late," Joey fretted.

"It's okay," Victoria said. "Just take your time."

He looked in dismay at the other children.

"Concentrate," Victoria said. "Do the course, like we
practised."

Joey started to cycle, wobbling precariously as he went

round the cones, squashing one under his bike's wheels. She corrected it quickly.

She glanced over at Belinda. She still had a child left to go, so Joey wasn't quite the last. Little Eloise whizzed round the course at breakneck speed.

"Again, please," Belinda said without humour. "This time with a little more care."

Eloise's eyebrows drew together. "Not fair!"

Belinda fixed her with an icy stare. "Life isn't fair."

Eloise's bottom lip shot out, but she wheeled her bike back to the start and duly began again. Imelda was going to be fuming when she heard.

Joey was still doing the course. He seemed uncertain about which way to go. Victoria couldn't understand this. It seemed blatantly obvious. She pointed him in the right direction. He continued, a little disheartened now. Eloise had peddled round again and he was still at it. He was going so slowly; he could barely stay on the bike. Victoria gave him a push and he sailed to the end.

"Well done!" she said, clapping her hands.

Belinda looked over at them. "Nicely done."

Miss Henley walked towards them and handed Joey his certificate. Any other child would have been pleased, but Victoria saw the change in his eyes. His face grew red. He stood unnaturally still. She jumped in, before he could erupt.

Taking Joey's bike, she grabbed his hand and walked him over to the bike rack.

"I didn't do it," he said, under his breath. "I didn't do it, I didn't do it . . ."

"Of course, you did it, Joey," she said. "You did a really good job."

So he'd squashed a few of the cones. What did that matter? He'd cycled so carefully. In fact, he'd been the most conscientious child she'd seen, but he was such a stickler for the rules.

"Didn't do it," he said louder.

"Wait there," she told him.

She jogged back onto the playground, past Belinda who was watching her with great interest.

"Miss Henley?" she called, almost out of breath as she caught up to her. "Joey isn't feeling well. I'm going to take him home, okay?"

Miss Henley blinked. "Oh dear! What's wrong with him? I thought he did so well . . ."

"I think he's got a migraine coming on," Victoria said, with an anxious look back at the bike rack. Joey was coming after her. She had to stop him before he started yelling.

She ran back to him, her heart hammering as she led him and his bike to the car. Thank God she'd brought the car! She bundled him in the back and climbed in herself. He objected loudly as she started to drive.

"Mum, stop! I haven't done my seat belt!"

"Well, do it then!"

"I can't!"

He was kicking, thrashing about in panic. She pulled up a few meters down the road and turned to look at him.

"Right, Joey, take a deep breath and . . ."

"I can't!"

He threw his water bottle, catching her cheek. Stars danced before her eyes. She hunched over the steering wheel, setting off the horn. Her face smarted with pain.

From the back seat, she could hear Joey twisting about: "Didn't do it! Didn't do it! Didn't do it!"

She took a moment to breathe through the pain. Then she turned and looked at him. He had curled himself up into a ball.

"Didn't do it."

She leaned over and kissed his damp hair, then fastened his seat belt correctly.

"It's okay, Joey. It's all going to be okay."

22

I didn't want to do bike training but Mum made me. Ricky didn't want to do it either. He told me his dad died riding his bike, then I got a tummy ache. I couldn't stop thinking about Ricky's dad. I didn't know him, but I picture him as a bigger, taller version of Ricky.

I didn't want to do the bike test either. I knew I wasn't going to be able to do it and I was right. I failed but Mum cheated and picked up the cones I knocked down. I felt hot all over when Miss Henley called my name out and gave me my certificate. I tried to tell her what happened but Mum made me go home early. I didn't even have time to sharpen my pencils. They're all going to be blunt tomorrow. I'll have to go in early so I can get my desk how I like it. I hope Mum doesn't make me late with all her talking.

I really should go to sleep now, but I can't stop thinking about the deer.

23

VICTORIA

V ictoria glared at her phone. She couldn't believe that awful Kayla woman was actually ringing her. What the hell did she want? Oh, for goodness' sake, and now she'd gone and left her a voicemail.

She pressed play and listened as Kayla babbled on, finally finishing with an invitation for a play date on Sunday afternoon. Victoria shuddered at the thought, but she texted her back to accept.

She checked her face in the mirror. Over the past few days, the bruise on her cheek had changed from red, to blue to a more muted yellow. It was looking better, but it still required a skilful application of concealer and she would still need to be vigilant to ensure it stayed covered.

She yawned and checked the lounge was tidy. Good job she had checked – the lamp was lying on its side from Joey's wobbler earlier. He'd been rather emotional in the days since the bike training, and increasingly unpredictable, up one minute, down the next. His eyes were a little red she thought, as though he wasn't getting enough rest. Perhaps it was time to up his dose of melatonin.

Joey had never been a good sleeper, even when he was a baby. She had taken him to the doctor aged three but she had been unconcerned, telling her all children were different and he would grow out of it. Joey did not grow out of it. He seemed to sleep less every night, wandering the house and getting into all sorts of mischief. One night he'd got into the cleaning cupboard and pulled out all the bottles. He hadn't managed to get any of the safety caps off, but it had been enough to give her a major fright. She'd doubled up on the baby proofing after that. And she'd turned to the Internet for a solution to his insomnia.

That was when she had discovered melatonin gummies. Parents in America could buy them as easily as candy. Joey's doctor was still refusing to prescribe anything, so Victoria circumvented her and bought melatonin online. Joey quite liked the gummies, which tasted like sweets. He just had to take one every night, and half an hour later he would become drowsy. Not only that, he slept longer in the mornings too. No longer was she woken at four because Joey wanted his breakfast. In fact, she sometimes had to wake him these days, because he was still asleep when she got up.

Joey was thrashing about in his room, cussing at the top of his voice. She didn't know where he'd heard such language. She and Kit were mindful about what they said around the children, although she knew Kit swore like a trooper at work – it was expected. She hoped to goodness Joey never let rip like this at school. She could just imagine the phone call she'd get from Miss Henley if Joey's behaviour was anything less than exemplary. The school had very high standards.

"Keep it down!" she yelled up the stairs. "Ricky will be here any minute."

"Shitbag! Shitting shit stirrer!" Joey seemed to be stuck on that word.

Victoria sat herself down at the piano and played the 1812 overture as passionately as she could, then she listened for a moment, but there was no one at the door. Joey was still ranting, letting out the odd "Shit!" She launched into "The Devil's Staircase".

By the time she'd finished the piece, Joey had quietened down. All was silent, punctuated by the occasional thud which she ought to be able to explain away. Knowing Joey, he'd probably thrown on his earphones the moment she started playing and was now listening to his own music. She was ashamed to realise she didn't even know what Joey liked these days.

She received a text from Anna, confirming that she was over at Maddie's. Victoria was happy to hear that. It meant that she wasn't going to be here to stir things up with Belinda.

She heard a car pull up outside and watched from the window as Belinda and Ricky walked up the path. Was it her imagination, or did Belinda linger just a fraction too long in front of the garage?

Belinda smiled when Victoria answered the door. "How's Joey?" she asked, looking around.

Victoria glanced up the stairs. "Joey? He's fine."

"Only, you left the bike workshop in such a hurry the other day . . ."

"Oh, that! He had a migraine coming on. I had to get some medicine into him."

Belinda looked troubled. "Poor Joey. I didn't know he suffered from migraines."

"Oh no, it's not a regular thing. I get them myself so I know to act fast."

Ricky made a beeline for the piano.

"It's good to see him focusing on something," Belinda said, watching him. "It's been a while."

Victoria kept her eyes on Ricky and tried not to see the

likeness to his father. "Okay, Ricky. Let's hear it from the beginning."

Belinda settled in her usual seat to watch. With Joey still upstairs, Victoria was ultra-aware of her presence. She thought Belinda might get bored and get her phone out, or else browse one of the many books on the shelf, but instead, she just sat and watched as if Ricky and Victoria were putting on a performance. She tried not to look at Belinda and concentrated instead on her student. When she did finally turn to look at her, just a casual glance, it seemed as though Belinda had edged her chair closer. Victoria turned back to Ricky once more. Her cheeks flushed hot and cold as she changed the sheet music and prompted him to play. She could feel Belinda's eyes boring into her back.

After the lesson, Joey came downstairs. Thankfully, he seemed calm and he and Ricky played together for a few minutes. Victoria kept a careful eye on him in case he lost his cool.

Belinda coughed.

"Would you like a glass of water, or maybe a cup of tea?" Victoria reluctantly offered.

"Thanks, but I need to get to Sainsbury's in a minute."

Victoria wondered if she should ask if Ricky wanted to stay again, but she didn't know how long Joey's good mood would last, and her own frazzled nerves demanded a break.

Belinda laid a hand on her arm. "I do appreciate the offer."

Victoria's skin fizzed where Belinda had touched her. Belinda gazed out the window, at the neatly manicured lawn.

"You know, when James died, people were kind at first, understanding. But as the months pass they seem to expect me to get over it. As if my grief has an expiry date."

Victoria opened and shut her mouth. She didn't know how to respond to this. If only her throat weren't so dry . . .

"James wasn't perfect. He was obstinate and grumpy. He could sulk for England and he was useless at saying sorry. But he was my husband and I . . . My life feels so dreary without him and I know that's a terrible thing to say because I still have Ricky, but that's just how I feel."

Belinda turned so that she was now looking straight at her. Victoria forced herself to meet her gaze.

"I'm sorry," she croaked.

"Why are you sorry?"

She got a flash of James Solomon with his neck bent the wrong way. She pictured the blood flowing from his body. She wasn't even sure if he'd really looked like that. Her memories had meshed with her nightmares and she no longer knew what was real.

"I'm sorry James died," her throat caught. "And I'm sorry if people haven't shown the compassion you deserve."

"Everyone but you," Belinda placed a hand on her shoulder. "That's the thing about tragedy. You soon learn who your friends are. You've been a good friend to me, Victoria, even though we haven't known each other long."

Victoria nodded. She had become a good friend to Belinda. The best friend Belinda could possibly have wished for. Perhaps that was the point to this whole mess.

VICTORIA CLOSED the dishwasher and snuggled up next to Kit on the sofa. He changed position and winced. The pills the doctor had given him were totally ineffective.

"Did you do your breathing exercises?" she asked.

He gave her such a look that she decided not to ask about the meditation too. What else had the doctor recommended? Her eye went to the beer in his right hand. Oh, yes. He was supposed to give up alcohol.

He caught her looking.

"I need it for the pain!"

"I know." She stopped herself from saying anything else.

She wanted to snuggle closer, but she didn't want to set off another painful spasm. She took her phone out, needing to cancel that wretched play date with Kayla and her snivelly child. She thought for a moment, before tapping out an excuse about visiting a sick friend. Kayla responded instantly, offering to make it next Sunday. Victoria rolled her eyes. Some people were so dense.

She turned her attention to Instagram and uploaded a picture of Joey playing the piano, careful to show him from the back.

#pianosofInstagram #musicalfamily #gratefulthankfulblessed.

Anna occupied the sofa opposite. She was so long now, sprawled out like a cat. When had she got so big? Victoria wondered. Time seemed to go faster with every passing year.

There were about five minutes left of the news bulletin. Having grown up in a big city where gun crime and stabbings were daily events, the local news always seemed charming by comparison. Last week there had been a feature on bike thefts after three local school kids had their bikes stolen.

"Oh, was that a bike thief update?" Victoria asked.

Kit nodded. "It turns out one of the three kids had just left his bike at the station."

Victoria howled with laughter as the boy's gran clipped him round the ear, live on television.

"And finally tonight, we are going to highlight a terrible accident which occurred back in February."

Belinda's face appeared on the screen and Victoria stopped laughing abruptly, all the muscles in her body tensed. She looked at Kit, but he was staring, open mouthed at the screen which now showed a reporter sitting beside Belinda on a soft blue sofa.

"Belinda Solomon's husband, James, had been cycling home from work on Friday, 9 February when he was tragically struck by a car and killed. Police later received an anonymous 999 call from a member of the public who told them where James could be found. This person did not identify themself or give any further details, nor have any witnesses come forward to say what happened so Belinda and her son, Ricky, are left without answers. James was a keen bike enthusiast for whom cycling was not only a hobby but also an important way to do his bit for the environment. Four months on, his family are still seeking answers."

Kit was very, very still. If he was breathing, he was doing it very softly. His chest barely moved. She rubbed her hand up and down his arm but got no reaction. She glanced across the room at Anna who stared back at her. The venom in her eyes was unreal.

"That was you, Mum!" she hissed. "You killed that man and left him to die."

Victoria glanced at the door, but Joey was still up in his room. Next to her, Kit's eyes swam with pain. The programme was still running. There was a clip of James on his bike followed by another of the road where he had died.

Belinda was talking again, appealing for witnesses: "If you know anything, no matter how insignificant, please get in touch. We deserve answers."

Another video of James came into view again, this time with Ricky as a baby. The little boy giggled and gurgled in his father's arms. Then a phone number came up on the screen.

"If you have any information on the death of James Solomon, call now."

Victoria caught the motion of Anna's fingers tapping on her phone. Was she taking down the number? An advert came on and Kit let out his breath in a long whoosh. Anna rose to her feet and headed towards the bathroom.

"What are we going to do?" Kit asked in desperation.

Victoria was already on her feet. She'd noticed Anna had left her phone on the arm of the sofa. She hurried over and picked it up.

"What are you doing?" said Kit.

"Just being a responsible parent."

It appeared that Anna had been texting Maddie about her homework. She scrolled back through the exchange but didn't see any cause for alarm. Apparently, Maddie had a crush on a boy called Martin but Martin liked some other girl. Poor Maddie. It might help if she stopped scraping her hair back into such a tight ponytail. She loaded up Anna's emails. There were hundreds, nearly all of them promos: vouchers off this, vouchers off that, interspersed with messages from school, reminding her about Sports Day, library books and uniform sales. She clicked on Anna's notes, but there was nothing but the name of a book Anna was reading for English and the rest of her apps appeared to be games.

She turned back to her husband. "Are you okay?"

His eyes narrowed. "Why would I be okay? Nothing about this is okay. It's eating me alive."

Victoria wanted to say something, but Anna was just coming out of the bathroom. She set the phone down where she'd found it and went to reason with her.

"You know, your dad and I could go to prison for a very long time if any of this comes out."

Anna wouldn't look at her. "I know."

"There would be no one to look after you and Joey. You'd both end up in care. Is that what you want?"

She shrugged in response. "They're going to find out anyway, eventually."

"They don't have to."

Anna nodded towards the lounge. "Dad's a total wreck."

"He just had a shock, seeing it on the news like that. I'll make us all a cup of tea. That will calm our nerves."

"That's your answer to everything, isn't it?"

Victoria ignored her and strode into the kitchen. Nobody would ever find out. She would see to that.

24

Ricky came round. He didn't say he was coming. He just came. I was in the middle of a game so I said he'd have to wait but Mum said that was rude. I don't get why. He never said he was coming, so if anything, he was the one who was rude.

I couldn't find my *Star Wars* T-shirt so Mum made me wear the shirt Anna bought me for my birthday. It says "Eat. Sleep. Chess" which makes no sense at all but Mum says I have to wear it because Anna paid for it out of her own money and we don't want to hurt her feelings. Ricky said it was a good T-shirt but Ricky doesn't know a king from a queen.

Once I was dressed, I asked Ricky what he wanted to do but instead of answering the question he said:

"It's a nice day."

I asked if he wanted to play on my computer but he said: "It's really sunny outside."

Then Mum said:

"Why don't you boys go out?"

She gave me some money and said we could and buy some Cokes and then go to the park. I've never been out without Mum before so I wasn't sure. She said as long as we looked when we crossed the road, we would be fine which isn't true because there could be a hurricane or a tornado or a kidnapper but Ricky said:

"Yes, Mrs Hill."

And Mum went a bit red and said:

"You boys have fun."

When we went in the shop, the shopkeeper handed me my Coke before I even got to the counter. I asked how he knew what I wanted but he just laughed. He couldn't guess what drink Ricky wanted though. He likes Sprite.

There were all these little kids at the playground so we went for a walk along the lake. While we walked, I told Ricky about the game I played earlier. Ricky is a really good listener. I asked him what games he liked playing, but instead of answering, he said he'd seen a report about his dad on TV. His mum told him that his dad's death was an accident but according to the news it was something called a hit and run.

"Your mum lied to you," I said.

Ricky said he had to go home then, even though we hadn't finished our walk. You're supposed to walk all the way round the lake but Ricky had a funny look on his face all the way home and when I asked if he wanted to come back to my house, he said no. I think he's upset because of his mum being a liar. It's a shame because I like his mum. Does this mean all adults lie?

25

ANNA

A strange man was walking down the path when Anna arrived home from school on Monday. She knew just from looking at him that he wasn't one of her mother's friends, not in those overalls.

"Mum!" she called, as she let herself in. "Mum!"

Victoria came out of the kitchen, an oven glove thrown casually over her shoulder.

"Mum, who was that man?"

"Oh, that was just the plumber."

"What was he doing here?"

"The toilet in our en suite was blocked."

"Can't Dad deal with that?"

"Apparently not. Anyway, it's fixed now." Victoria busied herself, setting the table for dinner. She'd gone to a lot of trouble tonight, laying out a white cloth and wine glasses.

"Hungry?" she asked, as Anna settled on the sofa with her homework.

"Yeah, I suppose."

Her mother brought out a bottle of wine and set it on the table.

"Who's coming to dinner?" She hoped to God it wasn't Eddie.

"No one." Victoria smiled like the effort was killing her, her lips pinched shut.

Anna's eyes flicked over the wine glasses but she said nothing.

Her dad was not home in time for dinner. There was nothing unusual about that. He didn't exactly work a nine-to-five job. Up until recently, Anna hadn't thought much of it. Now she knew he hated his job, she resented the fact that Eddie made him work late. Poor Dad. He was missing this lovely dinner.

Joey was talkative that evening, droning on and on about his game, so neither she nor her mum could get a word in edgeways. Victoria nodded attentively and every so often, she repeated something Joey had said. If you didn't know better, you might think she was paying attention to him, but Anna was wise to her. She probably didn't have a clue what he was going on about. Not that it interested her either. Joey could be a terrible bore. He didn't care in the slightest if anyone was interested in what he had to say, he just kept talking regardless.

Victoria took a sip of her wine.

"Can I try a bit of wine?" Anna asked.

A dark look crossed Victoria's brow, but then she smiled. "Why not? You are almost a grown up, after all, Anna. Perhaps it's about time you tried a little."

Anna's jaw dropped. "Are you serious?" Her mother never let her have wine. She was the only one of her friends who never got to try it. Even Maddie was allowed a little taster of a Sunday.

"You have to be eighteen to drink wine," said Joey.

Anna glared at him. "Shut up, idiot."

"I am not an idiot. I'm more intelligent than you are."

"Oh yeah, that's why you can't tie your own shoelaces?"

"I can ..."

"That's enough," said Victoria. "Do you want some wine or not, Anna?"

"Yes please!"

Victoria poured an inch of wine into her glass.

Anna took the glass and raised it to her lips. She took a careful sip, as if she didn't do this every Friday night, or whenever there was a decent party.

"Well?" Victoria demanded. "What do you think?"

"It's very nice. A bit strong but ..."

Victoria nodded. She seemed satisfied with this answer.

Joey continued to prattle on as they finished their dinner. Anna drank her wine slowly, and when she'd finished, Victoria leaned across the table and topped her up. Not just a little taster this time, but a proper glassful. Anna bit her lip to keep herself from smiling. Her mum was up to something. Was this another bribe? Was she trying to buy her silence with wine?

Joey slid to his feet. "May I leave the table?" he said and without waiting for an answer, he went to the freezer and helped himself to an ice lolly, which he took up to his room.

Anna looked across the table at her mum. Victoria didn't make any move to get up, even though she'd finished eating. They both just sat there, sipping their wine. Anna wracked her brain, but she couldn't think of anything to talk about. The wine was nice though, cool and flowery. She felt a pleasant glow in her cheeks, like she'd just been for a run.

"So, how was your day?" Victoria asked.

Anna hated that question for what it was: a lazy parental probe into her business.

"I got an A minus on my maths homework."

Victoria frowned. "Only an A minus?"

"That's good, Maddie got a B plus."

"Really?" Victoria looked pleased. It was pathetic. Her mother was in competition with Maddie. A competition Maddie knew nothing about.

Victoria drank a bit more wine so Anna did too. She had nearly finished it now and was wondering if she should sneak out to the garage and get another bottle to drink in her room. She didn't want to lose the buzz.

"A little more?" Victoria held up the bottle.

Anna's eyes widened. "Why not?"

She watched as Victoria refilled her glass. For all her mum knew, Anna had never had a proper drink before. She wished Bex was here to see this.

"It's so nice that we can do this," Victoria said smoothly, her long fingers laced around the stem of her glass.

Anna nodded uncertainly.

"That's one of the nice things about having a nearly grown-up daughter. Someone to talk to, woman to woman."

Woman to woman? Could she hear herself?

Anna chugged her wine, no longer enjoying it. Her mum was being weird and she had had enough. She didn't want to sit here and make conversation. She wanted to go up to her room so she could chat with her friends in peace, but Victoria seemed to have other ideas. No sooner had Anna finished her glass than Victoria promptly filled it up again.

What the hell was going on?

"It's been so hard for me, these past few months, having no one to talk to," Victoria said.

"You had Dad."

"Dad's never here."

"Whose fault is that?"

Victoria raised her perfectly groomed eyebrows, but said nothing, merely sipped her wine.

Anna toyed with her own glass. She was in half a mind not to drink any more, but how often did her mum just give it away like this? She was beginning to wonder how much she was going to give her. They'd nearly finished the bottle. Would she open another one, or would that be that? She took a big glug.

"It's been hard having to hide my feelings all the time, to keep everything together," Victoria went on. "I only want what's best for you, you know that, Anna? I want what's best for all of us. That's why I've worked so hard to keep our family together."

Her eyes lingered on Anna as if she was trying to assess whether her words were sinking in. Anna didn't know what to say so she kept on drinking.

"Now that you're older we should drink together sometimes," Victoria went on. "As long as you're mature about it. I get so lonely when your dad's at work. It's nice to have someone to talk to."

Victoria finished her glass and Anna said nothing. Victoria stood up abruptly and went into the kitchen, returning a moment later with a fresh bottle of wine. Unbelievable! Her glass was still half full but Victoria topped her up again. Anna pinched herself under the table. No, she wasn't dreaming. This was really happening.

Victoria was watching her closely, and Anna started to feel like a specimen under a microscope. She smiled to herself impishly. Maybe she should play along and pretend to be a little wasted. That seemed to be what Victoria wanted, the amount of wine she was plying her with.

"So, Anna. I was wondering how you were feeling . . . about the accident? I know you saw it on the news. That must have been unsettling for you?"

So that was what this was about. Her mother wanted to know if she was going to blab.

"Yes, it was unsettling," she said truthfully.

Victoria looked suddenly alert. "Because, you know, it's

Joey who will suffer if it all comes out. You would be separated for sure and he'd end up in some horrible home where they didn't understand him and his gifts. He's only nine, for goodness' sake, Anna. You wouldn't want that would you?"

"I'm not the one who committed a crime and covered it up." Anna suddenly burst out laughing. Maybe she was a little more drunk than she'd thought. She shouldn't have said that, should she?

Victoria leaned across the table. "You tell, and we all suffer. Do you understand, Anna? We're a family. This affects us all."

"What about Ricky Solomon? Doesn't he deserve to hear the truth?"

Victoria's face fell. "Why are you being like this, Anna?"

"I'm not being like anything. You should never have told me. Scratch that, you should never have done it."

"It was an accident!" Victoria protested.

"Yes, but you should have done the right thing!"

"If you think I'm going to let you destroy our family, you can think again."

Anna set her glass down on the table with a loud clink. It seemed her mother was done too. She screwed the lid back on the bottle and put it back in the fridge. Anna sat alone at the table, wondering what on earth had just happened. Had her mum just threatened her? At the very least, she'd got her drunk to extract information from her. Would she stop at nothing?

She slunk up the stairs and peered in at Joey. He was sitting up in bed waiting for his story. He still liked to have his favourite book read to him every night. Anna went in and settled herself next to him. He passed her the book.

"On a long twisty highway on a star speckled night . . ."

Joey smiled up at her and she pulled him closer as they

recited together: "The moon burst like a blister in the bright twilight..."

When she'd finished reading, Anna kissed Joey on the top of his head and tucked him in.

"You want the light on?" she asked.

Joey nodded. He always slept with the light on. Not just his night light, but the main bedroom light. He got freaked out if he woke up and it was dark.

She went into her own room and checked her burner phone. There was a long WhatsApp conversation between Bex and Dina, arguing about whether Dina should go on a second date with some boy from their school. It was at times like this that Anna really resented having to go to Godalming Grammar. It was hard to join in with a conversation when she didn't know the boy they were talking about. She wanted to tell them what had just happened, but it was so strange she hardly knew what to say. Besides, Harley and Dina would love it if their mums gave them wine. Not Bex though. Bex would say her mum was trying to buy her silence, and she would probably be right.

Maddie texted in a panic because she'd done the wrong chapter for English. Anna replied that she could copy the answers off her at break. Maddie got so worked up about this stuff. She really needed to lighten up. Anna sighed heavily. If only that was all she had to worry about. She settled down on her bed but there was no way she could sleep so she watched some video clips on her phone. Around midnight, she heard the front door bang. That meant Dad was finally home. He seemed to get in later and later. Probably avoiding her mum.

She could hear her parents talking, having a heated conversation, all in whispers. Victoria was getting louder, perhaps because she had drunk so much wine.

"You've got to call him," she was telling her dad.

"I don't know if we should..."

"What choice do we have? If we don't deal with this now . . ."

What were they talking about? It sounded important. She pressed pause on her video. Her parents' real-life drama was way too distracting. Perhaps she should go down there.

Then she heard the scream. Her heart pounded. What was that?

She bolted across the hallway.

"Joey?"

He was still in bed. His eyes were wide open, but she could see he wasn't awake.

He was still screaming, thrashing his arms and legs.

"Joey?" she said softly. "Joey? It's okay. You're having a dream."

Gently, she stroked his back. His chest heaved, his pulse was racing, his face sweaty.

"It's okay. You were having a nightmare. It's gone now. Whatever it was, it's gone."

His eyes were wide, startled. "Where's the deer?"

"The deer's gone, Joey. You can go to sleep now. You're safe."

She tucked him back in, wondering how her parents had missed this. She could still hear them downstairs. Their argument seemed to have lost its steam now, and she could hear her mother rattling the tea things in the kitchen. Was she seriously making tea at this hour?

She left Joey's door ajar and returned to her own room, wondering if she was ever going to get to sleep. Poor Joey. It was obvious what had brought this on. He was still worrying about the accident. Victoria's lies were damaging him. The more her mother pretended nothing had happened, she thought, the more the family would pay.

ANNA BURIED her face under the pillow until Victoria marched in and switched on the light.

"Time to get up," she barked. "You've got twenty minutes to get dressed and eat your breakfast."

Anna sat up wearily.

"Mum, I don't feel too good . . ."

She made herself look as feeble as possible. Winning a day off wasn't easy with Victoria. She'd sent her in with tonsillitis last year, only for the school to send her straight home.

Victoria regarded her coolly. "I expect you've got a bad head, have you?"

"And my stomach . . ."

Victoria nodded, as though she'd expected this. "I think we both drank a bit too much wine last night," she said.

Come to think of it, her mother did look a little pale.

"I don't want to be sick at school."

"No, I don't suppose you do."

Victoria trotted off without another word. Anna heard her helping Joey into his uniform. Joey ought to be more than capable of getting himself dressed for school but Victoria often gave him a helping hand. She seemed to think this was totally normal, but Anna found it weird. She didn't know why Joey didn't just get on with it. She couldn't imagine anything worse than still being dressed by her mother.

Anna slept until she was woken again by the sound of vacuuming. How the hell could her mother vacuum when she was hung-over? What was wrong with the woman? She checked her phone and found an irate message from Maddie, panicking because she needed to copy her homework. She didn't know why Maddie had to make such a drama of everything. She wished fervently that they could switch places. Her problems were nothing compared to the mess Anna was dealing with.

Her mum had finally finished vacuuming. She grabbed her phone and headed downstairs. Victoria insisted she charge it on the telephone table, no doubt so she could read her texts. She plugged it in and made her way to the kitchen to raid the fridge.

Victoria was arranging a vase of flowers on the kitchen table.

"Feeling a little better?"

"A little," Anna conceded, piling her plate high with bread, ham and cheese.

"Well, I've got a student coming in half an hour, so stay upstairs please."

So that explained the vacuuming. Her mother rarely vacuumed upstairs because no one ever went up there. But if they were having a guest of any sort, the downstairs had to look like a show home. They even had an old grandfather clock in the hallway – Victoria liked to tell an elaborate story about how it had been her great grandfather's but Anna knew for a fact that none of their family had two pennies to rub together, much less a priceless antique. She lied constantly, her mum, telling people whatever she thought they wanted to hear. No wonder Joey was so messed up.

Joey. All at once, she remembered his startled eyes.

"Mum, did you know Joey had a nightmare last night?"

"Did he?"

"Yes, it was about a deer. I think he must still be upset about the accident."

Victoria went on arranging the flowers.

"Do you think you should get him some counselling?"

"Yes, maybe. I'll see what I can do."

She looked Anna in the eye for just a little too long. Of course she wasn't going to take Joey to see a counsellor. Not when he might blab and land her in trouble. Anna picked up her plate of food.

"Maybe you could do a bit of Latin if you're feeling better?" Victoria suggested as Anna trudged back up the stairs. Anna chose not to hear her.

She sat on her bed while she ate and texted her friends but it wasn't a lot of fun since they were all at school. Dina texted her an emoji of a frog and she was about to ask if that was her new boyfriend when Victoria burst in. Anna shoved the burner phone under her pillow. She watched warily as her mum sat down on the end of her bed.

"How would you like to start learning to drive?"

"Mum, I'm fifteen!"

"I know, but there's a driving preparedness course you can take. They use dual-controlled cars on private land. It's perfectly safe and legal. Then, when you turn seventeen, you could take your test right away and . . ."

"You could boast about it to your friends."

Her mother flinched. "No! I just thought you might like it. I couldn't wait to learn when I was your age."

"So, what's the catch?"

"There's no catch. I just wanted to do something nice for you."

"Bribe me, you mean?"

Victoria pressed her lips together. "Why are you making this so hard?"

"Why won't you do the right thing? You should go to the police station and hand yourself in, Mum. Or at the very least, admit it to Belinda. Let her decide what to do with you. It isn't fair, the way you're just carrying on like nothing happened."

Victoria gritted her teeth. "What choice do I have? I have a family."

"Yeah, and some example you're setting us. I've a right mind to hand you in myself."

Victoria leaned closer. "I've tried asking you nicely, Anna.

Stop threatening me. I don't like it and it doesn't suit you. You know what the stakes are here. You know what could happen to you and Joey."

"Has it ever occurred to you that Joey might be better off in care?"

She saw the sting in her mother's eyes and shuffled back against the headboard. "This is not a joking matter."

"I'm not joking."

Victoria furrowed her brow and Anna waited for the inevitable tears. Her mother could turn them on and off at her own pleasing. Victoria rose from the bed and stood silently in the doorway, waiting for an apology that was never going to come. Anna's burner phone buzzed under her pillow.

"We're a family," Victoria said. Her eyes seemed to bore right into her skull. "I won't let you, or anyone, else tear us apart."

She walked out, shutting the door with such force the whole house shook. Anna listened as her mother's footsteps receded. Her breath came in dizzying rasps. She texted Bex:

If anything happens to me, tell the police it was my mum.

26

VICTORIA

Victoria left Anna's room and jogged back downstairs. She stood in front of the telephone table. Anna's phone was in the charger. But she'd definitely heard a little beep up in Anna's room. She replayed the sound in her head. Yes, definitely a beep.

She leaned against the wall as the realisation hit her.

Anna had a second phone.

It didn't make any sense. Why would Anna have a second phone? What could she possibly need it for?

She wandered into the kitchen and poured herself a glass of water. Then she glanced out the window and noticed someone on the pavement in front of the house, camouflaged behind a large golf umbrella, even though it was barely raining. The umbrella looked a bit unsteady, as though it was a bit too heavy. Victoria watched for a moment, until the figure raised the umbrella a little. It was Anna's unsuitable friend, the one who had called round that time. She steeled herself for a confrontation but by the time she got to the door, the girl was gone.

"Hello?"

Victoria pulled on some shoes and stepped out into the garden. She hurried up the path, but the road was clear now. Where had she got to and why wasn't she at school? She returned to the house and bolted the door behind her.

———

"Mum, why don't you drive your car anymore?" Joey asked over breakfast on Tuesday.

"Yeah, Mum," Anna said, feigning innocence. "Why don't you drive your car?"

Victoria shot her a look then turned to her son. "Well, you see, Joey. As the Environmental Ambassador for your school, I have to set an example."

"By not driving your car?"

Victoria set down her teacup. "That's right. It's more environmentally friendly to share Dad's car."

"Isn't it a waste, keeping a car you don't use?" Joey asked.

"Yes, well I'll probably get rid of it, eventually."

Anna sat up straight. "I'll tell you what, Mum, I can put an ad on Facebook if you like. How much do you want for it? I bet I can get someone to take it off your hands."

Victoria coloured. "Thank you, Anna, but I can take care of it myself. Now hurry up, both of you. We don't want to be late."

She rose from her chair and walked out of the room, cutting off any further conversation.

Kayla stood directly in front of the gates when they arrived at the school. Victoria grimaced and slowed her step.

"I think I just saw a slow worm," she said to Joey.

He looked down at the grass, distracted. Kayla's son, George, was doing a little dance on the spot. He was humming to himself and flapping his arms like a bird that was about to take off and Kayla made no attempt to rein him in. You'd never know that child was supposedly gifted.

Samantha and Zara arrived, and Victoria relaxed as they formed a huddle.

"Did you see that bit on the news?" Samantha asked. "About Belinda's husband?"

Victoria shook her head. "I was watching that new thriller on Netflix. Did you see . . ."

"Did they find out who did it?" Zara broke in.

"That's just the thing." Samantha was practically wagging her tail with excitement. "They're appealing for new witnesses to come forward. Someone must have seen something."

Victoria cast her eyes around the assembled parents, careful not to linger too long on Belinda, who stood off to one side.

Portia squeezed herself into the huddle.

"Poor Belinda," she said a little too loudly. "How does she sleep at night knowing any one of us could have done it?"

"Oh, come on . . ." Victoria protested.

"No, I mean it. Whoever did it is probably a local because no one else knows those small country roads."

Victoria tried to scoff. "Anyone could find them on satnav . . ."

Portia's eyes gleamed. "Imagine, the killer could be here right now, walking among us."

"Among Us? Isn't that one of the kids' computer games?" Victoria said.

Portia looked at her with consternation. "This isn't a laughing matter, Victoria. That poor woman is suffering. Think of little Ricky. He's been robbed of a dad. It's so tragic."

Victoria swallowed. If they didn't stop talking about the bloody accident she was going to throw up on her shoes.

Joey skidded to a halt in front of her, tripping over his

feet. She helped him catch himself quickly before anyone noticed. The boy was so clumsy at times. You'd think he had two left feet.

"If the driver was someone local, they've probably been acting suspiciously," Samantha speculated. "Like, they would have had to go the garage. Hitting a man would make a huge dent in your car."

"I think the police would have thought of that," Portia said dryly.

"Surely someone would have seen them," Samantha said. "I mean, this is a small town. How does a person drive around with a dented bumper without anyone noticing?"

"People probably did notice and they're keeping quiet. Maybe it was someone important."

Victoria thought again of Paul Schooner. Had he seen the news report? Had it jogged his memory? She looked down at her hand and pretended to examine her nails. Perhaps he was too removed from town gossip to have heard about James Solomon. Her eye flicked to Kayla, who looked so confident and self-satisfied, standing in front of the gate like that.

"You know, the way Kayla drives, I wouldn't be surprised if she's the one who mowed James down." The words were out of her mouth before she could stop them.

Portia's lips curved into a smile. She glanced over at Kayla and the distaste showed on her face.

Samantha turned and looked at her too. "She does like a drink."

Zara nodded. "You know, she had shaky hands last week. I saw her drop her keys . . ."

Samantha's eyes popped. "I saw that!"

"I think she likes to have a liquid lunch . . ."

"And breakfast by the looks of it," Portia said, looking her up and down.

"Do you really think it was Kayla?" Samantha asked.

Kayla must have caught her name because she glanced over in their direction. Victoria quickly turned to look at Joey.

Her friends closed ranks and Samantha burst out in raucous laughter. She wasn't being a bitch. That was just how she responded to pressure. Zara joined in, tilting her head back and laughing deliriously.

"Alright," Portia said under her breath. "What the fuck are you two laughing at?"

The minute Victoria got home from the school run, she marched straight up to Anna's room and began to tear it apart. The girl had a second phone. She was sure of it. Of course, it was quite possible she had taken it to school with her, but even so, if there was a second phone then it stood to reason that there was also a second charger, and that might still be in her room.

Under Anna's bed she found ticket stubs for an eighteen-rated horror film. When had she gone to see that? And who with? She couldn't imagine Maddie sitting through such a film. The girl had come out in hives when Anna put on *Coraline* at their last sleepover. Then she remembered the girl with the umbrella and frowned.

She looked through Anna's drawers and in the secret compartment in her teddy bear. When Anna was a small child, she always used to hide stuff there. But not anymore. Victoria swept back the curtains and found an envelope tucked between the pages of Anna's thesaurus. She gasped as she pulled out a pile of what appeared to be payslips. They all had Anna's name on them. Harry's Burgers she read, incredulously. Anna was working at the burger shop? What the hell?

She flopped down onto Anna's bed, tears flowing as she breathed in the scent. It seemed her daughter had a secret job and a secret life.

She reached for Anna's teddy bear and held it tight. She had thought she and Anna would always be close, unlike her own mother, who she couldn't talk to at all. But she'd been a fool. She didn't have a clue what was going on in her daughter's life. She didn't even know who she was anymore. She released the bear. To her surprise, one of its arms was hanging off. She had gripped it so tight, the stitching had come undone.

Victoria didn't know how long she lay on Anna's bed. Finally, she rose, aware that there was housework to be done. Why couldn't she just close her eyes and take a day off? There was always so much to do. And she had more piano lessons to teach later. She couldn't afford to cancel those. People would say she was unreliable, and she had a reputation to uphold.

She dragged herself downstairs and made a start on the laundry. Technically, Anna was old enough to do her own washing by now, but Victoria wanted to make things easy for her. Her schoolwork was so important, she'd rather Anna focused on that. She didn't want her stretched by unnecessary chores, but apparently, Anna thought she could do a job on top of all the studying she had to do. How did she find the time? Victoria was genuinely puzzled. Between studying at the library and working on her homework, it wasn't as if Anna had much time to spare. Was she bunking off school? Was that what was going on? But no, that nice headteacher of hers would ring if Anna was absent on a regular basis. Maybe he had. She found the number for Harry's Burger House.

"I'd like to speak to the manager," she said, without preamble.

"Can I ask what it's concerning?" said the young lad who took her call.

"No, you can't," Victoria told him.

"Okay, please hold."

She waited a full hour before she hung up, by which time, she was incensed. She had a legitimate complaint and they couldn't be bothered to talk to her. She would go down there.

No, she would write a letter. No, an email. Then there would be a record. And she'd copy in her MP.

She felt a little better, once she'd decided this. She stepped into the kitchen to boil the kettle. Out the window, she could see a little dog who seemed intent on digging up her lawn.

"We'll see about that," she muttered.

She stepped outside, and approached the dog, who slobbered happily at her feet. She took him by the collar and stepped out into the street, straight into the path of Paul Schooner.

"Oh! I'm sorry. Diego slipped his lead . . ."

Paul stopped and stared at her. He must have realised who she was. And if he didn't know before, he now knew exactly where she lived.

"It's Victoria, isn't it? I've been meaning to talk to you."

He bent down to clip the dog's lead back on. Victoria felt a tightness in her throat, as if she was the one wearing the lead, rather than the dog.

"I don't know if you heard but there was an accident, just up the road from my house?"

Victoria couldn't speak. He looked at her closely.

"I can't help thinking you might have seen something? You were at my house just before it happened."

Victoria willed her hands not to shake. "Er, yes I did hear, actually. I spoke to the police as soon as I heard, but I wasn't able to be of much use."

She stood her ground and waited for him to challenge her version of reality. He ran a hand through his thick blond hair.

"Are you sure because . . ."

She thought fast. "You know, I've got a nice juicy bone for

your dog, if you'd like? And perhaps a cup of tea for you?" She forced herself to smile. "You know, I'm famous around here for my tea."

It felt ridiculous to say this to someone who was actually famous, but her nerves had turned her into a blabbering idiot.

Paul hesitated.

"Come on, Diego!" she called, then she turned and headed back towards the house, wiggling her hips as she walked across the lawn. Paul stood there for a moment then followed.

Once inside, Victoria couldn't help but stare a little. Paul Schooner. In her kitchen. He'd been handsome once, before he lost his front teeth and broke his nose. There had been a girl in her class at school who had his picture in her locker. Then he'd lost England that match, and the poster came down.

She opened the fridge and moved a few things around. Since she didn't really have a bone for the dog, she fed him one of Joey's sausages.

"Er . . . Diego shouldn't really be having those. The missus put him on a strict diet."

She smiled winningly. "I'm sure it won't hurt just this once. It'll be our little secret." She switched on the kettle. "I'll just make that tea."

"Coffee for me, if you don't mind."

"Coffee it is."

She located the coffee and a couple of mugs.

"Milk and sugar?"

"Whisky, if you have it."

"No problem."

She reached behind him, gently brushing his shoulder as she opened the cabinet. She felt his eyes upon her as she pulled out a small bottle of Talisker and two glasses.

It felt strange, pouring alcohol so early in the day, but Paul seemed to think it was normal. She poured herself a glass too, even though she had no intention of drinking it. In her experience, drinkers liked company. She handed him his glass and their fingers connected. She met his eyes and glanced away. He raised his glass to his lips and took a sip.

"How are you settling into the neighbourhood?" she asked, leaning back against the counter.

"We should really talk about the accident. I know you said you'd been to the police, but I feel like I should go too, just to set the story straight."

She looked at him curiously. "Why didn't you go before?"

He examined his hands. "I meant to go. I was just busy. And then a couple of weeks passed, and I thought, well, I really should have gone by now. I felt bad, but it honestly slipped my mind. I've been so preoccupied doing up my house. It's like a full-time job, dealing with the builders, plasterers and decorators. It doesn't even feel like my house anymore." He laughed. "Does that sound ridiculous? I mean, they were supposed to be finished by the end of March and what is it now, June? I can't tell you what a relief it is to get out of the house."

She nodded with sympathy. "Silly me, I forgot to make the coffee!" She busied herself, scooping out grounds from the canister. "Hmm, that smells so nice. That's my favourite thing about coffee, the smell."

He stepped closer. "You smell pretty good yourself."

She darted him a glance then looked away. He tossed back the rest of his whisky while she finished making the coffee. She immediately topped him up. He threw her an appreciative smile. His eyes were a little glazed. She bit her lower lip and let her attention wander to the window.

"Paul . . ." Her low, throaty voice sounded silly to her own ears. "Do you really think you should go to the police? You might get in trouble for not coming forward sooner."

"The thing is, what if my statement helps them catch whoever did it?"

"How would it? I've already told them all there is to tell."

"But what if you got the time wrong or something?"

"I'm sure of the timing. I have a clock in my car."

"You were driving a Volvo, weren't you, just like the . . ."

She leaned forward and pressed her lips to his. "You drive me crazy," she told him. She forced herself to look him in the eyes.

When he didn't resist, she took his hand and led him upstairs to the bedroom. His little dog bounded ahead of them, excited at the chance to explore. In the bedroom, she dropped his hand and drew the curtains. Then she shooed Diego into the en suite where he whined and whimpered.

"Won't be long," she whispered as she shut the door.

Paul sat on the bed and pulled his T-shirt over his head.

Oh Lord! At least his chest was muscular. He was far more ripped than Kit, who had always struggled to gain weight.

"Paul, this is all happening so fast. I really think we should get to know each other better first. Why don't we . . ."

"Stop talking, woman."

He was shedding his trousers now. His legs were thick and hairy but his calf muscles were impressive.

"Don't mind if I keep my socks on, do you? I have poor circulation."

Victoria looked at Kit's nightstand. His pint glass still contained an inch of water from this morning, and his book sat waiting for him beside the bed.

Forgive me.

She wriggled under the duvet and waited. She was too embarrassed to get naked in front of this perfect stranger. She couldn't look at him, so she stared up at the ceiling and imagined he was Kit.

Paul clawed and fumbled at her clothes. In all her life, she'd never been with anyone but Kit. She hadn't missed much. He was rough and clumsy, and with his extra bulk, she felt like he was suffocating her.

"You like that, baby?"

"Hmm . . ."

Come on, just get it over with.

She closed her eyes and imagined what the girls at school would say if they could see her now, lying in bed with one of England's most famous football stars. After a few minutes, he stopped.

"I'm sorry," he said. "I probably shouldn't have drunk so much."

"That's okay."

He rolled off her and rested his head wearily against Kit's pillow. He was puffing and panting under his breath. She turned away, a little revolted now.

They lay in bed together for a while and he told her all about his problems. Such silly, pointless problems that were barely problems at all.

"You're a really good listener," he told her.

Eventually, he closed his eyes and she reached for her phone which she'd left on the nightstand. She took her chance and snapped a selfie of the two of them in bed together.

His eyes flew open. "What are you doing?"

Victoria smiled. "I don't think you'll be going to the police now."

He sat up. "What? What are you talking about?"

She showed him the picture she'd just taken. He went to grab the phone off her, but she shook her head.

"I've already emailed that picture to myself."

"Wait . . . What? You're married too, aren't you?"

"That's true, but I hear you're on your last chance with your wife. So I'm telling you, don't go to the police. Or she'll be getting a copy of these photos."

He stared at her. "You're insane!"

He scrambled from the bed and pulled his clothes back on almost as fast as he'd taken them off. "You've also got really freaky eyes, you know that?"

She took no notice. Kit had always said her eyes were her best feature.

"Don't forget your dog," she called after him.

She took a lingering glance at the photo before she deleted it. She couldn't run the risk of Kit seeing it. Even though she'd done this for them, she wasn't sure he'd understand.

28

VICTORIA

"I'd like to start by asking you a few questions before I go and observe Joey at school," said Darren Mills, the terribly expensive educational psychologist she'd booked to assess Joey.

"Well, nobody knows him better than me!" Victoria said with confidence.

She plumped down opposite Darren in the lounge and listened as seriously as she could. Darren had a habit of pushing his glasses up the bridge of his nose. As Victoria watched, they would slowly slide down again until he did it again. It was very distracting. They had just slid down his nose for the third time when she heard someone at the door.

"That will just be my daughter, Anna, coming home for lunch," she said.

She really wished Anna would stick to some kind of schedule. She had made her a packed lunch that morning in the full expectation that Anna would eat at school, but it seemed her daughter had other ideas.

Anna bounced into the lounge and dumped her bag down on the sofa.

"Hello," she said when she saw Darren.

He pushed his glasses up his nose again. "Hi. My name's Darren. I'm here to see your mum about the difficulties your brother's been having."

"About bloody time."

"You go have your lunch," Victoria said sternly.

"Actually, it might be helpful to get your daughter's perspective," Darren said. "Anna, why don't you take a seat?"

Victoria bristled. It felt like they were ganging up on her.

Darren ran briefly through Joey's early childhood development again, with Victoria listing as many of his achievements as she could think of.

"He knew all his numbers by the time he was two," she said proudly. "And he was playing simple tunes on the piano by the time he was three."

She glanced at Anna, daring her to contradict her but Anna said nothing. She probably didn't remember. Victoria continued to run through his accomplishments. If only she could make Darren see what a gifted child Joey was, they could call off this ridiculous autism nonsense and they could all return to normal.

"He was ahead with all his developmental milestones," she said in conclusion.

"He didn't wave though, did he?" Anna pointed out. "Not until he was four, and then he did this funny, stiff-armed wave, kind of like a robot."

Victoria shot her a look. The educational psychologist didn't need to hear about that. That was just Joey messing around, being quirky.

"He was talking in sentences before he was two," she said. "He had an excellent vocabulary. One of his very first words was antelope."

Darren smiled and glanced at his notes. "So how is Joey at sitting still and concentrating?"

"Excellent," she said. "When he's playing the piano or chess, he's laser focused."

"And what about other times? During dinner for example?"

"He's either silent or won't shut up," Anna said. "He goes on and on about his computer games but if you try to talk to him about anything he's not interested in, he just switches off."

Victoria frowned. "Kids get bored," she said. "I can understand that, especially when Kit is talking about work. He works in the city," she couldn't help adding.

"And what does your husband think about Joey? Does he think he's doing okay?"

Victoria glanced at Anna. "He's not around much because he works such long hours."

"He wishes Joey were better at sports," Anna said. "He can't catch a ball to save his life."

"Right," said Darren with another smile. "The next step is for me to go in and observe Joey in class. And I'll speak to his teacher as well to get her take on this."

Victoria nodded miserably. She just hoped Joey was going to give it his best today.

"I'll write up my report afterwards and send you a copy," Darren said, pushing his glasses up his nose one last time.

She nodded. "Thank you for coming and sorry to take up your time." She walked Darren to the door, watched as he got into his car, then turned and looked at Anna. "We need to talk."

"I need to get back to school."

"What about your lunch?"

"I'll eat on the way."

"Oh, no you don't. Sit down."

She produced the payslips and looked triumphantly at her daughter.

"I earnt them," Anna said, totally deadpan.

"You . . . you can't just take a job without asking. You're a child, Anna. You can't work without permission."

"I knew you'd say no," Anna said sulkily. "You never let me do anything. I need some money so I can have a life of my own."

"You get pocket money."

"I want to save up."

Victoria crossed her arms. Perhaps it was admirable, the urge to work and earn her own money. "But why the burger place? Why not Waitrose? Or Marks and Spencer?"

"You're such a snob, Mum."

"You can't just take any old job, Anna. If you wanted to work, I could have got you something more . . . suitable, respectable. Something that would look good on your CV."

"I don't even have a bloody CV. I'm fifteen!" Anna burst out. "You should hear yourself, Mum. You're ridiculous! What the hell does it matter where I work? I'm earning money and it's fun. I like working there. They're good people. We have a laugh."

"A . . . laugh? Is that what you think this is?" Victoria felt the hands of time twisting backwards. All the work she'd done, all the sacrifices so her children could have a better life than she'd had.

"Mum, I really have to go. I'll be late for maths."

"I'll give you a lift. We can talk some more on the way."

Anna fidgeted about in the passenger seat. She could never just sit still, she always had to be doing something, tapping her foot or fidgeting with the glovebox.

"Mum, that man who came today. Does he think Joey is autistic?"

Victoria sighed. "There's nothing wrong with Joey. People just don't understand him because he's gifted. So they want to pigeonhole him."

"He might be, though, Mum. I mean, I read that leaflet and I think it fits."

Victoria gripped the steering wheel tighter. "Just leave it, Anna. Let's talk about something else. How's Maddie these days? I haven't seen her in a while."

"Maddie's a stress head. She doesn't want to do anything except revise."

"Sensible girl. It's good that she takes her studies seriously."

"I wish that was all I had to worry about."

"What do you mean?"

"What do you think I mean?" Anna snapped. "The accident, of course. How can you just carry on, like nothing happened?"

Victoria paused at the traffic lights. "I've been thinking about this, Anna, and if it hadn't been me who hit James, I think it would have been someone else."

"You *what*?"

"You should have seen the way he rode. You'd think he was training for the Tour de France or something, the way he tore about the roads. He was always weaving in and out of traffic. He was one of *those* people."

"What people?"

"You know, adrenaline junkies. They get off on taking risks. Why else would he be riding down a dark lane like that? He could have taken another, safer route that night. It was his choice to go that way, so I don't think I can be entirely blamed."

Anna opened and closed her mouth. "I can't believe I'm hearing this."

"I'm just stating the facts, Anna. I'm sorry that he died but he has to take some of the responsibility too."

"Except, he's the one who's dead, and you're the one who got off scot-free."

A CHILL BREEZE blew across the playground when Victoria arrived to pick up Joey from school. She wrapped her cardigan around her shoulders. Was it her imagination, or had all the groups closed ranks? The Reception mothers formed a tight circle with their buggies and two of the sporty mums were doing press-ups against the wall. Victoria positioned herself between Portia and Samantha. Imelda Daniels was just in front of them, talking to one of the career mothers, and Portia was edging closer, so as to be in their periphery.

There was a woman smoking quite blatantly in front of the gates. Victoria caught a nostalgic whiff. She had been an avid smoker back in her teens. Back then, everyone smoked and nobody thought anything of it. Now, it made you a social outcast, lower than people who tested on animals, or had botched cosmetic surgery on their lips.

Standing next to this loser was Kayla, grinning brightly as if everything were absolutely fine. But it wasn't fine because everyone was talking about her. The wind stirred with the rumours, and although she looked her usual perky self, Victoria noticed that the very tips of her ears were tinged pink.

"Look at her, grinning her arse off because she thinks she's got away with it," Samantha muttered.

They all shot little glances at Kayla. She did look guilty. And the more people looked at her, the guiltier she looked.

Imelda Daniels finished her terribly important conversation and turned towards them.

"What was that?" she said.

Portia leaned forward. "Haven't you heard? Kayla is the one who ran down James Solomon. Apparently, she had one too many the night it happened."

"She was seen leaving All Bar One at midnight " Zara said.

Victoria nodded. The accident had happened in the early evening, but she wasn't about to let the facts get in the way of a good rumour.

"I heard she left George home alone," the words were out of her mouth before she'd even known she was going to say them. She clapped a hand over her mouth, wondering if she'd gone too far, but Imelda was drinking it in. Her eyes danced with delight.

"It's disgusting she's allowed to get away with it," she said.

Kayla looked their way and they all looked down at their phones. They wouldn't dream of saying anything to her face.

There was a lightness to Victoria's step as she walked back home with Joey. She hoped she hadn't pushed things too far with that detail about George, but boy, Imelda had loved it. Perhaps she would think of Victoria when she was making the volunteer rota for the school fete. Victoria had been landed with the tombola the last time, and it had been absolute mayhem. She would take anything rather than do that again.

29

JOEY'S DIARY

Lies people have told today:

1. Ricky said his mum is not a liar.
2. Miss Henley said Ricky's mum is not a liar.
3. Dad told Mum he didn't know about Anna's job.

30

W hen Darren rang the bell, Victoria had the silliest compulsion not to answer. She felt ridiculous, hiding in the upstairs bedroom, but there she was, squatting down low, the way she had sometimes done as a child when the big burly man came round to collect the money her parents owed.

She remembered her mother's frantic warnings: "Get down, Victoria. Stop gawking. He'll see you."

The rattling of the letter box. The rattling of her own heart, thumping so loud she was sure it would give them away. And then the relief as the footsteps receded.

"Not yet!" She remembered her mother pulling her back. And then one last rattle before they were gone.

"I know you're in there!" the big man would call out.

But Darren had better manners than to go yelling through people's letter boxes, even if he suspected she might be in. She heard the envelope drop onto the mat, but she waited the requisite five minutes before she crept downstairs to grab it. She couldn't deal with it just yet. She popped it in the kitchen drawer under all the other junk she didn't want anyone to see.

———

BELINDA AND RICKY were slightly early for the next piano lesson. They caught Victoria off-guard as she was vacuuming the lounge. She bit back her irritation and shoved the vacuum into the cupboard. Belinda had an unreadable look on her face as Victoria showed them into the room.

The lesson itself was unremarkable. Ricky was a little less fired up than he'd been before. He seemed a little deflated, Victoria thought, but it wasn't her place to pry. Besides, she could hardly talk to the boy with his mother sitting not three feet behind him.

Joey was quiet too. He thrashed Belinda at chess but seemed to take no enjoyment from it. He seemed tired of her company now, as if he only played to please her. Why did Belinda insist on hanging around for the duration of the lesson? Victoria couldn't kick the feeling that she stayed so she could keep an eye on her.

Just as they were leaving, Anna made an appearance in the living room. She'd been in her room studying for the duration of the lesson and Victoria had rather hoped she'd stay there.

"I saw you getting your car towed last week," she said to Belinda.

Belinda nodded. "We broke down outside the Co-op. So embarrassing! We held up the traffic for a good half an hour while we waited to get towed."

"Oh no, how awful," Victoria said.

"Yeah, it was mortifying," Belinda said. "All those other drivers beeping and yelling at me to move but the engine was just dead."

"I don't know why they do that," Victoria said. "It seems so unnecessary."

Belinda looked at her steadily. "Yes, for some reason, people are completely different when they get behind the wheel."

Anna coughed. "If you need a new car, my mum's selling hers."

Belinda looked at Victoria. "Are you?"

"I..."

"Do you want to see it?" Anna asked. "It's in really good condition."

Belinda's mouth twitched slightly. "Then why are you selling it?"

"Mum doesn't use it anymore. She's trying to be more environmentally friendly."

Victoria forced herself to speak: "Stop it, Anna. I'm sure Belinda doesn't want to ..."

"Actually, I do need a new car," Belinda said. "Maybe I should take a look."

There was something false in that smile of hers, but there was little Victoria could do as Anna fished in the drawer for the keys.

Victoria swayed and clutched at the shoe cupboard. She ought to say something. She needed to stop this, but her lips felt as though they were stuck with glue. Anna was already at the door. She darted a rebellious glance at Victoria before stepping outside. Everyone, except Joey followed.

Anna unlocked the garage door and it whined in protest. Clink, clank, clunk. The door opened slowly, painfully, dragging out the inevitable.

"How many miles did you say it's done?" Belinda asked as they waited.

"I don't know," Anna's voice wobbled slightly. "We've only had it a few years."

Victoria sank down onto the front step and waited. Her legs would no longer carry her, and she was weak from the pretence. She watched as Belinda took a step closer, ready to inspect the car, and she held her breath.

31

Now that the moment had come, Anna was petrified. A huge lump rose in her throat as she prepared herself for Belinda's reaction. She half expected Victoria to jump in front of the car or fake a heart attack, anything to divert the woman from seeing what she had done. Instead, her mother seemed to have shrivelled like a pumpkin left over from Halloween. She had folded herself onto the step, and sat as if gazing out at the warm, balmy evening. As if her life wasn't about to change forever.

Belinda took a step forward, then moved around the side. She circled the car a couple of times, checking out the paintwork. Anna moved closer and saw that the car was pristine. The glass on the windscreen was all in one piece, not a single chip. The headlight that had been smashed up looked good as new, and there was not a scratch to be seen on the front bumper. Anna couldn't move. It was as if her mind had disappeared into a fog. Her mouth was filled with words and recriminations, but she couldn't spit them out.

She ran her fingertips over the bonnet, wondering if her mother had somehow created an illusion. If she had ever wondered if Victoria was a witch, this was the proof. Where was the badly crumpled metal? The shattered window, with the cobweb of glass in the centre. Was this in fact her mother's car at all? She checked the number plate. It looked the same. It appeared to be the same make and model. But it could not be her car because this car looked perfect, whereas Victoria's car was a wreck.

Belinda stepped out of the garage and gave her a gentle nod.

"It's very nice," she said. "Probably a bit too nice to use as a runabout."

She met her eyes and Anna had the sudden urge to scream but only a faint squeak came out. Belinda didn't notice. She waved to Victoria, then she led Ricky out of the garden and out to the road where her own unreliable car was parked.

Anna's eyes whirled back to Victoria, who smiled wanly. To the uninitiated, her mother looked chilled out, relaxed. Anna knew better. Victoria was on the verge of collapse.

The muscles in the back of Anna's neck burned as she strode towards her.

"What the hell happened?" she hissed.

Victoria glanced out at the street. They both heard Belinda's car start. Anna shook with rage. She ought to run after Belinda and tell her that they'd all been had, that this was not the car she'd intended to show her. Not the car Belinda needed to see.

She turned back to Victoria. "What kind of witch are you?"

Victoria gave the faintest of smiles and hung her head, as though it physically pained her to carry it around.

Joey came outside and sat on the step beside Victoria and she sat there, caressing him like a baby. It infuriated Anna, the way they hugged each other. He was making her feel better, and their mother didn't deserve to feel better. She needed to face up to what she had done.

After a while, Joey went back inside. Victoria went to get up, but Anna stopped her.

"What the hell happened?"

Her mother looked at her with defiance. "I took care of it, like I take care of everything."

"Is that even the same car?"

Victoria gave her a superior look.

"What did you do, Mum? Change the number plates?"

"No, no. It's all above board."

"Does Dad know?"

Her mother met her gaze. "Dad arranged it."

"Yeah, right."

"I'm serious. He called an old classmate. Someone we went to school with."

"When? I haven't seen anyone here."

"Oh, well you and Joey were both at school. Besides, he's not the type of person you'd want to meet."

"He's a criminal, you mean?"

"No, I wouldn't call him that but he's very . . . discreet."

"Lucky for you."

Her mother looked at her sharply. "You do realise that if Belinda had seen the car as it was, it would all have been over?" She held up her fingers to show a space an inch wide. "You came this close to destroying our family, Anna."

Anna got right in her face. "No, Mum, you're doing that on your own."

ANNA WAS SCROLLING through her mother's Instagram feed on Sunday morning. There was a carefully positioned selfie of

Victoria holding a cactus, and another of her pretending to water a tomato plant.

#plantsofInstagram #schoolfete #SurreyStBernards.

The kitchen table was loaded with plants. Victoria had bought dozens of little pots of tomato plants, sweet peas, foxgloves and geraniums. Not to mention a substantial number of cactus plants.

"Cactuses are always popular with parents since they're virtually impossible to kill," Victoria told Anna. She lowered her voice. "Unless you're Joey, that is. Joey has had three and somehow he's managed to kill them all."

Anna did not smile. Her mother was trying to be all buddy-buddy, acting as though nothing had happened.

They carried the trays and boxes down to the car.

"I'll have to drive extra slowly," Victoria said. "Precious cargo onboard."

She shut the boot and marched back to the house.

"Come on, everyone in the car! We don't want to be late."

"*You* don't want to be late," Kit grumbled as he pulled on his trainers. "I'd be quite happy to stay in bed."

"We need to be there early. Imelda Daniels is counting on me."

Anna snorted.

"No one had better tell me the results of the footy or I'm going to be fuming," her dad said. "I can't believe I'm going to miss the match just so I can sell plants to a bunch of people who probably don't even want them."

Victoria laid a hand on his shoulder, the way she always did when she wanted something. "Your sacrifice is acknowledged."

"Are you sure you've got the right day?" Kit asked when they arrived at the school. There was a row of tables out on the field and a few stacks of chairs but little else. There was no bunting, no signage and no one manning the car park.

Victoria hurried over to a woman with big hair. She must be the Queen Bee, Anna decided. She was the only one sitting down, while all the other adults buzzed about, following her orders.

"Reporting for duty!" Victoria announced.

The Queen Bee took a moment to look up from the papers she was holding, then she smiled with all her teeth.

"Victoria. So glad you made it! And you brought the family too!"

Her eyes drifted from Joey to Anna before settling on Kit.

"Where is everybody?" Victoria asked. Portia had texted that morning to say that Ariadne had a vomiting bug. She hoped it wasn't going around.

"Haven't you heard? There's an important match on this morning."

"No one had better tell me the result," Kit growled.

The Queen Bee burst out laughing then stopped abruptly. "Victoria, can I ask you to run the tombola today as well as the plant stall?"

"Oh, but I was on the tombola last year . . ."

"And did an excellent job I hear. The stalls are right next to each other so I'm sure you and your family can manage it between you."

Anna's dad shrugged. "In for a penny, in for a pound."

The toothy grin returned. "That's the spirit. You're on tables eight and nine."

They walked onto the field. The grass had that freshly mowed smell and the sun peeked through the clouds. Perhaps this would be the year it didn't rain. Tables eight and nine were far too small, so they had to put half of the plants on the ground.

"Aren't you worried people will tread on them?" Anna asked.

Her mother shrugged. "If we don't put them out, people

won't buy them. I don't want to be left with a ton of plants to take home."

"So speaks the school Environmental Ambassador!"

Anna looked up to see a round-faced woman, who was dragging a small suitcase behind her. She wore chunky red glasses and a sparkly gold dress. If Anna had to guess, she'd say this woman was the magic act. She glanced at her mother and saw her grimace. The woman stopped in front of the stall to her left.

"Hey, Vicky, looks like we're neighbours!"

Anna giggled. Her mother hated being called Vicky. She had a feeling this woman knew it too.

"For crying out loud!" Victoria said under her breath.

"Who is that?" Anna whispered.

"Oh, that's just Kayla."

"Why don't you like her?"

"I didn't say I didn't like her."

Anna raised a brow. "Could have fooled me."

She glanced at Kayla again. She was humming to herself as she set up her stall, dabbing her hand with an experimental swatch of silver glitter. She seemed fun. Her son, by contrast, was very quiet. He crawled under the table with his iPad and stayed there, amusing himself with his games.

Anna finished setting up the plant stall and moved to help her dad and Joey with the tombola. Joey stood on his tiptoes, nudging their dad as he tried to attach tickets to the prizes.

"Why don't you take a look around the stalls?" Kit said, handing him a couple of quid.

"I don't think they're ready yet," Anna said.

Kit gave her a look. "He can still have a look, can't he?"

Joey pocketed the money and began a slow amble around the field.

"Right," Kit said. "I reckon we've got about fifteen minutes to get this lot sorted."

A voice came through the loudspeaker. It was the Queen Bee. She blethered on for ages, while all around her, the volunteers scrambled to finish setting up.

"And now for our special guest, Paul Schooner!"

"Mum, our friend Paul is here!" Anna said.

Her mother continued with what she was doing, but Anna noticed the pink tinge to her cheeks. She listened as Paul made a short speech and then someone handed him a giant pair of scissors so that he could snip through the thick red ribbon.

A loud cheer went up and the crowd surged onto the field. She caught her mum darting little glances at Paul as he visited each of the stalls, accompanied by his wife and children. When they reached the plant stall, his wife bought the largest, spikiest cactus.

"That's what he calls me, his little cactus," she told Victoria with a wink.

"Why's that?"

"Because I might be small, but I'm fucking prickly . . ."

"Where are we going to put that thing?" Paul cut in.

"You'll find somewhere," his wife said. She was smiling, but Anna didn't miss the glint in her eye.

For the next half hour, they were rushed off their feet. The tombola drew the most interest, and it was a mad scramble to match the winners with the prizes. A girl handed over a winning ticket – 205 – and Anna scanned the table until she found a bottle of rum.

"Here you go - 205!"

Her dad looked up with a frown. "Anna!"

"Yeah?"

"Was she over eighteen?"

"What?"

"That young woman . . ."

Anna's hand flew to her mouth. "Oh, shit!"

"Never mind, she's gone now. Just make sure you check in future."

Kayla's face painting stall had no customers at all. Anna couldn't understand it. When she was little, she had loved having her face painted. She'd always asked for a big strawberry on each cheek. She wouldn't be seen dead with a painted face now of course, but those little kids . . .

She watched for a moment as one woman steered her children past Kayla's stall. What was all that about? Perhaps she didn't want her kids to get messy.

Joey came running over.

"Mum! Dad! Miss Henley's wearing jeans!"

Kit smiled. "You know, Joey, teachers do have a life outside of school."

Joey looked at him doubtfully. "Oh yeah, Dad. You can have this back." He handed over the money he'd been given.

"Didn't you buy anything?"

"Couldn't make my mind up. Can we go home now?"

"Afraid not, son. We're here till the bitter end."

"You've got orchestra at one," Victoria reminded him.

"Yeah, I know but . . ."

The Queen Bee made another announcement over the loudspeaker and Joey covered his ears with his hands. Kayla handed her son a pair of ear defenders, which he wore quite happily, to drown out the noise.

"You should get Joey some of them," Anna said.

"Thank you, Anna, but you can leave the parenting to me," Victoria said and she handed Joey her phone to play with.

There was another rush for the tombola. Kit took the money and Anna raced up and down, locating the winning items. At one point the queue was five people deep. Gradually the rush died down and Anna drank her can of Coke in one go.

"Good work!" Kit said, sinking back into his chair.

The tombola looked like it had been hit by a plague of locusts. There were strips of paper all over the place and they were down to the last few prizes.

Anna glanced over at her mum, Victoria had dirt down the front of her shirt and under her fingernails. She stifled a giggle. Her mother hated to look anything but pristine when she was out in public.

Now that the tombola prizes were gone, they had a flurry of customers for the plant stall. There were small children wanting plants for their rooms and more serious gardeners snapping up the bargains. Once Victoria had dealt with them all, the Queen Bee flounced over.

"Haven't we been busy?"

It was pathetic, the way her mother glowed with pride.

"You haven't done anything," Anna muttered under her breath. "It was all us."

The Queen Bee did not appear to hear. "Would you mind awfully if I borrow your husband?"

"Be my guest."

Kit raised his head. "Er, what exactly do you need me for?"

"I just need some crates of drink brought off the van."

Kit and Victoria looked at each other.

"Er . . ."

"He can't," Anna told her. "He's got a bad back."

The Queen Bee hid her teeth. "Where are all the men when I need them?"

"I can do it," Kayla called from her stall.

The Queen Bee looked at her. "Oh, no. I need you right there, thank you."

"Oh yes, I'm rushed off my feet here."

Kayla shot Victoria a comical look which she didn't return.

Her mum really was a bit of a bitch, Anna concluded. She turned and noticed Mrs Solomon, sheltering below a willow tree with Ricky. She had a knack of camouflaging herself, blending in with the background. Silent and observing.

"Mum, can I play with Ricky?" Joey said.

"Okay, but you've got to be back here by one."

"Alright, Mum."

Anna raised an eyebrow. Brilliant as Joey was, he couldn't keep track of time to save his life.

"I think it's time for a burger," Kit announced. He stood and stretched slowly, painfully. Anna wished she could make his back pain go away.

"Can you get me a Coke?" Victoria asked.

"I'll have a hot dog," Anna said.

Kit nodded and walked away.

Miss Henley came over and looked at her mother's plants.

"Are you buying?" Victoria asked curtly.

"We must have a talk about Joey," Miss Henley said. "I do feel he needs more support than he's currently getting . . ."

Victoria rubbed her head. "I'd really rather wait until the assessment process is completed. We don't want to jump the gun, do we?"

"No, but there are some practical things we can do now. I think he would benefit from more support at break times, but we'd have to make a case for . . ."

"I can do Thursday," Victoria said abruptly.

Miss Henley blinked. "Okay then. Thursday after drop off?"

"Wonderful, I look forward to seeing you then."

Victoria waited until Miss Henley walked off to another stall.

"Interfering cow," she muttered under her breath.

"Um, Mum. I think you've got another customer."

There was a man coming towards them. As he got closer, she saw that all his teeth were worn out on one side, causing his jaw to slant to the left. Anna smiled nervously but he didn't smile back. He wasn't looking at her. His eyes were locked on Victoria with an intensity that made her shiver.

Her mum staggered to her feet, palms pressed down on the flimsy table. The plants wobbled perilously. For one ridiculous moment, Anna thought it was an earthquake.

"Mum? What's happening?"

"Anna, can you mind the stall a minute?"

Anna watched open mouthed as her mother scurried off in the direction of the car park. The rough looking man went after her, his long legs closing the distance between them in no time. Anna scanned the field for her dad but he was nowhere to be seen.

Shit, what should she do? She pulled out her phone. "Come on, Dad, answer."

But Kit did not pick up. Minutes ticked by and Anna felt sweat building on her brow.

"How much are the azaleas?" a woman asked.

"On the house! Take them!" Anna said. She pushed the plants towards the dumbfounded woman and took off. Her stomach lurched as she ran towards the car park.

"Mum!"

She spotted her by the car. The strange man stood very close to her, almost as if he wanted to kiss her but the body language was all wrong. Her mother had her back pressed against the car, like she was trying to get away from him, and he had one hand just above her shoulder, resting on the roof of the car. His other hand was balled into a fist.

She only caught three words.

"You owe me."

"Mum!" she yelled across the car park.

The man turned and looked at her. He gave her a wink, then released her mother and swaggered off towards his own car.

"Mum? Who was that? What did he want?"

"Oh, Anna!"

Victoria looked ready to cry. "He's just . . . an old friend. I didn't expect to see him here, that's all."

Anna narrowed her eyes. He'd been familiar somehow, though she couldn't quite place him. She was pretty sure she'd seen him at their house that time. Hadn't Victoria said he was the plumber? She touched her mother's hand. It was shaking. "Are you sure you're okay, Mum?"

Victoria was silent for a moment. She closed her eyes and when she opened them again, all signs of tension were gone. She looked back at the field, where the school fete continued without them.

"What are you doing away from the stall, Anna? You can't just walk off like that!"

"What did he say to you exactly?" Kit asked when he returned from the burger stall.

"Nothing much," Victoria said, with a glance at Anna. "We can talk about this later."

A couple of kids ran over to the tombola.

"Can you serve them?" Kit said to Anna. "I'm still eating."

Anna took the children's money and searched for their prize.

"He wants more money," Victoria murmured. "He got wind of the news report and now he thinks the job is worth double."

"Double! The cheeky sod!"

"Shh! This is serious, Kit. He was really nasty."

"Where are we supposed to get that sort of money? We're maxed out as it is. I told you we should have had the car scrapped."

"And I told you that would have been too obvious. People would have asked questions."

"So what are we going to do about Nigel? We don't have that sort of money."

"I don't know. I'll have a think. I always think of something."

"Yes," he agreed, taking a bite of his burger. "You always do."

The fete dragged on. Joey was late for his solo, but then he performed so well that he was instantly forgiven. Normally, Victoria would have glowed with pride, but today her mind was elsewhere. She was still a little shaken from her encounter with Nigel. He seemed under the impression that she had money to throw around. People always did that: they took one look at her beautiful house and they thought she was loaded. They didn't see the loans and credit card debts that mounted up, month after month.

"Oh, they're going to draw the raffle!" Kayla said.

Victoria turned and looked. Sure enough, Imelda Daniels was back up on stage, reminding everyone that the grand prize was a night away at a luxury spa.

"Please welcome back our local celebrity, Paul Schooner, to draw the lucky raffle winner."

Paul put his hand in the barrel and drew out a piece of paper.

"And the winner is . . . Imelda Daniels!"

There was a slow handclap. Somebody booed. It might have been Kayla. Imelda coloured and held up her hands.

"Draw again. I insist. It won't do for the chair of the PTA to snag the top prize!"

With a shrug, Paul dipped his hand in again. "Eve Henley."

It was Miss Henley's turn to shake her head. "Redraw!"

Paul stuck his hand in for a third time. Some little nobody won. One of the Reception mums with a double buggy and too many dogs. Victoria was glad she hadn't won because the thought of turning down a luxury night away was too much to contemplate. Especially now, when they needed the money.

She cast her eyes over tables eight and nine. The tombola had sold out and they were left with just the sorriest looking plants. She and Anna counted up the money, while Kit and Joey started on the clean-up. Most of the other volunteers had scarpered.

It was only a short drive home, but the traffic in town was ridiculous. Apparently, everyone had been to the pub to watch the game.

"Three-nil!" a group of lads yelled out of their car window.

"Oh, for fuck's sake!" said Kit.

"They didn't say who won," Victoria said.

He lifted his eyebrows and she promptly shut up.

It was raining by the time they got home, and they all got drenched in the dash from the car to the house. Victoria threw on her dressing gown and warmed up some ready meals to eat in front of the TV, since Kit wanted to watch the match. Anna and Joey wolfed down their food and scrambled up to their rooms.

They ate quickly, shovelling the food into their mouths. Victoria wasn't even sure what flavour her ready meal was supposed to be but she ate every bite. She pushed her tray away and rested her head against Kit's shoulders.

"How did I get so lucky?" she whispered.

"Huh?"

He turned and looked at her. He had a bit of tomato sauce smeared across his cheek. Victoria reached up and rubbed it off.

A little later, Anna came downstairs.

"Dad, can I go out?"

Why was she asking Kit?

"Have you finished your homework?" Victoria enquired.

"Most of it."

"What about your Latin?"

"Mum, I've told you. I'm dropping Latin."

"Then the answer's no."

As Anna hovered in the doorway, the football match ended and the local news came on.

"Police are investigating dozens of new leads on the Godalming hit and run. It is believed that the car that hit local cyclist, James Solomon, was a Volvo. Once again, if you have any information on the incident, no matter how trivial, please ring the number on the screen."

Victoria's shoulders tensed. She felt as though her body had been sucked into the sofa.

"They know," Kit breathed. "They bloody know."

"No, they don't," Victoria said firmly. "It's fine, Kit. Loads of people drive Volvos."

"Loads of people don't live just up the road from the scene of the crime."

"If they knew, they would have come knocking."

"They probably will now."

"And if they do, we've got it covered."

She glanced at the door, but Anna was no longer standing there. The little minx had taken the opportunity to slip out.

"What the hell does she think she's playing at?" Victoria asked when a search of the house confirmed that Anna had indeed gone out.

"She's got her phone, hasn't she?"

"She'd better have."

She started to dial.

"Wait, let me do it," Kit said.

"Why?"

"It'll be less . . . confrontational."

Victoria set her jaw. She didn't need this right now. She couldn't understand it. Anna used to be such a sweet little girl. No trouble at all. She couldn't believe she had changed so much in such a short space of time.

"Anna? This is Dad. Can you call or text when you get this? I just want to know where you are and if you'll be needing a lift home."

Kit hung up the phone. Victoria was far from satisfied.

"Where the hell is she? Why isn't she answering?" She thought for a moment. "Hey, I bet she's gone to the Burger House!"

Kit shook his head. "No, she doesn't work Saturdays."

Victoria stared at him.

"She's probably with Bex."

"Who the hell is Bex?"

"Her best friend."

"No, Maddie's her best friend!"

"Not anymore."

"Wait, is that the girl with the . . . piercings?"

"She does have one piercing, if I recall." His phone beeped. He smiled as he read the text. "It's okay, she's at Bex's. I'll pick her up at ten."

"Ten? That's a bit bloody late, isn't it?"

"She's fifteen. We've got to let her have a life. Besides I'd rather she's hanging out at a friend's house than trying to get into some pub or club."

"Anna's not like that."

"They're all like that," Kit said. "They're teenagers."

Victoria settled back onto the sofa. "How did you know she doesn't work Saturdays?"

Kit looked uncomfortable.

"You've known all along, haven't you? How could you do that and not tell me?"

"You give the kid a hard time," Kit said. "I know you only do it because you want to protect her but I feel like she needs to breathe a bit. I also think if she wants a job, she should have one. We both worked at her age."

Victoria looked out the window. "I don't want her to be like us! I want things to be better for her. For both of them."

"And they will be," he said. "If we can just keep ourselves out of prison."

VICTORIA WAS TOO angry to talk to Anna when she came home. Instead, she went upstairs and began getting ready for bed. As she stood brushing her teeth, she noticed a fresh crease in the middle of her forehead. She was sure that hadn't been there that morning. She ignored it and continued to brush her teeth. She must have brushed a little too vigorously because the sink was spattered with blood. Instantly, she was transported back to that cold February night. She saw the glare of the headlights, the ribbons of blood in the road and the noise – the unexpected onslaught of her own agonised screams.

She turned on both taps and watched as the water swirled round and round in the plughole. What if the police were coming for her? What was she going to do?

SHE EMPTIED the sink and crawled into bed, bone-tired but still unable to relax. She pulled a notebook from her bedside drawer and started to brainstorm. There had to be some way she could get her hands on that money. The only thing she could think of was to teach more lessons, but she had already filled the popular four o'clock slots and few parents wanted their children's lessons to go on later in the evening. What about the summer holidays though? Parents were always looking for somewhere to send their little horrors. She could offer intensive lessons. Half a day at a time.

Where had Kit got to? She'd thought he'd come straight up to bed, but instead she heard him and Anna in the kitchen: the sound of cupboards opening and closing. The smell of toast being made. Anna burst out laughing. Anna never laughed like that with her anymore.

"Mum!"

Joey stood in the doorway, his little face peering in.

"What is it, darling? Did Anna wake you?"

"Mum, I want to sleep in your bed."

"Oh, Joey, you're much too old for this nonsense!"

His bottom lip came out and Victoria folded him into her arms.

"Come on, let's get you back to bed."

She led him back to his room and pulled back the covers. Then she felt the dampness. The slightly sour smell . . .

"Oh, Joey!" She opened his chest of drawers and pulled out some clean underwear and pyjamas. "Here, have a wash and put these on."

"It wasn't me," he said in a small voice.

"Well, who was it then?" She began peeling off the sheets. It had gone right through the mattress protector.

"It was the deer."

Victoria gripped his shoulders tightly. "It was just a dream, got it? You've got to forget about that nonsense."

Joey pulled away. "Stop it. You're hurting me!"

"Can't I give my son a hug?"

Joey didn't answer. He sat down on the floor and began pulling chess pieces out of his drawer. He positioned them on the board.

"Right, well, I'm going to get you some clean sheets," Victoria said briskly.

She went downstairs to the utility room.

"Is Joey awake?" Kit asked.

"He wet the bed."

"Oh dear. Do you need a hand?"

"No, I can manage, thank you." Her eyes flickered to Anna, standing in the hallway, her long blonde hair was now styled in a sophisticated updo and she wore lipstick and mascara. Not clown make-up. She'd taken care to apply it properly. Or perhaps this friend of hers had done it for her.

"So you were with Bex tonight?" she said, as she hunted for bedding.

"Yes."

"What about Maddie?"

"What about her?"

"I like Maddie."

"You be friends with her then."

Victoria yanked out a duvet cover. It had little ballerina mice on it. One of Anna's old ones. It would have to do.

"So Maddie's out and Bex is in?"

"Harsh, Mum. I'm still friends with Maddie. I just prefer Bex."

"Is that why you're dropping Latin?"

"No, you're why I'm dropping Latin."

"Come on, Anna," Kit called from the kitchen. "Finish your toast. It's getting late."

Victoria carried the sheets up the stairs and remade Joey's bed. He'd put his pyjamas on the wrong way round but she didn't bother to correct him.

"I'm sorry, Mum," he said as she tucked him into bed.

"You've got nothing to be sorry for, Joey. You're a good boy."

She left the light on, the way he liked it. Then she

returned to her room and brought up the calculator function on her phone. Great, so she just needed to teach three children a day for three hours each in order to make . . . nowhere close to the amount of money she needed. She felt like banging her head against a brick wall. What the hell was she going to do?

33

Am I

1. A good friend; or
2. A bad friend?

I took the quiz in Anna's magazine but the questions didn't make any sense.
Ricky says I'm a good friend, but he might just be saying that. People never say what they mean. Sometimes he laughs at my jokes, other times he goes all quiet and grumpy. I don't mean to upset him about his dad. I know what I want to say in my head, but when I open my mouth, the wrong words come out.
p.s. I'm going to stay awake for the rest of the night. That way the deer won't get me.

34

VICTORIA

Victoria kept her eyes down when she spotted Kayla in the playground on Monday morning. She couldn't help but notice the way George walked, up on his toes like a ballerina. She walked past quickly and pretended to wave to a friend in the crowd.

"Don't forget we're meeting on Thursday," Miss Henley said brightly, when she delivered Joey to the classroom door.

"Yes, I haven't forgotten." There was something in the teacher's tone that always rubbed her up the wrong way. She spoke to her like she was speaking to one of the children. She turned to leave and saw that Imelda Daniels was waving to her. She checked behind her to make sure she wasn't mistaken, but no, it was her Imelda wanted. She scurried across the playground.

"Hi, Imelda."

"Victoria, have you seen Portia today?"

"Er, yes, I saw her drop Ariadne just a minute ago."

"Ah, good. People have been talking, you know."

"About what?"

Imelda cast her gaze around the playground. "Some people are questioning Portia's commitment to the PTA."

Victoria tilted her head. "Why's that?" But she already knew why. Portia hadn't helped out at the school fete, and she'd been absent from the last two PTA meetings. They bored the pants off her, she'd admitted as much to Victoria.

"She's definitely coming to the next fundraiser," Victoria said. "She's on my quiz team. And we've both put our names down to help out with the refreshments for the open evening."

Imelda smiled. "You're a good friend, Victoria. No one is questioning your commitment. Sometimes, I can't help thinking you'd be a better fit for vice chair."

Victoria's mouth fell open, but before she could say anything, Imelda spotted the head teacher.

"Sorry, Victoria, I must go. We need to discuss requirements for the new school minibus."

Victoria nodded, her head held high as she walked out of the school. Imelda Daniels thought she'd make a good vice chair! She couldn't believe it.

On the way home, Victoria stopped off at the local shop for a few essentials. She didn't want to be seen buying frozen pizza, but Joey would eat little else at the moment and he'd already rejected the one she had in the freezer. It had to be his usual brand or nothing at all.

As she stood in front of the frozen cabinet, she heard a strangled sob. She looked up and saw Belinda Solomon. She froze, attempting to be as invisible as possible. If she were the one sobbing into the frozen cheesecakes, she wouldn't thank anyone for drawing attention to it.

She picked up Joey's pizza and attempted to squeeze past but Belinda grabbed her arm.

"Victoria?"

"Oh, Belinda!" She glanced over at the door.

"It's all too much," Belinda sobbed into her shoulder.

Victoria stood uncomfortably still and patted Belinda on the back. She was still clutching the pizza with her other hand so the whole manoeuvre was really uncomfortable.

"It's that bloody news programme," Belinda said with a gasp. "It's made me so paranoid. It's got me suspecting everybody. That's . . . that's why I agreed to look at your car. Can you believe it?"

"My . . . my car?"

"The detectives told me they thought the person who killed James was driving a Volvo, so now I suspect everyone who drives one."

Victoria forced out a laugh. "Lots of people drive a Volvo."

"I know! I'm ridiculous!"

She wracked her brains, trying to think what car Kayla drove. It was one of those little Renaults, wasn't it? So that was her off the hook.

She gestured to the pizza.

"Let me just pay for this and I'll walk you out to your car."

"Oh, Victoria, you've been such a good friend to me," Belinda said through her tears.

Victoria extracted herself from Belinda's tentacles and made her way to the till. She couldn't even remember what else she'd come in for. The shopkeeper smiled.

"How's your boy?"

"He's fine thanks."

He continued to talk as he rang up her purchase, but she was in no mood to chit-chat. What was going on with Belinda? Was she genuinely feeling overwhelmed or was this some ploy to trip her up?

In the time it took Victoria to pay, Belinda had pulled herself together. They chatted amiably as they walked to Belinda's car.

"Would you like a lift?" Belinda asked.

"Oh no," Victoria said, her heart in her mouth. "I'm the school's Environmental Ambassador, remember?"

She walked on, unable to look at Belinda a moment longer. She scurried along the pavements, wishing she could get home faster. She couldn't bear to see anyone, couldn't bear to . . .

Damn! There was Paul Schooner and his wretched dog. She quickened her step, almost tripping over the curb. Diego spotted her and started yapping. Victoria did not look back.

The keys rattled in her hands as she unlocked the front door. She watched from behind the curtain as Diego sniffed at her garden. To her consternation, Paul let him off the lead and the little dog charged onto her lawn, where he proceeded to dig up the flower beds. Was he . . . yes, he was, he was marking her garden! She wanted to bang on the window, but she didn't want to get into a confrontation with Paul. Her phone beeped with a new text:

I need that money by Saturday, 6pm.

What did he expect her to do? Sell a kidney?

She started to dial Kit but then she set the phone down. Kit would be busy with work. She needed to sort this out for herself. She caught her reflection in the hall mirror and a grim smile formed on her lips. She would do what she had to do.

She hadn't lied when she'd told Anna that Nigel was an old friend. Okay, friend was probably stretching it, but they knew him from way back, when they used to play marbles in the playground. He wasn't the sharpest tool in the box, if exam results were to be believed, and yet, he'd had an uncanny knack of winning everyone's marbles, including hers.

Nigel had never left the old neighbourhood. He still lived

in the house he'd grown up in and he ran his business from his old garage. Victoria couldn't understand why he had never moved away. He was doing alright for himself by the sound of it.

THE JOURNEY WAS ABOUT forty-five minutes by car and probably twice that by public transport, but she didn't fancy driving into the city. She texted the student she was supposed to be teaching that morning and cancelled their lesson. Then she caught the next train to London.

Victoria hadn't been on a train in years. She'd forgotten how crowded and dirty they could be. She hopped off at Waterloo and changed for a tube train that propelled her through dark tunnels and out onto busy platforms where everybody seemed to know where they were going and everybody was in a rush.

She wasn't quite prepared for the sensation she felt as she walked out of the station. She hadn't been home in fifteen years and she felt a lump in her throat as she took in the familiar surroundings. She allowed herself a small smile as she passed the chemist shop where she'd once held a Saturday job and increased her pace as she neared the flats where she'd lived as a child. Wet washing hung from the grimy balconies and a group of teenagers huddled in the doorway. One of them gave her the eye so she kept on walking. Yep, it still stank of piss and weed, and she was glad to be out of it.

Nigel's house looked as shit as it always had. For someone who was apparently doing well for himself, he hadn't spent any of it on the outside of his house. The paint was peeling off the front door, and the windows were smeared with dirt.

She walked round to the back, listening for voices. The

garage door was open, the radio on, belting out music. A red Peugeot sat up on a ramp, suspended above the ground. Nigel leaned against his workbench and sipped a mug of tea. She closed her eyes for a minute and psyched herself up.

"Hi, Nigel."

"Victoria?" he swung round to look at her. "I take it you've got my money?"

"Not yet," she admitted, "but perhaps we could come to some alternative arrangement?"

"Like what?"

"I don't know. Perhaps I could do some work for you? Sort out your admin? Everybody hates filling in forms. I can do bookkeeping too."

He took a gulp of his tea. "No thanks. I'd rather have the money."

"You're not being reasonable. I've already paid you what I owe you. If you want more then you need to give me more time."

"What about your other motor? That would do nicely."

"I'm not . . . I can't just give you my car."

"The way I see it, you ain't got much choice."

Slowly, she undid her top button. "What if we came to a different arrangement?"

He looked her up and down. It was impossible to tell if he was smiling or sneering because of that lopsided jaw of his.

"Stop dicking around. I want the money."

For a moment, she was floored. The way he dismissed her was insulting.

"You're not even listening to what I have to offer."

"Too right I ain't. You're going to pay me what you owe me, and if I don't get it today, then the price is going up."

"You can't do that!"

"I can do what I bloody well like. You're a wanted woman, from what I hear. Now if you'll excuse me, I have work to do."

He set down his mug and turned the music up louder. Victoria watched as he slid back under the car. She walked out of the garage and stood in the doorway. The gall of the man, whistling while he worked.

She glanced at her phone. If she left now, she should make the next train back home. Instead, she walked back into the garage and had a good look around. Her eye went to the little table where he kept his tea things. She walked over and lifted the lid of the tea caddy. He had teabags, the philistine. She had a look at his workbench. There was a container of engine oil. Would he notice if she squirted some of that onto his teabags? Probably.

She turned and looked at the car he was working on. Her eyes widened as she saw the key in the ignition.

"Nigel?" He didn't answer. Probably, he couldn't hear her. "You asked for it!" she yelled.

"What?"

She walked over to the stereo and changed the dreadful pop music to Classic FM. It was a piece by Mahler but it would have to do. She reached into the car, turned the key in the ignition and put the car in gear. Then she let off the hand-brake. She felt the vehicle roll.

She ignored his blood curdling screams as he was pinned under the wheels. She heard the sound of flesh squelching, the crunch of bones breaking, saw the puddle of bright red blood that leaked like oil from under the car. He was still screaming as she walked away. She glanced around, checking that no one had seen her. She might still make that train if she hurried.

35

I was too tired for History. I asked Miss H if I could go home, but she couldn't get through to Mum so I had to stay until home time. Miss H let me sleep in her office. It was nice in there. I curled up on the bean bag and dreamed about hamsters.

p.s. Mum put vitamins in Anna's tea. I don't know whether to tell Anna or not. I'm always getting things wrong.

Maddie kept nudging Anna during maths.

"Anna!"

"What?"

"You're falling asleep! What were you doing last night?"

"Not a lot."

"Then why are you so tired?"

"I dunno. I ..."

"Oh my God, have you got a boyfriend?"

"What? No!"

Maddie narrowed her eyes. "Then why do you look so sus?"

"I don't know ..."

"But you'd tell me if you did?"

"Maddie, of course I would!"

"Because I feel like you don't tell me anything anymore."

Maddie's eyes filled with tears and Anna grimaced. God, this was awkward.

"We really need to listen," she said. Anna rubbed her eyes and tried to concentrate as the teacher blathered on about isosceles triangles. She blinked at the symbols on the board. They didn't make the slightest bit of sense to her.

"Anna!"

She felt pain in her rib. She lifted her head and realised Maddie was glaring at her.

"You fell asleep again," she hissed.

Anna sat up sharply. It was weird. She'd done a shift at the burger shop yesterday and then she'd gone straight home. It had hardly been a wild one.

She looked at her watch. She had double art after this, which she normally loved, but there was no way she could make it through. She'd have to go home and take a nap. What did it matter if she missed one lesson anyway? It was hardly the end of the world.

"I thought you were having lunch with me?" Maddie said, as she walked towards the gates.

"I'm sorry. I have to go home. I'm really knackered."

"Can I come?"

"Oh, Maddie . . . no, I'm sorry I really need to sleep."

"Yeah, right. Tell your boyfriend I said 'hi'."

Anna sighed and shoved her books back in her locker. She didn't have the energy to argue.

The house was quiet when she arrived home. Good thing she had her key. It was a pleasant surprise to find her mother out. She didn't feel like dealing with her questions. She went into the kitchen to make herself some tea – that's what Mum always did when she was feeling under the weather.

As she was looking for a teaspoon, she noticed that there was an enveloped stuffed down the back of the drawer. She drew it out curiously. It was addressed to her parents, but it was still sealed shut. She wondered why they hadn't opened it. There was a girl in her class whose mum got into massive debt and no one had known until she found a stash of letters hidden in the shoe cupboard. Those letters had turned out to be unpaid bills. Anna swallowed. Perhaps she'd better open this one just in case.

The kettle had boiled so she steamed it open using a life-hack she'd seen on YouTube. The envelope was a little damp but she got it open, and pulled out the letter. It was the report from that Darren guy. The one she'd met that day. Her eyes skimmed the page. There was a brief synopsis of everything they'd discussed, followed by the outcome of his discussion with Joey's teacher, and his own observations of Joey. Right at the end were his conclusions: "Joey is clearly a highly intelligent child with significant social and communication struggles, as well as sensory needs which are not currently being met. I recommend that Joey is referred immediately for evaluation for Autistic Spectrum Disorder and he may well benefit from an Education, Health and Care Plan."

Instinctively, she agreed with this assessment. No wonder Joey was so eccentric. She forgot all about her tea and carried the letter through to the lounge. She now understood why the envelope hadn't been opened. Her mum had been so weird and unhelpful when Darren was here. Apparently, autism didn't fit with her vision for the family. Her dad would get it though. She spotted his book lying on the coffee table and slipped it between the pages for him to find. Her bed was calling. She sloped upstairs and when she reached her room, she flopped down on the bed and slept instantly.

She had no idea how many hours passed, but she could hear her parents downstairs which meant her dad was already home. What time was it?

"What are we going to do about Nigel?" he asked.

There was a slight pause and then Victoria said. "I don't think we need to worry about him anymore."

"Why? What do you mean?"

"I heard something about him today. He had an accident at work. A bad one."

Another pause.

"What sort of accident?"

"A car fell on him. He's severely brain damaged."

Another pause.

"Look me in the eyes and tell me you had nothing to do with it."

"Of course I didn't! How could I make a car fall on someone? Can you hear yourself?"

"For fuck's sake, Victoria. My number is in his contacts and we both went to school with him."

"Relax. Like I said, it was an accident. The police aren't looking for anyone."

Anna rose from her bed and crept out onto the landing just in time to see her father grab his keys and walk outside, slamming the door behind him.

"Dad!"

She started down the stairs, pushed past her mother and bolted to the door but it was too late. Her father was already in the car. He roared off down the street.

She turned and glared at Victoria. "This is all your fault!"

"Anna!"

She ran back upstairs to her room and grabbed her phone.

"Bex!" she whispered. "Oh God, Bex, what am I going to do?"

Kit was gone three long hours and, in that time, Victoria took her anger out on the house. She polished and scrubbed until everything sparkled. There was literally nothing left to clean. The dryer beeped, indicating the wash load was done. Victoria went to take it out, but Joey got there first. He pulled out a warm towel and wrapped it around his neck like a scarf, leaving a heap of clean laundry on the floor.

"Oh, for goodness' sake, Joey."

She scooped up all the clothes and carried them upstairs to her bed to sort. She stopped when she came across Kit's football shirt. She buried her face in it but it just smelt of detergent.

"Where are you, Kit?" she whispered softly.

Anna stood in the doorway. "Is he ever coming back?"

"Of course, he's coming back!" Victoria said, smoothly. But the truth was, she didn't know. Kit had never walked out on her before. They'd always had their arguments, but not like this. It was getting late, and she was getting worried.

Still, she carried on as normal, grilling lamb chops for

dinner. She made mashed potatoes and roast vegetables for her and Anna. Pepperoni pizza for Joey.

As she dished up the chops, she recalled her mother often going without so she would have a good portion of meat. Anna and Joey never went without, and nor did she or Kit. There was always good food on her table. Always warm beds to sleep in and decent clothes to wear. She and Kit provided for their family. That was important, and Kit was a good father. That's why he had to come back.

The atmosphere at dinner was frosty. Anna barely said a word. Victoria couldn't believe her lovely girl was becoming so bitter. Once she was older, she would understand that everything she did was for them, for their family.

"How can you eat like that?" Anna asked, once Joey had left the table.

Victoria looked at her in surprise. "I've done a lot of housework," she said. "It's given me quite the appetite."

Anna pushed her plate away and stormed up the stairs. Victoria continued to eat. It was strange, she'd have thought she'd feel bad about what she'd done to Nigel but she didn't. He shouldn't have been so greedy. She'd had to stand up to him. When she'd heard he was badly brain damaged, it was a relief. She'd had so much to worry about lately, it felt good to be taking back control. She'd got her family into this mess, and she was going to get them out. She just had to convince them of that.

They were all in bed when she heard the creak of the front door and her heart leapt. Minutes passed but Kit did not come upstairs. Eventually, she tiptoed down and found him flat out on the sofa, fast asleep. She took a blanket and pulled it over him. Sleeping downstairs like this was a disaster for his back, but now that he was asleep, she knew not to wake him. Besides, he might still be angry. He was bound to see things differently in the morning.

All that housework made for a good night sleep and Victoria awoke just before her alarm in the morning. She jogged downstairs to find Kit in exactly the same position as she had left him.

"Kit? Time to wake up for work."

He opened one eye and looked at her with thinly veiled contempt. They didn't exchange a single word as he got ready and he didn't make any move to kiss her as he went to the door.

"What was I supposed to do?" she demanded to his retreating back. "He would have kept demanding more and more money."

Kit shook his head. "You can justify anything, can't you, Victoria? Just as long as it suits you."

"That's not fair."

He closed his eyes and stood very still for a moment, one hand on the door frame.

"Are you alright? Is it a spasm?"

She longed to feel the pressure of his hand on hers. There had been so many times, when the pain had gripped him and he had clung to her. She had enjoyed that closeness, that feeling that he needed her. He waited a moment before he spoke. "We'll talk tonight, okay, Victoria?"

It was only after he'd left that she saw the flask of coffee she'd made him, sitting on the telephone table.

Joey came downstairs and she went through the motions of making breakfast.

"Did Dad come home?" Anna asked. Victoria turned and saw her in the doorway. She felt as though she didn't know her daughter. She looked like Anna, but oh-so serious: the way she held herself. The tension in her face.

"Of course, he did," Victoria said popping some toast in the toaster. "Now, have you done all your homework?"

"No, but I'm sure you have."

"Well, I did make a few adjustments when I typed up your history essay. It's on the printer."

Anna picked up the papers without a word and stuffed them into her backpack.

"Careful, darling, you don't want to crease them."

She left the children to eat their breakfast, then helped Joey into his school clothes. He always looked so smart in his uniform.

"Joey, will you get your shoes on?"

"My legs won't work," Joey said, folding his arms.

"Oh, for goodness' sake!" She reached for his shoes and placed them on his feet. "You have to sink your feet into them."

Anna came and stood by Joey. "Mum, he's nine years old. He's perfectly capable of putting his own shoes on."

"Piss off, Anna!" Joey snarled.

"Now, now!" Victoria pressed Joey's left foot into his shoe, followed by the right and then they were ready to go. She grabbed her keys and . . .

"Joey, where are you going?"

"Just a minute, I forgot something!"

She watched in exasperation as Joey disappeared up to his room, tracking dirt over her neatly hoovered stairs.

Anna picked up her bag. "Right, I'm going to go."

Victoria nodded. "Yes, of course. Have a lovely day, darling." She moved to kiss her daughter, but Anna dodged and flew out the door.

Two Reception dads stood in the centre of the playground. They were the types that rode bikes with trailers on the back for their kids. James Solomon had probably ridden one of those, Victoria thought with a pang.

She steered Joey towards his classroom. He was yapping on and on about his computer game.

"Joey, time to go in. Joey!"

He didn't appear to hear her. She pressed her lips together and gave Joey a little push in the direction of his classroom. He stopped talking and blinked, like a vampire coming out into the sunlight.

"Morning, Joey," Miss Henley said, a little too slowly for Victoria's liking. He was already being treated differently. *She had to get him out of this school.* She headed to the office to pick up her tickets for that evening's fundraiser. She and Kit always enjoyed the school quiz nights. Kit got a chance to show off his sports knowledge and Victoria liked catching up on all the latest gossip.

There was a cluster of mums talking and laughing outside the front gate. Imelda Daniels was there, talking to Portia. Samantha and Zara stood close by, hanging on her every word.

"And then she drives off at the speed of . . . I don't know. I swear I could see dust."

Victoria nudged Portia. "Who are we talking about?"

"Kayla," Portia whispered. "Imelda tried to corner her about the accident, but she drove off."

"Guilty conscience?" Victoria said.

"Got to be," Imelda said. Zara and Samantha were like nodding dogs.

"What did you actually say to her?" Portia pressed.

"Well . . ." Imelda leaned in closer. "I told her the police were still looking for the culprit and I mentioned that she'd been seen drinking . . ."

She stopped abruptly and straightened up. Victoria turned and saw Belinda just behind them.

"It wasn't Kayla," Belinda said.

Victoria dropped her eyes to the floor. Imelda removed herself from the group and slinked up to Belinda.

"She was seen drinking on the night it happened," Imelda said softly.

"It wasn't her," Belinda reiterated. "She doesn't drive a Volvo."

The group fell silent. They all looked at each other as if trying to think of a new line of argument. They'd all been so convinced. Belinda turned and walked towards her car. Victoria scurried after her.

"Belinda, wait!"

"It's just gossip," Belinda said. "Nasty childish gossip. They don't like Kayla, so they want her to be guilty."

"Yes," Victoria agreed. "You're right of course."

"Sometimes I think I'll never find out who did it," she said. "Ricky will never get any answers. It's so hard to lay it all to rest. We're stuck in limbo, Victoria. I can't turn back time, but I'd give anything, *anything* to know the truth."

Victoria swallowed. She felt like she should say something, but she couldn't force out the words.

"I . . . hope you get your answers," she said lamely, before returning to the group.

"She alright?" Samantha asked.

Victoria glanced back at Belinda, just to check she was out of earshot.

"To be honest, I think she's losing the plot."

Imelda leaned closer. "What makes you say that?"

"I don't know, she seems really desperate. Do you know I found her sobbing into the freezer cabinets at the shop the other day? She was such a mess. I don't think she can cope. I mean, it's not surprising given all she's been through but . . ."

"It must be so hard for her," Imelda said.

"Poor bitch," Portia said.

"I wish someone would knock down my husband," Zara muttered.

Samantha gave her a wink. "Maybe Kayla would do it if you paid her enough."

Portia looked at her sternly. "It wasn't her, remember?"

"Oh yeah."

Victoria went straight from school to Louisa's house for her weekly lesson. It started to rain as she made the long walk back down Farncombe hill. Ever since she'd given up her car, it had been raining an abnormal amount. Sometimes she felt as though the storm clouds were purposely targeting her. She ran the last few metres, up the path to the house.

She fumbled for her keys. Where were they? Where the hell were they?

She was still searching when the door swung open.

"Kit! What are you doing home?"

His jaw was clenched, his lips tight. "They sent me home."

"What do you mean?" She followed him into the lounge.

"I messed up big time."

She shook her head. "How . . . how bad?"

"I lost the client five million pounds, Vic. Eddie said it was the last straw."

"Oh, Kit!"

She stepped towards him, but his body was as rigid as stone.

"I lost the client five million pounds and all I could think was, what will Victoria say?"

She swallowed, gulping down her own fears, her own horror. "I say we'll get through this, Kit. You'll get another job, another bank . . ."

He exploded with harsh laughter. "Are you kidding me? After this, I'll never work again." He sank down onto the sofa. She could almost hear his heart beating from across the room. "You know what the sad part is? I don't even care. I hated that job. It sucked the life out of me. I hate who it made me."

She tasted acid in her throat.

"You'll find something else," she resolved. "Something better. You can freelance. Work for yourself."

Already, her brain was checking off tasks: update his LinkedIn profile, contact old friends and acquaintances, speak to anyone who might be able to give Kit a job.

"You're not listening, Victoria. No one is going to hire me. I'm done."

She hated him then, the way he just accepted it. "We do not give up," she said through clenched teeth.

"I do," he said.

Victoria closed her eyes. She couldn't believe this was happening. Everything they'd worked for, this life, this house . . . She began doing the calculations in her head. They could sell Kit's car. She could put up her hourly rate and work longer hours. They could take out more credit cards, but that wouldn't work forever. At some point, they'd have to pay it all back. And as for Joey, they could never afford a private school now. She didn't know what they were going to do.

Kit lay back against the sofa pillows. His shoulders relaxed, his face softened. Was that a smile? What the hell did he have to smile about?

"I'm not going to think about it," he said. "I'm going to take a day or two to relax. Maybe longer. The doctor said I shouldn't be working. Maybe I'll finally take his advice."

"But what are we going to do for money?"

"What would anybody else do in my situation? They'd sign on."

Her cheeks burned with humiliation. This was like her dad all over again. "You can't. You just can't."

Kit ignored her and reached for the book on the coffee table. As he did so, an envelope fell out. "What's this?" he asked. She felt a shift in her stomach. It was the envelope containing the educational psychologist's report.

Her mind was racing, wondering how the envelope had got there. It had to be Anna. That scheming little madam must have found it and put it there for him to find.

"Give me that!"

Kit was already tearing into it. His eyes darted quickly across the page. He glanced at her, then back at the report.

"Well?" she demanded.

"Have you even read this?"

"Not yet."

"Why not?"

"I . . . I couldn't."

His face went as red as a boiled lobster. "It backs up what Joey's teacher was saying. It looks like he's autistic."

"But he can't be! Have you seen the state of his room? Autistic people are obsessively tidy, everything in its place."

Kit looked at her incredulously. "That's just a stereotype, Vic. They're not all like that. Each one is different. If you did the least bit of research, you'd know that."

What had got into him? Kit had always been such a soft-hearted man, a gentle giant but now he was looking at her like he wanted to kill her.

She collapsed on the sofa beside him, sobbing genuine tears of despair. She didn't want Joey to have autism. She didn't want Kit to lose his job, but most of all she couldn't bear to have him hate her. They were in this together. Always had been. Why couldn't she make him see things her way?

She felt his arms around her and the relief was immense. She sobbed into his chest, soaking his shirt with her tears and he held her in a way he hadn't done in weeks. His heartbeat against hers and her breath slowly returned to normal. Finally, he pulled away and she saw that his eyes were red and puffy.

"I just don't know if I can do this anymore, Vic. I feel like I'm losing my mind."

She clung on tight. "It'll be alright, Kit. Just remember we're in this together. I won't let anyone come between us."

38

VICTORIA

"It's only one report," Victoria said, as she set the tea tray down on the table. "We need to get a second opinion. We need to be sure because Joey is so gifted..."

Kit grimaced slightly, but he was nodding. "Of course, that makes sense, but this bloke seems pretty convinced..."

She watched intently as he drank his tea. Kit always drank hot drinks faster than she did. She liked to wait for them to cool. He set down his cup and a great yawn escaped him. He sprawled out on the sofa.

"I might take a nap," he said with another yawn. "I know we need to talk, but I'm so tired I can barely keep my eyes open."

Victoria nodded her agreement. He really did need the rest. She went and got the blanket and covered him up. He really should have gone up to bed. He would likely be out for hours. They had that fundraiser at the school tonight, but it was probably best if she went alone.

When the children came home, she explained their dad was tired and they dutifully tiptoed around him. She made a quick dinner of chicken nuggets and chips and read Joey his nighttime story.

"Please check in on him before you go to bed," she said to Anna. "I know Dad's home but he'll be sleeping."

"So you said."

"Anna, he left his job today. He's not going back."

Anna's face lit up. "Oh, really? I think that's for the best."

Victoria clasped her hands together and reminded herself that Anna was just a child. She didn't know what she was talking about. "Alright, well, have a good evening."

"You too, Mum."

Anna smiled, but there was no real warmth in her face. It made Victoria feel uneasy as she slipped out into the night and walked towards the school. There was always plenty of booze at these things so driving was out of the question.

She spotted a group of teenagers, hanging around outside the shop. She wasn't sure but she thought one of them was that friend of Anna's. The girl glared at her. If she'd been on her own, Victoria might have approached her, but she wasn't going to take her on when she was with her friends.

Her phone rang. It was Portia.

"Hi, Portia, I'm just on my way."

"Victoria, I'm sorry but Ariadne has come down with a temperature. I can't possibly leave her."

"Oh no! I hope she feels better soon!" She tried to sound sympathetic, but this was a real blow. Now she was two team mates down and Portia knew all the soaps. If they got a question on *Coronation Street*, they'd be screwed.

She was about to say goodbye when she heard Ariadne giggling in the background. Portia shushed her but Victoria heard her alright.

"Sounds like she's feeling a little better?" she said pointedly.

"She still has a temperature," Portia shot back.

Victoria set her jaw. Ariadne sounded fine. She knew Portia just couldn't be arsed.

THE SCHOOL HALL was buzzing when she arrived for the fundraiser. The wine was flowing, and all the parents looked happy and relaxed. The stage had been decorated with crepe paper pineapples and flamingos. What that had to do with the donkeys they were raising money for, Victoria had no idea, but at the centre of it all was Imelda Daniels. Her teeth were so impossibly white that she'd clearly had work done, not that she would admit to it. Especially not while she had the microphone pinned to her little black dress.

Samantha had bagged them a table and Victoria walked over to join her, slipping out of her jacket. Even with all the windows open, the hall was like a sauna.

"Hey, where's your other half?"

"He had to work," Samantha said. "Where's yours?"

"Same." She tapped her nails against the table.

Great, they were three people down now. Zara had better be on her way.

Samantha nudged her. "Look who's here!"

She turned and saw Belinda walk in. She looked around the busy, bustling room then she marched over to the bar and bought two bottles of wine.

"She's on a mission," Samantha said.

Victoria nodded. She didn't recall the last time Belinda had attended a school quiz. She kept her head down as Belinda searched for somewhere to sit. Inevitably, she headed straight for their table.

"Do you have room on your team?"

Samantha eyed her two bottles of wine greedily.

"Absolutely!"

Victoria looked up and forced herself to nod.

"Good." Belinda scooted in next to Victoria.

Imelda tapped her glass and smiled down on them all. "Welcome to the seventh annual St Bernard's quiz night . . ."

Zara came scuttling in and sat down next to Samantha. "What have I missed?"

"Nothing. Imelda's just sucking up to the teachers," Belinda said.

They all stared at her for a moment. Then Zara giggled.

Samantha turned her attention to Zara and the two of them had a natter whilst Victoria and Belinda did their best to answer the questions. There was a football round that Victoria was sure Kit could have answered, but she didn't regret leaving him at home. So much had gone on in the last few days, she didn't want to risk him coming undone in public. She couldn't have him sobbing into his pint and telling everyone he'd lost his job.

"And now for the general knowledge round: Greta Thunberg, Daryl Hannah and Elon Musk. What do these three people have in common?"

Belinda and Victoria looked at each other blankly.

Samantha looked up from her wine. "They're all autistic."

Victoria blinked. "Seriously?"

"Yup."

Victoria narrowed her eyes. "Who wrote this quiz?"

She glanced around the hall and caught sight of Miss Henley sitting next to Imelda on the stage.

"We're all on the autistic spectrum somewhere, aren't we?" said Zara.

"No," Victoria said, fists balled. "We most certainly are not."

Imelda came over to talk to them at half time. She looked around the table and her eyes narrowed.

"Where's Portia tonight?"

"Oh, she was going to come but Ariadne's ill."

"Poor Ariadne," Imelda said. "I hope she's better in time for her birthday."

"I'm sure she will be," Victoria said, taking a sip of her wine.

"If you want any more drinks, you'd better go and get them now. The bar's closing in ten minutes."

Zara didn't need telling twice, she scuttled off to the front.

"She's poison, that woman," Belinda observed, watching Imelda walk over to the teacher's table.

"She's alright," Victoria said. "She does a lot for the school."

Belinda snorted. "She does a lot for herself."

Zara and Samantha returned to the table with another two bottles of wine and a truckload of gossip.

"Have you heard the latest about Paul Schooner? Apparently, he's been putting it about again. There are rumours that he's been getting it on with some bored housewife."

Zara sighed. "He can come and visit me anytime."

"I don't believe a word of it," Victoria said. "I actually know Paul and he's dedicated to his wife. Very dedicated."

"Really?" Samantha was eyeing her with interest. "You know Paul? You never said."

"Well, we are neighbours."

"I know Paul too. Lovely man, isn't he? He plays tennis with my cousin."

Victoria wanted to laugh. Samantha was talking out of her arse of course, but that was fine. Anything to take the focus off her.

The quiz resumed, and there was a mad scramble to find the pen, which had apparently rolled under the table during the break.

"Damn. Missed the question."

"Oh, well." Zara took another sip of her wine.

Victoria was aware that she hadn't bought a bottle yet, but they were getting through it fast. Zara was very giggly, and Belinda was speaking into her chin.

"I'm so glad Ricky and Joey are friends," Belinda said.

Victoria reached for the wine bottle.

"Oh, me too."

"He's quite the character, your Joey. Do you know, he told Ricky the strangest story, about hitting a deer that wasn't a deer."

The bottle slipped, and now she was pouring wine all over the table. She knew she was doing it, but she couldn't seem to make herself stop. All the air had rushed from her lungs and she could hear the screech of the brakes. The sound of her own screams filled her ears.

Samantha grabbed the bottle off her and blotted the stain with a paper napkin.

Victoria needed to say something. She needed to say it now, but she felt as though her throat was closing up . . .

"We . . . we watched a nature programme the other night," she burst out. "There was a deer in it. Joey was quite . . . struck by it."

Samantha topped up their glasses. Victoria grabbed hers and slugged it back.

Belinda's eyes glazed over.

"A deer that wasn't a deer," she said again.

ONE OF THE Reception mums heaved into the flower beds when Victoria dropped Joey off the next day. She wasn't the only one who looked a bit ropey. Two of the career mums were wearing sunglasses, and a third was as pale as raw pastry. Normally, Victoria would have quite enjoyed this spectacle, but today she had more important things on her mind. She spotted Belinda and hurried over to her.

"How are you feeling?"

"My head's beating like a drum," Belinda groaned. "I take it we had a good night?"

"As far as I remember."

She eyed Belinda warily. How much did she actually remember? She herself recalled everything vividly, including the moment Zara won the raffle, and then tripped over her handbag and face-planted the floor.

"Would you . . . like to come round for a cup of tea?" she asked casually.

She knew Belinda worked, but she was fairly certain this was her day off.

Belinda eyed her steadily. "That would be lovely. I've got a few errands to run, but I could be with you about eleven if that suits?"

Victoria bit her lip. She had Louisa's piano lesson at eleven.

"That would be fine," she agreed. She'd have to cancel Louisa. And her dental appointment after that.

Kit had gone to his first physio appointment this morning. She had given him clear instructions that he wasn't to let anyone see him. She couldn't have the other mums gossiping about what was wrong with him. The bank would continue to pay him for a little while at least. Hopefully she'd find him a new job before the money ran out.

She dashed back home and threw on some Mozart. From the cupboard under the sink, she pulled out a series of Tupperware boxes: washing powder, baking soda, crème of tartare, ah, there was her special concoction. Carefully, she opened the lid and measured out four teaspoons which she added to the tea caddy.

She gave it a good stir. Did it look too obvious? The white

powder was clearly visible, against the dark brown tea. She stirred it more vigorously. There, that was better.

Satisfied, she replaced the Tupperware boxes and returned the caddy to the cupboard. She pulled out a series of cleaning products and a pair of disposable gloves then looked around for somewhere to stash them. Her eye fell on the oversized handbag Anna had given her for Christmas. It was a little too garish for her tastes, but now, finally she had a use for it.

Was it just her or was it getting stuffy in here? She opened the window and wiped a hand across her brow. The church clocked chimed the hour. Eleven o'clock. She paced around the room, making little adjustments until the clock chimed again. Quarter past.

Come on, Belinda.

The doorbell rang and she clapped her hands together, filled with a kind of sick excitement. She was about to find out exactly how much Belinda knew.

39

ANNA

Anna was shattered. She'd had to cancel her shift at the burger shop last night and gone to bed before nine but she was still feeling sleepy. Her dad looked the same way, listlessly stirring his cornflakes this morning. He might have liked to stay in bed if only Mum would let him. Poor Dad. She'd told him how proud she was that he'd chucked in his job. She didn't care what her mother thought. Life was too short to be unhappy.

Science was hard going that morning and if it weren't for Maddie, Anna would have flunked the test. Luckily, she could see Maddie's paper easily enough to copy some of her answers. She caught on and gave her evils but Maddie was no rat, so it was all good.

As she walked home at lunchtime, she prepared her speech for Victoria. She really needed the afternoon off. If she had to sit through geography, she was definitely going to fall asleep again. Geography was brutal. She'd have to pretend to be worse than she was. Feeling tired wasn't going to cut it. Perhaps she should tell her mum she'd been sick, but then she wouldn't get any lunch and she really was starving. A headache then. A really bad one. She unlocked the front door and went in. It was quiet. Could her mum be out on an errand? She could only hope.

"Mum?" she called. "Mum, I . . ."

She stopped. There was a woman sprawled out on the sofa. Anna took a step closer. It was Mrs Solomon! Her hair had fallen across her face and she was drooling like a dog.

"Ah, Anna. I'm glad you're home," her mother said, with a worried look. "Belinda has come down with a virus or something. I need you to help me get her to her car."

Anna looked at Mrs Solomon again. She looked totally out of it.

"What happened?"

"I don't know," Victoria said. "She seemed wobbly and then she sort of collapsed on the sofa."

"Where's Dad?"

"I'm afraid he's out this morning. It's just you and me."

Anna watched Mrs Solomon. She didn't move at all.

"Can you just wait with her, while I go and get her car? I'm going to bring it right up to the house. That way we won't have so far to carry her."

"Why don't we just use your car?"

"Your dad's taken it this morning, and I don't want to use the Volvo."

"No, of course not."

Victoria did as she'd proposed. She parked right on the front lawn and came back inside.

"So . . . how are we going to do this?"

"You take one side, I'll take the other," Victoria said, as if Mrs Solomon were just a mattress they were lugging down the street. "Support her under the arm, Anna."

It was awkward, getting her to her feet. She did nothing to support herself, so she was a dead weight.

Anna felt a bit icky about touching Mrs Solomon, but her

mother held her right under the shoulder, so Anna did the same. Her bare arm felt cold and doughy. There was something unnatural about the way she didn't wake.

She looked at Victoria. "She's not going to chuck up, is she?"

Victoria grimaced. "I hope not. Careful, we don't want to tear her clothes."

"It's alright, Mrs Solomon. We're going to get you home now," Anna said. She hoped to god her own mother never drank this much. She'd be totally mortified.

They half carried, half dragged Mrs Solomon out to her car and placed her in the back seat. Anna tried to sit her up, but she kept flopping down again so in the end they lay her on the back seat and pulled a seat belt around her middle.

"Are you sure she's alright?" Anna asked.

"She'll be fine," Victoria said. "I just need to get her home."

"You don't think we'd better go to the doctor's?"

"Oh, no, I'm sure she just needs bed rest."

"I'd better come with you. You'll need help getting her into her house."

Victoria's eyes flickered. "I'm sure she'll start to come round by the time I get her home. Besides, you need to get back to school."

Anna looked at her mother more closely. "Why don't you take her to the doctor's?"

"Alright, I'll level with you. She's not ill, she's drunk. Belinda has a serious drinking problem."

"Yeah? Well, she's probably really depressed about you killing her husband."

Instinctively, Anna opened the passenger door and climbed in.

"What are you doing?"

"I'm coming with you. I want to make sure Mrs Solomon is alright."

"Very well then." Victoria got in and started the car.

Anna had never been to Mrs Solomon's house, but she knew, as soon as they reached the town centre, that that was not where they were going. They stopped at the lights and her mother pulled her wallet from her bag.

"Anna, why don't you take my credit card and go and buy yourself a new outfit? I hear there's a sale at that boutique you like."

Anna turned and looked out the window. "No, thank you."

"Are you sure? You could get yourself some new sandals. Didn't you want those black ones with the sparkly straps?"

"I thought Dad left his job?"

"He did."

"So money must be tight. Turn the car around, Mum. We need to take Mrs Solomon home."

Victoria glanced in the mirror.

"When you're older, you'll understand," she said, accelerating as she headed out of town. "I have a vision for this family, a wonderful, perfect vision. We have a very bright future ahead of us. You and Joey are going to be happy and successful. You'll never want for anything, and people will always respect you. You may not understand now, but in time, you will, Anna. Everything I do, I do it for you and Joey. I want you to be happy. I want you to succeed."

"Mum . . ."

"One day we'll live in a big house, even bigger than the one we have now. It will be grand beyond our wildest dreams. Joey will go to a wonderful school where he can be nurtured the way he deserves, and you, my darling, will go to one of the best universities in the country."

"Stop it, Mum. I don't even know if I want to go to

university."

Victoria looked aghast. "Of course, you do. If you don't go to university, you won't get a good job."

"Are you talking about yourself or me now?" She knew her mother had sacrificed her own career to support Kit so that he could study.

"Anna, you deserve the best in life and I'm going to make sure that you get it." Victoria picked up her phone. "Hi, darling, can you come and get me in an hour? I need you to pick me up from Havant train station. Yes, don't ask! PTA business..."

Anna loosened her seat belt. "What's going on, Mum?"

"Shush, darling, I need to concentrate on the road."

Victoria took a sharp left, and they went off the main road, heading down a long, windy lane. It appeared the conversation was over. Victoria put on some Beethoven and Anna nodded off for a while. When she awoke, she could see a strange object on the horizon. Was that a ship?

"I can see the sea!"

"Yes, isn't it beautiful?" The water glittered in front of them and she tasted the salty sea air in her mouth.

"Mum, what the hell is going on? Where are you taking us?"

She glanced at Mrs Solomon in the back. "Are you okay there, Mrs Solomon?"

Anna reached over and nudged her. She responded groggily but didn't open her eyes. Anna couldn't believe she was still so out of it. She'd dealt with drunk people before. Her friend Dina had got extremely drunk one time and Anna had been really worried. But even Dina hadn't been unconscious this long, and certainly not in the middle of the day.

They followed a steep road that led up and up. Victoria was driving so fast that for a moment, Anna thought she wasn't going to stop. She stared out the window at the tall, gleaming white cliffs. In the distance she could see a red and white striped lighthouse.

"Mum, what is this place?"

Victoria smiled. "Your dad and I used to drive up to this spot when we were young. We'd sit here for hours and watch the ocean. It was so secluded we rarely saw anyone. I always thought it was terribly romantic, watching the waves rush in and out. In fact, you were conceived not far from here."

"Oh, gross, Mum!"

They lurched to a halt right at the top of the cliff. A flimsy piece of barbed wire was all that separated them from the massive drop below.

Anna let out a long breath.

"Mum, it's just beautiful here but it's hardly the time to take selfies. We need to get Mrs Solomon home, and I'm supposed to be at school. I'll get a detention if I miss geography."

All at once, the thought of school was very appealing. How she longed to sit with Maddie and whisper and giggle and chew gum. Victoria was unbuckling her seat belt. She had a very determined look on her face, her tongue twisted slightly as she opened the car door. There was no one around. Not even a hiker, though it looked like the sort of place people might come for a picnic. Anna's stomach gurgled a little and she felt like she might be sick.

"Mum, what's going on? Why have you brought us here?"

"I didn't want to bring you. You wouldn't get out of the car." Victoria had opened the back door. Mrs Solomon groaned slightly. "We need to get her into the driver's seat."

"Mum, no!"

"It's the only way, Anna. Come on, help me."

Victoria was smiling. Anna stared at the silver shimmering flecks in her eyes. She was serious. She was really going to do this.

The wind whipped through her hair as she opened the car door.

"Mum!"

Anna gulped down the sea air and fought her way to the back seat.

"That's it! You get the legs."

"No!"

"Come on, you can do this."

"Mum! No!"

"Very well, I'll just have to do it myself."

Anna blinked back tears as her mother yanked Mrs Solomon from the car and dragged her across the chalky ground. Mrs Solomon lurched about in her sleep.

"Jesus, she's heavy!"

Even without Anna's help, Victoria somehow managed to get Mrs Solomon into the driver's seat. She sat unnaturally forward, flopped over the steering wheel, arms down by her sides.

Her mother closed the driver's door with great difficulty because one of Mrs Solomon's arms kept getting in the way. Instinctively, Anna climbed in the back.

Victoria turned and stared at her.

"Come on, Anna. Out you hop."

Anna folded her arms and realised she was shaking. "No, Mum. Think of Ricky! That poor little boy has already lost his dad."

She met her mother's stare and felt a fresh wave of alarm. There was something very unsettling about her expression. Each side of her face seemed to show a different emotion, one side anger and the other fear.

"Anna, I'm asking you for the last time. I need you to get out."

Anna gripped the door handle so tight her knuckles hurt. "If you want to kill her, you'll have to kill me too."

"Get out of the car, Anna."

Victoria's heart pulsated in her ears. She glanced around again, terrified someone would stumble upon them. She needed to do this now, before she lost her nerve. She yanked Anna's car door open and attempted to pull her out, but the child was strong and wilful. She kicked and bucked, landing a powerful blow to Victoria's chest.

"Hey, that hurt!" Her hand flew to her breastbone and Anna used the opportunity to slam the car door shut. There was a click as she locked it from the inside.

Victoria rapped on the window.

"Anna, get out! I have to do this."

"You can't, Mum, you'll kill us both!"

"Not you. Just her."

"No, Mum. If you do this, you're a murderer. Even more of a murderer than you were before!"

Victoria opened the driver's door and disabled the locks. She opened Anna's door again. This time, Anna punched her in the face. The force of the blow had her staggering backwards, skidding in her heels. Once again, Anna slammed the door.

"Right, I'm not taking any more of this!" Victoria leaned across Belinda to get at the controls. She put it into drive. Anna's cries rose in pitch.

"Mum, you can't do this! You can't!"

"Get out of the car!"

"Mum, no!"

Victoria shut her eyes for a moment. Beethoven was playing softly, a slow poignant movement. She breathed in the music, then tugged at the handbrake.

"Quick, get out. It's going to roll."

The car jolted forward. Anna dived for the handbrake, pushing it back.

"Get out of the fucking car!" Victoria screamed.

Belinda shifted in her sleep. "James! James, is that you?"

The car jolted again and scraped against barbed wire.

"Anna, you have to get out!"

Her daughter's hands became claws that clasped her tightly and dug into her flesh.

"Mum, you have to stop this. You're going to kill us all!"

Victoria's hands shook. She held on to the handbrake and tried to concentrate on the music. The car made an ominous creaking sound. They both froze. Victoria was afraid to breathe.

"Anna, get out!" she pleaded one last time.

Anna didn't move. The car shook with her sobs.

Victoria closed her eyes. "Okay!" she finally relented. She reached down and put the car in reverse. To her horror, she felt the back wheels lift off the ground. "Shit!"

She and Anna pushed together, forcing the handbrake down. Victoria was lying across Belinda's lap now. If the car went over, she was going too. The car continued to skid. She couldn't tell, but she thought Belinda's foot might be on the pedals.

"Get out!" she begged her daughter.

"Together," Anna said. Slowly, she opened her car door.

She did not get out right away but shuffled across until she could sit with her feet on the ground.

Victoria wriggled out of Belinda's lap, knowing that any sudden movement could send the car crashing over the edge. Once she was out, she bent down and tried to get a look under Belinda's feet. She felt the car shudder. She saw with a quick glance that Anna had finally got out of the car. She reached across Belinda for the handbrake, but Anna got there first. She hoisted herself into the passenger seat, tears streaming down her face.

"Come on, Mum. You don't have to do this. Take her home. Take me home."

Together, they pulled Belinda out of the car and laid her down on the ground. Once Belinda was out of the way, Victoria got back in the car.

"Careful!" Anna called as she backed away from the cliff edge. The car jolted forward once more, and Victoria stared down into oblivion. Then the car seemed to right itself, shooting back to safety.

Getting Belinda back into the car was harder than it had been the first time. Victoria was tired and bruised and Belinda's arms and legs jerked erratically, landing a kick to Victoria's groin. They laid the unconscious woman across the back seat. She looked so peaceful like that. All her worry lines relaxed, her mouth smiling slightly, and Victoria couldn't help but wonder if she would have been better off if Anna had let her carry out her plan. At least she'd be free of her grief.

Victoria had just refastened her seat belt when they heard voices in the distance. A couple of hikers emerged. Then more and more. Soon an entire scout troupe filled the area. It seemed this place wasn't as secluded as she'd thought.

"Can we go now?" Anna said.

"Just a minute."

She unfastened her seat belt, walked to the edge of the cliff and peered down at the sea. The roar of the waves was louder than she remembered. She watched for a while as the waves thrashed against the rocks. She had planned it all so carefully, dropping a trail of hints like breadcrumbs as she spoke to the other mums at school. It didn't take much. She only had to ask if Samantha thought Belinda looked okay. Or if Portia had noticed that Belinda had forgotten to put her make-up on. She'd set it all up so perfectly. If the police asked around, everyone would agree that yes, Belinda had seemed a little depressed. It was only to be expected. She had lost her husband after all, it must all have been terribly hard for her. But none of them had known it was this bad. None of them had expected her to take her own life . . .

She rang Kit. "Change of plans," she said, keeping her tone as light as she could. "Can you collect Joey and Ricky from school at three?"

"What? Belinda's Ricky?"

"That's the one. I'm with her now. She's not feeling well. But she'll call the school to let them know it's alright. Thank you. I'll text you her address. We'll see you there."

She set down the phone.

"How's she going to call the school, Mum? She's totally out of it."

"She should start to come round by the time we get back to Godalming. If not, I'll call and pretend to be her."

Anna scratched her head. "So the effects of the drugs will start to wear off by then?"

Victoria didn't answer.

"What did you give her, Mum? Was it the same stuff you give Joey to make him sleep?"

"Of course not! I would never give Joey anything that might hurt him."

Victoria started the car. Now that they weren't going to off Belinda, she was desperate to get her home.

Belinda did not stir, even when they carried her into her living room. Victoria went into the kitchen and made some strong coffee. That should do the trick.

Anna gently shook Belinda. "Mrs Solomon? Wake up, you're home now. Ricky will be coming home from school soon."

Belinda's eyes shot open.

"Where . . . who are you?"

"It's me, Anna. Victoria Hill's daughter. You weren't well. We've been . . . looking after you."

Victoria hurried over to her and placed the coffee on the table beside her.

"Belinda, thank goodness! We were getting quite worried. Here, drink this. You need to perk yourself up."

Belinda looked at her with slightly unfocused eyes. "Ricky?"

"It's okay, my husband will drop him off. You just need to ring the school and tell them that's okay."

Belinda tried to get off the sofa, but she immediately sank back down again. "What's wrong with me? Why am I so weak?"

"I think you had a bad reaction to the wine last night."

Belinda shook her head as if trying to dislodge the fuzziness. "Can . . . can you hand me my phone?"

Victoria dialled for her. Belinda was slurring her words horribly and she wondered what the receptionist must think.

"Here, drink the coffee." Victoria gave a little laugh. "Don't worry, you're not the only one. Half the parents have massive hangovers after last night. I think that batch of wines must have been dodgy."

Belinda frowned into her cup. "I didn't feel this bad this morning."

"Really? I felt awful. I could barely keep my eyes open."

Belinda nodded thoughtfully. "I've got a banging headache. Would you mind getting me a couple of paracetamols? There should be some in the kitchen cupboard."

Victoria hopped up and searched for the pills. She didn't like to leave Belinda alone with Anna. You never knew what she might say.

Belinda swallowed the pills and sat back, exhausted. She was shivering horribly so Victoria brought her the duvet off her bed. They sat with her for half an hour or so, just to be sure she was getting better.

"I'm fine, honestly," Belinda insisted, after Victoria offered to make her a second cup of coffee.

"Are you sure?" Victoria said. "Only, you were asleep for a really long time."

Belinda rubbed her eyes. "I don't know how I'm going to sleep tonight. Perhaps I'll catch up on all the things I was supposed to do today."

"Why don't you just take it easy? Watch a film or something. We all need a duvet day once in a while."

Belinda reached for her hand. "Thank you, Victoria. You've been such a good friend."

Anna rose to her feet abruptly. "Is it okay if I use your loo?"

Belinda shifted her attention. "Yes, of course. It's the blue door next to the kitchen."

"Hello? I'm home!"

"Ricky!" Belinda broke into a smile as her son charged into the room.

"Hi, Mum. Guess what? Our class raised £200 for the

donkeys. We were the top fundraisers in the whole school. That means we get to watch a film with popcorn next Friday."

"That's wonderful!" Her eyes tracked Kit, standing just inside the door. "Come in!" she called but Kit lingered in the doorway, twisting his hands together and biting down on his lower lip. "Thank you for bringing him home," she said.

"Er, no problem."

"I'm making us all dinner!" Ricky offered. "Who likes marmite sandwiches?"

"Thank you, Ricky, but we need to get home," Victoria said.

She heard the chain flush and Anna came out of the bathroom. She whispered something to Kit.

"Right, we need to get going," he said. "Joey's waiting in the car."

"Thank you for everything!" Belinda called after them.

"It was nothing," Victoria said. They all made for the door.

"Is she on drugs or something?" Kit asked when they got outside.

"Probably," Victoria said. "She looked pretty wrecked."

She glanced at Anna, expecting a wisecrack but her daughter was subdued.

Kit went straight upstairs for a nap when they got home.

"I should go and do my homework," Anna muttered, as Victoria made a pot of tea.

"No, wait. Come and sit with me a minute, let me explain."

Anna gave her such a look that Victoria thought she would refuse but then she slumped down at the table, too tired to object. Victoria poured tea for both of them, but Anna refused to drink.

"I know what you did today," she said in a low voice. "You

came this close to killing me." She held her thumb and fore-finger an inch apart to demonstrate the distance.

"Anna, you know I love you. More than anything . . ."

"What about Mrs Solomon? If I hadn't been there, you would have done it, wouldn't you?"

"You have to understand. Everything I do, I do it for you and Joey."

Anna leaned closer. "All I know is you ran a man over and left him for dead."

"It wasn't Mum."

They both jumped. Joey stood in the doorway. He looked so small with his school shirt hanging out of his trousers, one sock up and one sock down.

"Joey . . ."

"I remember what happened, Mum. It wasn't your fault, was it? It was mine."

Anna looked at her little brother. "What do you mean, Joey?"

Joey took a step forward. "It was the night we were supposed to go to the Greek restaurant, only Mum wanted to stop at that football player's house on the way. Mum talked to him for ages and I was really bored. I told her but she wouldn't listen. By the time we got back to the car, I was really hungry and I was worried there wouldn't be any food left. I think Mum was hungry too because she was driving quite fast down the country road, the one that bends round in a W. Dad had the radio on. We'd heard they were doing a broadcast live from the restaurant and we didn't want to miss it. Then The Song came on and it was like my brain was on fire. I felt it bouncing around in my skull so I ripped off my seat belt and lurched forward to turn it off. Mum and Dad both turned and looked at me and then there was a big crunch. I saw something hit the front of the car, but it happened too fast to see. Then Mum was screaming and screaming. Dad opened his door and took a look. He said it was a deer, only it wasn't a deer, was it? Because deer don't ride bicycles."

He took a deep breath, and let the air rush from his lungs.

Victoria reached for her son and held his sweaty body against her breast. "No, Joey, it wasn't you, it was me. I was the one driving. It was a deer. Really, just a deer."

Anna pinched the bridge of her nose. "Tell him the truth, Mum. He deserves to know."

Victoria stared at her, and tried to hold on to Joey, but he was slipping from her grasp now, running off, bounding up the stairs.

"Why don't you just tell him?" Anna asked again. "Why all the lies, Mum?"

Victoria's eyes were like steel. "How can I protect him if I tell him the truth?"

Anna left her mother at the table, with two full cups of tea that were by now undoubtably cold. She went upstairs to Joey's room. He'd left the door slightly ajar. She peered in and saw that he was writing frantically in his diary.

She went in and rested a hand on his shoulder.

"It's going to be okay now, Joey," she told him. But she had no idea if that was true.

42

VICTORIA

Victoria watched as Anna came out of Joey's room and walked across to her own room and shut the door. What had she said to him? No doubt she'd be straight on the phone to that unsuitable friend of hers. Anna was like a loose cannon. You never knew what she would do next. Victoria hugged herself. Her body felt cold and hot at the same time. Was it the guilt that made her feel this way? Or the fear of being found out? She couldn't go to jail, she just couldn't. She'd worked so hard, and everything was falling apart.

She caught a glimpse of herself in the hall mirror. The whites of her eyes gleamed back at her and she felt her mind and body separate. She set to work clearing away the tea things while her brain worked through countless possibilities. What was she going to do now? And most of all, did Belinda have any idea what she had done?

She went into the lounge and found Kit resting on the sofa, where Belinda had laid hours before.

"I want you to drive over to Belinda's and see if she's alright."

Kit rubbed his eyes. "Why wouldn't she be?"

He looked at her and stilled, holding her gaze for a long time before twisting his body away from her in disgust.

"Victoria, this has got to stop. You've got to leave that woman alone."

"I am leaving her alone. I just want to check she's alright. She was so out of it."

"Why don't you just call her?"

"You can't tell much from a phone call."

She picked her keys up from the telephone table.

"Victoria, don't!"

"Why?"

"Because you're acting crazy. You need to stop all this. You need to calm the hell down."

She let the keys fall back down on the table. For once, Kit was right. If she played it cool, the storm might blow over, and if it didn't, she needed to think very carefully about what she was going to say to the police. There was still no evidence against her. Nothing to prove she'd done anything wrong. After all, Kit had been the one to make the 999 call. She would do everything in her power to protect him but if it came down to it, there was no sense in Joey losing both his parents. Their son needed her now more than ever.

THE SKY WAS dusty pink when Victoria padded into the kitchen on Thursday morning. It was painfully early, but her heart was racing, her mind too busy to sleep. She switched on the kettle and without thinking, reached for the caddy. She had the lid open and was spooning tea into the pot before she stopped herself. She tipped it back in and opened the spare caddy, where the normal tea was.

There was no sense in putting herself back to sleep. She

needed to keep her wits about her. It was doing Kit good though. He had slept soundly beside her last night. He had no idea what had gone on with Belinda but she still felt his anger over Joey. She had meant what she had said, she was going to have several other experts come and see him and she wouldn't rest until she found one who agreed with her own opinion.

Kit was still going on about Nigel too, but there had been no developments on that score. Nigel was irreversibly brain damaged and the incident was still being reported as an accident. She wondered if he had been blackmailing anybody else for money. It wouldn't surprise her. She'd done the world a favour. Nigel had got what he deserved. It was Belinda they needed to worry about.

Victoria took her tea and walked into the lounge where she sat down at the piano. She so rarely played for pleasure anymore. She closed her eyes and let herself feel the music, playing with such intensity and feeling that she began to wonder if Joey had got his gift from her after all. The longer she played, the better it sounded. Her fingers flew over the keys and the music swirled around her, pulling her into another world.

"Victoria?"

She blinked. Kit was standing in front of her in his dressing gown, hands on his hips.

"What the hell are you doing? It's five in the bloody morning."

Victoria looked up from the piano. Her fingertips were painful and callused. "I was just playing . . ."

He backed away. "Alright, just keep it down, okay?"

Belinda wasn't on the school run that morning. Victoria kept an eye out, but she didn't spot Ricky either. Perhaps they'd overslept. It wouldn't surprise her, the state Belinda had been in.

"Good morning, Joey. Victoria, are you ready for our meeting?"

"Was that today?" Victoria blinked at Miss Henley. "Oh, I'm really sorry but I have a family emergency."

Miss Henley's face fell. "I'm sorry to hear that. We really do need to discuss getting Joey some extra support. When would be a better . . . ?"

"I'll have to let you know," Victoria said. She backed away, almost colliding with Samantha. "I really have to go now."

She turned on her heel and hurried across the playground, overtaking one of the sporty mums. Someone whistled at her. She didn't turn around to see who it was. She had to get away from Miss Henley and all her questions.

Paul Schooner was outside the shop when she passed so she quickly crossed the road. She kept on walking, faster and faster. She was pretty sure this was the quickest she had ever made it home, and she was wearing some of her highest heels.

Back home, she found Kit in the lounge. He was munching on a slice of toast and watching daytime TV. She badly wanted to switch it off but she needed to tread carefully. Let him have today. She'd make sure he started the job search properly on Monday.

"I'll get Joey from school today," he said. "Save you a journey."

She smiled then stopped. If he did, then he'd have to talk to Miss Henley, wouldn't he? What if she mentioned their supposed family emergency? Worse still, what if he went and sat down with her and had her stupid meeting? Kit might not see the harm in Joey having a bit of extra help in class, but Victoria was horrified at the idea. Joey would never fit in if the other kids thought he had special needs. She picked up her phone and texted Belinda.

Victoria: Hope you're feeling better?

She waited a moment, but there was no reply, so she went into the kitchen and began cleaning. She was on a mission today, clearing out all the cupboards and turning the packets and tins so they faced the right way. She cleaned and cleaned, checking her phone whenever she remembered but there was no reply.

Kit was fast asleep when it was time for the school run. He'd barely left the sofa all day. She picked up his teacup and took it through to the kitchen with the others. He could collect Joey another day. Best to let him sleep.

There were only a couple of other parents in the playground when she arrived for pick up, neither of whom she had any desire to speak to. Suddenly, Miss Henley bolted out of the school doors, waving at her frantically.

"Mrs Hill! I need you to come with me."

"Why?" she asked, startled. "What's going on?"

"I don't want you to worry but I'm afraid there's been a bit of an incident."

She felt a prickle of unease. "What sort of an incident?"

"Please, come with me." Miss Henley ushered her across the playground.

Victoria looked around. "Where's Joey?"

Miss Henley pointed upwards. Victoria looked up and saw Joey standing on the roof of the old library building. The roof was approximately fifteen feet off the ground and Joey was standing there, balancing with his arms, not even holding on.

Victoria's hands flew to her face. "Joey! Oh God, Joey! Get down this minute!"

Joey didn't respond.

"Get down!" she yelled even louder but Joey didn't even look in her direction.

"I don't understand how he got up there," Miss Henley said. "We were coming back from assembly when I realised he wasn't with us anymore." She glanced behind her. "Mr Jackson's gone to get a ladder."

Victoria cupped her hands around her mouth. "Get down, Joey!"

"I don't think he can hear you."

"Why not?"

"I think he's having a meltdown."

"Joey!" Victoria yelled again, determined to prove her wrong. "Joey!" She rounded on Miss Henley. "How did he even get up there?"

"I think he must have used the window ledges."

Victoria swallowed. "I need to go to him."

"Mrs Hill, I really don't advise you . . ."

But Victoria was already kicking off her heels.

"Stay there, Joey! Mummy's coming!"

It was a tough climb up to the roof and she was surprised Joey had managed it. He wasn't the most agile. She hadn't climbed in years, but as a child she had spent hours climbing in the woods behind her house. She found a foothold and hoisted herself up. She just hoped the old building could take her weight.

"Joey!" she said, as she reached the roof. She was afraid of startling him.

Joey didn't answer her. He rocked back and forth on the balls of his feet. Victoria crept closer, pulling herself up as far as she could reach.

"Joey, I've come to take you home."

Joey kept rocking and she was tempted to grab his ankle and pull him down to safety. But what if he fought her, the way he did at home? There was no room to manoeuvre up here. She couldn't afford to make a mistake.

"Joey, is this about the accident?"

He turned and looked at her, his eyes wide and unseeing. He wobbled slightly and started to stagger backwards. She reached for him but only succeeded in grabbing his shoe. It fell to the ground with a thump.

"Joey!"

"Got him!" the caretaker called. He appeared on the ladder and Victoria's shoulders sagged as he put his arms out. Joey allowed himself to be helped down, not seeming to mind at all.

"You wait there, Mrs Hill!" the caretaker yelled. "I'll come back for you."

It was all a little undignified, but Victoria no longer cared. Joey was safe. That was all that mattered.

Ten minutes later, Joey sat on Victoria's lap in Miss Henley's office.

"I don't understand what happened," Miss Henley said. "Did something upset you, Joey?"

Joey shook his head. "Everyone was being noisy. I just wanted to be on my own."

"So you climbed up onto the roof?"

Victoria shook her head. "That doesn't make any sense."

"I guess it does to Joey," Miss Henley replied.

Miss Henley gave Joey a drink and some biscuits and made Victoria a cup of tea. They sat quietly for a few minutes. Victoria couldn't stop thinking about how scared she had been, seeing Joey up there. She pressed her lips together and watched Miss Henley. How could she let this happen?

"I want to go home now," Joey said, once he'd finished his drink. The colour had come back to his cheeks and he looked much more like himself.

"You take care," Miss Henley said, as they left the classroom.

Joey gave her a little wave.

The playground was deserted now. The caretaker let them out through the gate and Victoria thanked him again and they walked home in silence.

"We won't say anything to your father," she said to Joey. "It would only upset him."

Joey nodded.

K ayla stepped in front of Victoria the following morning.

"Oh my God, Vicky! Are you okay?"

Victoria narrowed her eyes. "Why wouldn't I be?"

"I heard about Joey climbing up on the roof. That must have been terrifying for you."

Victoria ignored her and nudged Joey forward. "Come on, let's get you to class."

Miss Henley wasn't at the classroom door. Instead, they were met by the head.

"Where's Miss Henley?" Joey asked, eyes wide.

"Miss Henley is off sick today."

"What's wrong with her?"

"Into class, Joey, you don't want to be late for the register."

Joey stood his ground. "I don't mind."

Victoria touched his shoulder. "You have to go and sit down. There will be a different teacher today. It will be okay."

A teacher Victoria had never seen before came forward to take Joey into class. Joey stared at her in dismay. "I want Miss Henley!"

The other teacher didn't seem fazed. "Miss Henley's off sick. I'll be teaching your class today."

Joey shook his head. "No. I want Miss Henley."

"Let's step outside and take a walk around the playground," the head said. "Joey clearly needs time to adjust."

"Where is Miss Henley?" Victoria asked. The gates were locked now, and she felt a little claustrophobic being on school grounds after all the other parents had gone.

"Miss Henley is off with stress. To be honest with you, I don't think she'll be back before the end of the week."

It dawned on Victoria that Miss Henley might have been put on gardening leave after the roof incident. Well, it was her fault.

Another teacher came out and asked Joey if he wanted to help with the school garden, which he gladly agreed to. He went off without so much as a glance back at her. As if he'd forgotten she was there.

"I don't want to exclude Joey in any way," the head said. "But we will have to do a risk assessment based on what happened yesterday. We need to be sure we can keep him safe."

Victoria nodded numbly. You would think Joey was a terrorist or something, not an innocent little boy.

At pick up time later that day, she caught snatches of conversation from the mums around her. She kept her head down and walked quickly towards her group.

"They're calling him roof boy," she complained to them.

"How original," Portia said.

Was she imagining it, or was Zara standing at a slight distance? She moved a little closer. Zara didn't move, but she didn't smile either. She was waving at Imelda on the other side of the playground.

"Don't worry about it," Portia said. "They'll soon find something else to talk about."

"Yeah, there's always juicier gossip," Samantha agreed. "Did you hear? Paul Schooner was seen snogging some woman behind the church."

Victoria smiled nervously. If there was any truth in these rumours, she was in even bigger shit. The hold she had over Paul depended on him not getting caught by his wife. What the hell was he playing at? Of course, it might all be malicious gossip . . . It seemed an odd sort of place for a rendezvous.

"Hey, has anyone seen Belinda?" she asked.

Portia pulled her hair back into a ponytail. "Ricky was dropped off by a neighbour this morning, so I assume Belinda must still be ill."

"Belinda always looks ill," Samantha said.

"What do you mean?"

"I don't know. I just find it a bit creepy the way she stands there, like all the joy has been sucked out of her."

Portia frowned. "It probably has."

Victoria squared her shoulders. "She's still got Ricky, hasn't she?"

The classroom door opened, and the substitute teacher stepped out.

"Ariadne is going to be giving out sweets for her birthday in a minute. If anyone would not like their children to have sweets, please step forward and you can leave first."

The parents exchanged amused looks. As if any of them would be brave enough to drag their children away from sweets.

Ariadne came out, wearing a large sparkly badge with "Birthday chic" written on it. She positioned herself on the ramp so she could hand out little bags of sweets to her classmates as they left. Victoria half expected them all to curtsey.

She waited until the last child had come out, but Joey did not emerge.

"Mum!" She looked across the playground and saw Joey walking towards her with the head.

"Joey's just been helping me with some tricky maths problems," she said. "He has a really good understanding of algebra."

Joey grinned from ear to ear, but Victoria found it unsettling. Had Joey spent all day out of the classroom? Were they segregating him? She glanced around for Ariadne, but the little girl had already left. She hoped Joey hadn't heard about the sweets.

"Will Joey be returning to his class tomorrow?" she asked.

"Soon," she promised. "We just need to be sure that we have everything in place."

"What exactly do you need to put in place?"

"We need to be sure we know where he is at all times, so I'd like to keep him in at break times, for the time being."

How could she refuse? She didn't want Joey ending up on the roof again. But neither did she want him segregated, like there was something wrong with him. It made her heart ache.

Joey spotted something sparkly on the ground. "Hey what's that?"

Victoria bent down and picked it up. "It's Ariadne's badge. We'd better get this back to her."

Joey talked non-stop as they walked across the playground. Victoria led him to the overflow car park where she had left the car.

"Why have you brought the car, Mum?"

"Because."

"I thought you were supposed to be setting an example?"

"Well sometimes I don't feel like setting an example. Sometimes I just want to get home."

"Then why are we going this way?"

"I thought we could just pop Ariadne's badge back to her. She might be missing it."

She waited but Joey didn't object, so she kept driving, up the hill and past the vicarage. Portia lived near Louisa, up on Farncombe Hill. She had a beautiful house, with a spectacular view, overlooking the town. She was glad to have an excuse to pop in. She was in need of a friend right now. Perhaps Portia would invite them in for a cup of tea. A bit of mindless chat was just what she needed.

There were three cars parked in Portia's driveway so Victoria had to park in the bay across the road. She held the sparkly badge in one hand and Joey's hand in the other. There were pink and purple balloons tied to Portia's front door for Ariadne's birthday.

No one came to the door, so she walked round to the back. Perhaps they were in the hot tub. She heard voices. Giggling and laughing. Samantha's voice. Zara's. She pushed open the gate and her jaw dropped. Portia was having a party. Everyone was there, all the mums from their class at school.

Portia was dressed as Princess Leia. She looked amazing. Ariadne was Yoda. She spotted Imelda Daniels with a glass in her hand. Eloise was holding a light sabre. Victoria stumbled backwards, her cheeks hot with humiliation. Portia was having a party, and she hadn't invited her. Hadn't invited Joey.

Even Kayla was there, painting the children's faces.

"Come on," Victoria whispered to Joey. "Let's go."

"Why are you whispering?" Joey said loudly.

Portia turned and stared. *Oh God, this was awful*, but Victoria held her ground.

"I see you're having a party?"

"Victoria!"

Portia took a step towards them. Her face was pleading. "It was a last-minute thing. I was going to take her to Legoland, but this morning she decided she really wanted a party. And I thought . . . I mean, Joey doesn't even like parties."

"I like *Star Wars* parties," Joey said.

Portia forced a smile. "You're welcome to stay."

Victoria shook her head. "No thank you. We know when we're not wanted."

Portia threw up her hands. "Don't be so melodramatic. I just thought . . . You always have piano lessons after school!"

"I could have cancelled, or Kit could have brought him. It would have been nice to be invited."

Annoyance flashed in Portia's eyes. "I'm sorry, Victoria, I just didn't think . . ."

She looked at Joey and couldn't finish her sentence, but Victoria knew exactly what she meant. She took his hand and fled. She thought Joey might kick up a fuss, but he followed her without a word. Mahler was playing on the radio as she reversed out of the parking bay. She heard shrieks of joy from Portia's house. It sounded like the party was just getting started. She switched the radio off and drove home in silence, hands clenched on the steering wheel.

"Kit!" she yelled as they walked through the door. "Kit, are you home?"

She almost tripped over Anna's bag, left lying in the hallway. As she moved it out of the way, she caught a glint of silver in one of the side pockets. She glanced up the stairs, then pulled it out. At last. Anna's secret phone.

It was an old model. Her cheeks flushed as she realised it was Kit's old phone. Had Anna stolen it, and bought herself a new sim card? It seemed more likely that Kit had given it to her. But why?

She switched it on and looked through the list of contacts. There were dozens of names, none of which she recognised. Who were all these people?

She checked Anna's text messages.

Bex: What R you going to do about your mum?

Anna: Don't know.

Bex: U can't let her get away with murder.

Anna: I have to think of my family. What about Joey?

Bex: Your mum is evil.

Anna: I know . . .

Bex: If U don't do something, I will.

Fear gripped Victoria's heart. She had to shut this down. She watched as Joey grabbed a packet of crisps from the cupboard. He stomped upstairs to his room with it and moments later she heard the sounds of his computer game. Her fingers gripped Anna's phone. What should she say?

Anna: Please don't tell. My mum's not that bad.

The reply came straight away.

Bex: U wot?

Anna: I know I said all that stuff, but she's still my mum.

Bex: U alright bae?

Shit, she needed to sound more like a teenager. She searched her vocabulary for something more colloquial. What was it they said these days? Everything was sic, wasn't it? Or was that already out of fashion? The phone beeped again.

*Bex: Maybe U should ring Childline? They'll know what
2 do.*

Anna: Don't stress. I'm going to talk to her.

Bex: Who?

*Anna: My mum. She's really quite reasonable if you get to
know her.*

Bex: Well, hello, Mrs Hill.

She dropped the phone. Shit. Her fingers trembled as she searched for the right reply, then she heard a noise from upstairs. Quickly, she deleted the whole exchange. She was going to have to deal with this Bex girl. She couldn't have her getting to Anna like this. She wasn't going to stand for it.

The doorbell rang and her heart leapt. It was four o'clock. Ricky's lesson. She hadn't thought they'd come.

Belinda stood unsmiling on the doorstep. She was still a little pale, even now.

"Have you seen Ricky?"

"No?"

"Oh, Victoria, I don't know where he is! He's been so upset about his dad. He's not coping very well at the moment, and I thought perhaps he and Joey . . ."

"Come on in. I'll see if Joey has any idea where he might have gone. Joey?" she yelled.

Joey didn't answer. She hurried up the stairs and burst into his room. The window was wide open and the curtains flapped in the breeze.

"Joey!"

44

Victoria's first thought was that he must have got up onto the roof. She ran outside, but there was no sign of him.

"Joey!"

She ran around the house, frantically checking every room but he wasn't anywhere to be found.

"He's gone," she told Belinda breathlessly. "They must have gone off somewhere together."

Victoria ran back up to Joey's room. He'd never gone off like this before. She found it almost impossible to believe he wasn't just hiding somewhere, being silly. She looked in all the obvious places: under the bed, inside the wardrobe. She opened his desk drawer and found her old biscuit tin. She'd wondered where that had gone. She lifted the lid. Inside were dozens of Joey's melatonin gummies. What was going on? When had he stopped taking them? She thought Joey told her everything. He was such a talkative boy when he wasn't in a temper. He chattered on about any and everything that came into his mind, an endless stream of consciousness, but he hadn't told her this.

"Any sign of him?" Belinda called from downstairs.

"No. He's not in the house."

"I'm going to drive around, see if I can find them. Call me if you hear anything."

"Of course." She paused at the top of the stairs. "Don't worry. We'll find them."

Without really knowing what she was looking for, Victoria continued to search Joey's room. Under his bed, she found a box of rotting leaves and twigs. Ugh. She'd clean that up once she'd found him. She rifled through his desk drawers and opened the wardrobe. It was neat and tidy, the clothes and shoes arranged just as she'd left them. Her eyes wondered upwards. The shelf above the wardrobe looked empty, but she had a feeling there might be something up there. She ran a finger over the wood. She didn't feel anything, but it wasn't dusty either.

She dragged Joey's chair across the room and hopped up onto it. He still had the box his school shoes had come in. She pulled it down and peered inside. She found a collection of chess pieces, just the bishops, and a notebook she'd never seen before. She opened it and found herself looking at Joey's diary. She hadn't even known he kept one.

She flicked through the pages, lingering briefly to read what was written there. It took her a moment to decipher Joey's squiggly writing. She flipped to the final entry.

45

Reasons to hate myself.

1. I made Miss Henley leave. Eloise said she's not coming back and it's all because of me.
2. I made Mum miss the party. She said she didn't care but I know she does.
3. I killed Ricky's Dad.

When Ricky finds out he's going to hate me forever but I have to be a man and do the right thing. I'm going to do it now, before the caterpillars start crawling around in my stomach. Mum calls them butterflies, but they're much more like caterpillars. They don't fly, they creep and crawl and send shivers down my back. I'm going to meet Ricky in a minute. I haven't told him what the plan is, but I need somebody there with me. Even though he'll hate me in the end. It will be worth it. The truth will set us free.

46

Victoria's fingers felt like they were on fire. *What are you going to do, Joey?*

She pulled out her phone. "Kit? Where are you?"

"I'm just taking a walk."

"Why?"

"Because I needed to stretch my legs."

"Well, I need you to find Joey."

"What do you mean? What's going on?" She could hear the alarm in his voice.

"He's snuck out of the house. Ricky's missing too. We think they're together."

"Should we call the police?"

Victoria froze. The police station. Was Joey going to confess?

"I need you to check the bus stop and the train station," she said.

"You think they might have caught a train?"

"No, but I want you to check just in case. Tell the ticket man to keep a look out for them, then come home in case they come back here. Belinda's driving around looking for them and I'll get Anna out looking too."

"What are you going to do?"

"I'm going to the police. Make sure you have your phone on."

"Okay . . . I love you."

The nearest police station was in Guildford, four miles away. It was a long way for two young boys to travel but Victoria knew not to underestimate Joey. He had a fair bit of money saved up, so it was quite possible he'd taken public transport, or even a taxi.

She kept her eyes peeled as she drove. She hoped to God he wasn't foolish enough to try and walk there. She couldn't bear to think of the boys trying to cross some of those country roads. The cars went so fast . . .

As she navigated the roundabout, Victoria felt a little light-headed, like she was breathing through a squashed straw. A car beeped from behind and she responded in kind. She couldn't believe this was happening. It was as if she had no control over her family anymore. They were like a bag of marbles, all rolling off in different directions and no sooner had she caught one than another would go rolling off another way.

When she reached the police station, she parked as close as she could and hurried up to the building. Two uniformed officers stood outside. They watched warily as she passed. For all she knew, these very same officers had studied grainy CCTV footage with her image on it. Perhaps coming here wasn't such a good idea after all.

The desk sergeant looked up with interest. "Can I help you?"

"Yes, have two young boys been in? My son and his friend wandered off and I thought they might have come in here?" She pulled up a picture of Joey on her phone. "This is my son,

Joey. He's a very bright boy." She didn't know why she was telling him this. It was just second nature to brag about her kids.

The sergeant's brow furrowed. "I saw a pair of kids not long ago. They didn't come right in, they just stood in the doorway and ran off again. I couldn't swear to it but one of them might have been your son."

"Thank you," Victoria said. The pressure on her chest eased a little and she found herself able to breathe again.

"Alright, well let me know if you need . . ."

She hurried out the door, her breath coming easier now she knew Joey hadn't blabbed. But she still needed to find him. She needed to know he was okay.

As she walked back to the car, her phone beeped.

Kit: They're not at the train station. No one's seen them.

Anna: The school's all locked up now. Bex says they're not at the skate park.

Belinda: Any news?

She started to reply, then thought better of it. She didn't want Belinda asking why they'd been to the police station. Where would they go now? She drove slowly through the town centre, hoping to see them outside one of the shops. She didn't know about Ricky, but Joey wasn't that interested in shopping. Perhaps they'd just head home.

Her phone beeped again as she was driving back towards Godalming. She glanced at the message.

Anna: They bought a couple of Cokes from the shop. I only just missed them.

She grinned broadly. Getting closer. She was coming up for the last roundabout. To the left was her house and to the right, the park. She chose the park. Joey always insisted on bringing a drink to the park. He said all that playing made him thirsty.

The car park was almost empty. Victoria parked as close as she could and hurried along the footpath. There were only a few children in the playground, all of them younger than Joey. She kept moving, following the path. Joey liked to do things in a certain order. He would take the path left around the lake. She walked past an angler, reeling in his catch.

Her phone buzzed in her pocket. That was probably Belinda again, but she wanted to keep going. She had a feeling she was going to find . . .

"Mum!"

Was she imagining it, or was that really him?

"Mum!" His voice was louder this time, unmistakably Joey.

"I'm coming, Joey! Where are you?"

She jogged along the path. She couldn't see him yet, but she was certain it was him she had heard.

She rounded the corner and there he was sitting on the bank. She threw her arms around him. "Oh, Joey, I was so worried . . ."

He was stiff in her arms. "You have to help Ricky."

"Where is he?"

"Someone dumped a shopping trolley in the lake. I was worried the ducks would get trapped in it. Plus it's bad for the environment. It's a pollutant."

"Yes, but where's Ricky?"

Joey pointed at the water. "He waded out to get it."

"He did *what*?"

She looked out at the murky water. Only now did she notice the boy. It wasn't a big lake and she didn't think it was that deep but there was something eerie about his silence. He had his head tilted back, like he was trying to float, but there was no splashing, no movement. He looked like he was losing the fight.

She watched for a moment then handed Joey her phone.

"You call Dad. I'm going in."

nna's phone vibrated. She looked at the display.

"It's my mum."

Bex folded her arms. "The psycho," she muttered.

Anna pressed her lips together. If Bex knew what had happened with Mrs Solomon, her head would explode.

"Hello?"

"It's me, Joey!"

"Joey?"

"Ricky's in the water."

"What water? Where are you?"

"I'm sitting next to the water."

"Where?"

"Broadwater Lake."

Anna pursed her lips. It was just a small lake, more of a duck pond. She'd never actually seen anyone swimming in it.

"Where's Mum?"

"In the water with Ricky."

"Joey, are they okay?"

"I don't know."

"Stay right there, Joey. I'm calling 999."

"I'll call," Bex offered. "You stay on the phone with your brother."

Broadwater Lake was just up the road. Bex slowed to make the call while Anna moved to the edge of the pavement. If only there weren't so many cars racing by. She spotted a break in the traffic and raced across to the island. More cars were coming the other way.

"Come on, get out of the way!"

She lost precious minutes as she waited for more cars to pass. Then she dashed across the road to the park.

"Joey!" she yelled. "Joey!"

She ran around the lake, trying to spot Joey or her mother. She couldn't see anyone in the water. Maybe they were out now. Maybe they were . . .

"Anna!"

She found Joey sitting alone on a log, his legs dangling into the water.

"Where are they?" she asked, leaning against a tree as she waited to get her breath back.

"There!"

She followed his gaze and saw Victoria rise up out of the water. She had hold of Ricky but he was panicking, thrashing and flailing about.

As Anna watched, they both went under.

"Oh, for fuck's sake, it's not even that deep!"

She began pulling off her shoes, getting ready to wade in. Bex came running up to her and grabbed her arm.

"Anna, don't! Help is on the way."

Her mother and Ricky bobbed back up to the surface. Ricky's hair hung over his eyes.

He was frantic, trying to climb Victoria like she was a ladder.

"Hey there!" Anna heard a voice from a little along the bank. An angler, she thought. There were usually a few of them about.

"Here!"

Whoever it was had found a life ring and thrown it into the lake. Victoria moved towards it. It had landed close, but Ricky was still thrashing about, clearly in a panic.

A couple of anglers were in the water, wading towards them. One found the ring and threw it to Victoria again. She grabbed onto it to catch her breath while they took charge of Ricky between them, carrying the frightened boy to the bank.

"It's okay, you're safe now."

A crowd had gathered. There were anglers, joggers and dog walkers now, and everyone wanted to help. Someone wrapped Ricky in their coat and he lay on the riverbank, coughing up water.

Someone else ran to the waffle van to get some hot drinks. Another woman gave her coat to Victoria who was also soaked from head to foot. The anglers had their own coats and towels to dry off with. They seemed prepared for every eventuality.

"If everyone's okay, I'll cancel the ambulance," Bex said. She walked off to get a better signal.

"You're Belinda Solomon's kid, aren't you?" said one of the joggers. "I know your mum. I'll call her for you, shall I?"

Ricky smiled weakly as he rang Belinda. "She'll be here in a jiffy," he said.

"Are you alright, Joey?" Anna asked. Her brother was still and silent. Most unlike him.

"It's all my fault," he whispered. "I thought they were going to drown."

"Oh, Joey!" she pulled him to her. His body was so cold. It must be the shock.

"She's a real hero, your mum," said one of the anglers. "It's bloody cold in that water, I can tell you."

Anna saw her mother smile but didn't reply. It wasn't like her to ignore a compliment. Victoria loved it when people paid her attention. Victoria sat quietly beside her, gazing out at the water. She wondered what she was thinking. Her eyes seemed a little misty. Perhaps she was trying not to cry.

"Ricky!" Belinda came running along the path. "Where is he? Where's my boy?"

"Right here, Mum." Ricky fell into his mother's arms.

The hot drinks came. Ricky hugged his gladly and watched the steam rise off the cup.

More people arrived. There was a reporter from the local news, who wanted to interview everyone about what had happened.

"I wouldn't be surprised if you make the front page," the reporter told Victoria.

She lifted her head. "Don't take my picture. I'll give you my Instagram. I have much better ones on there."

Bex let out a snort. "For fuck's sake. This woman is not a hero. Tell them what she's really like, Anna! She doesn't deserve to go on the front page."

Victoria coughed and Anna patted her on the back

"Mum?"

"She's putting it on," said Bex in disgust.

Blood trickled from Victoria's nostril. She wiped it away.

Joey looked at her with concern. "Mum?"

"I'm fine."

Victoria laid her head on Anna's shoulder and closed her eyes.

Bex prodded her with her boot. "Mrs Hill?"

"She's not breathing," Anna said. Her voice seemed to be coming from a long way away. "Someone do something! She's not breathing!"

The reporter crouched down beside her mother and ran his fingers along the side of her wrist, just under her thumb.

"Someone help me!" he yelled.

"What's wrong with her??" Anna said. Her voice sounded shrill in her ears.

"I don't understand what's happening! I can't feel a pulse."

ANNA

Anna clung to Joey and watched as they performed CPR on their mum. A woman was breathing into her mouth, the reporter pressing down on her chest. Joey's counting was loud and repetitive. Thirty compressions, two breaths, thirty compressions, two breaths. Over and over.

Joey covered his ears as the ambulance siren grew louder. He looked desperately at Anna. "What's happening? Are they going to take her away?"

Anna took his hand and squeezed it as the tears dripped down her chin.

Mrs Solomon held Ricky closer. She shook from head to toe as Victoria was lifted into the ambulance.

Someone must have rung Kit because he arrived soon after and drove Anna and Joey to the hospital. They sat in a waiting room, while the doctors worked on Victoria.

"It doesn't make sense – the water's not even that deep," her dad was muttering to himself.

Joey sat on the floor and wrapped himself around Anna's leg. Anna wanted to comfort him, but she didn't know what to say. She felt like she was in a dream and any minute she would wake up and her mum would be bugging her about her Latin.

Familia Supra Omnia. Family over everything.

A tall, lanky doctor approached them. Kit covered his face with his hands and turned away.

"I'm very sorry," the doctor said, "but we couldn't save her."

Joey looked at Anna, and it was down to her to speak for the whole family.

"We . . . we don't understand what happened? She was fine."

The doctor sat down on the coffee table and rested one leg on his knee. "We think your mother had a delayed reaction to inhaling the water from the lake."

Joey narrowed his eyes. "Is that even possible?"

"It's possible," the doctor said. "But it's very rare. The water, or possibly the dirt from the water must have irritated your mother's lungs, preventing them from transferring enough oxygen into the bloodstream."

"I don't get it."

The doctor watched him for a moment. "Would it help if I draw you a diagram?"

"Yes, it would," Joey agreed.

EVERYONE WAS IN SHOCK. They had received flowers from just about everyone they knew, and a few people they didn't. A huge bouquet came from Paul Schooner and his wife. Another from Miss Henley. No one cared when Joey traipsed mud all over the carpet anymore, and no one picked up the bags from the hallway. Their coats all sat in an untidy heap on the table. The house felt all wrong. It even smelled different. Possibly because no one was constantly cleaning it anymore. The house was too quiet, too messy, too still.

Anna was in no rush to get back to school. Bex popped round most days and distracted her with amusing stories. She didn't find them as funny as she once had, but she appreciated the effort.

Joey, on the other hand, didn't like being off school. On Monday, he got up at the usual time and put on his uniform. He looked a mess, one sock up and one sock down, with his hair sticking up on one side.

"You don't have to go in," Kit told him. "We've all had a big shock. It's going to take a while for it to sink in. Why don't you wait until after the funeral? See how you feel."

But Joey was adamant. "I want to go back. I want to look at my tray and all my pencils. I want to see Miss Henley."

In the end, Kit gave in and drove him to school.

Halfway through the morning there was a knock at the door. Kit answered it wearily. Mrs Solomon was standing there, holding a casserole.

"I'm so terribly sorry," she said. Her hands shook as she handed it over.

Anna thought she would leave after that, but her dad invited her in.

"I imagine you, more than anyone, can understand how this feels," he said.

Mrs Solomon nodded, her eyes travelling to the piano. Victoria had left some sheet music there. The last song she had ever played.

"I still can't believe she's gone," she said softly. "I'm so thankful to Victoria for what she did for Ricky but . . . I still really want to know what happened the night James died. I've gathered some of it from Joey but I need to know the full story. You were there, weren't you? Will you tell me?"

Kit drew a long breath. "I suppose you'd better sit down."

Anna crept out into the kitchen and switched on the kettle. She opened the cupboard and reached for her mother's tea caddy. She lifted the lid, while listening closely to the conversation in the other room.

He was telling her. He was actually telling her the truth. She felt a shiver run through her. It was both exhilarating and petrifying. It felt as though they had been prisoners to the secret for so long.

Kit got to the bit where the music came on and Joey distracted Victoria. He told Mrs Solomon how awful he felt, how he wished they could have reacted differently.

"Why didn't you help him, that's what I don't understand? Why did you just leave him there, in the road?"

Kit mumbled something Anna couldn't hear.

"Didn't you search for a pulse?"

"I hurt my back. It was so bad I could barely walk. I couldn't bend down."

"You know, he was in and out of consciousness by the time the ambulance reached him. I feel like . . . it would have been something if we could just have heard his last words. He was a wonderful father – he and Ricky were so close. It would have meant so much to us if we could have said goodbye to him. You robbed us of that choice, Kit. By leaving him there, you took that away from us."

Kit hung his head. "I'm so sorry," he said again. "I should have spoken up. I . . . I was a coward but Victoria told me to get back in the car, and then she just drove off. I felt like the decision had been made."

"You still could have rung 999."

"I did . . ."

"Not until sometime later. You might have been able to save him. But you let him die."

Kit nodded. "There isn't a day that goes by when I don't think about that, but Victoria was such a powerful personality," he explained. "I loved her deeply but there were times when I found it almost impossible to go against her. It was like I was under her spell. She was always so certain of everything. She had a vision for our family, you see, and she just wouldn't let anything get in the way."

Mrs Solomon was talking again now. She didn't say much about Victoria but concentrated on Joey. "He's just a child," she said. "And I know James wouldn't want him to suffer any more than he already has. I'm also grateful that you've finally found the courage to tell me the truth. It's up to you to make peace with it. Your children have already suffered so much for your actions, so I'm not going to report you. I can't do that to Joey and Anna, especially after what Victoria did for Ricky. I think we've all been through enough."

Anna smiled with relief and dumped the contents of her mother's tea caddy into the bin. They wouldn't need it anymore anyway. She couldn't be bothered with all that faffing around. They would use teabags from now on.

EPILOGUE

ANNA

"As you can see, Hansford House is set in thirty acres of beautiful parkland. It has its own private swimming pool, a tennis court and stables."

The visitors nodded eagerly. "Can you tell us when it was built?"

"The house itself is Edwardian, but the park has been here a lot longer than that, in fact the earliest mention of it is in the Domesday book back in 1066."

This went down well. The visitors got out their cameras and snapped pictures from all angles.

"Can you take one of the two of us?" an elderly couple asked.

Anna jumped up to take the camera.

Kit shot her a grateful smile.

Her dad seemed to be enjoying his new job, all things considered. It was quite a change from working in the city, but he seemed to be relishing his new role, showing visitors around the grand house and maintaining the grounds. In fact, she often heard him whistle while he worked.

The best perk of the job was that they got to live in. They got to enjoy the amazing house with its sprawling lawn and tennis courts. Of course, the manager was there pretty often too. She dealt with the stables and ran conferences and away days on the grounds. It had taken Anna a little while to remember where she knew her from, until she'd offered to paint Joey's face.

Joey had said no, of course. But he enjoyed playing with George when he came to visit. And her dad got along really well with Kayla. It seemed they had a lot in common.

Joey had left his old school now. With Miss Henley's help, they'd applied for a scholarship to a prestigious boarding school. The school was close enough that Joey was able to attend as a day pupil, but the small class sizes made life easier for him, and the high staff ratios meant they were more able to accommodate his needs. He was still in the process of being assessed for autistic spectrum disorder, but he was calmer than he had been in years.

They were still having counselling to help with the loss of Victoria and found that they enjoyed taking long walks as a family. It was a big shift. Life felt less pressured, less goal-oriented. A world away from the fast-paced life they'd lived before.

"HERE, I GOT THIS FOR YOU," Kayla said, handing Anna a brochure.

"Thanks."

Anna sat down on the swing seat and flipped through the glossy pages, smiling as she found a pottery course at the community college. This looked right up her street.

Joey and George sat huddled over a chessboard. It was a little challenging for Joey, having a friend who was his intellectual equal, but it made for far more interesting games. Joey's shoulders tensed as George captured his queen and Anna braced herself for his reaction.

There had been a time when Joey had responded to every loss by tipping over the table and throwing himself on the floor. But then he would win a couple of games and his anxiety would reduce. Gradually, he was getting to the point where he could just get up and walk away if needed. He might have to take his anger out on a cushion or a hay bale, but then he'd return and play again.

"You ready to play?" George asked.

Joey concentrated hard on a spot on the floor. "Give me a minute. I need to finish my anger."

Kayla caught Kit's eye and smiled.

"What have you got on this afternoon?" he asked as the visitors finished taking their photos.

"I've got a hunting party." She looked at the boys. "It might get a little loud."

Joey and George nodded. Joey was still a little freaked out when he saw deer on the estate. One day, he had been sitting quietly, when a deer had walked right up to him. It had looked at him over the table, tipped its head at him then slowly backed away.

Anna set down her brochure and her eye fell on the paper, lying on the table.

"Oh, did you see? Mum made the news." She passed the paper over to Kayla. It detailed how Victoria had received a posthumous medal for her bravery.

"We've been invited to Buckingham Palace," she said proudly. "It's going to be presented by the Queen."

Kayla smiled. "Your mum would have loved that. Make sure you get a selfie."

Anna nodded. "You know what? We can get it framed and

put it on the mantelpiece. That's what Mum would have done."

She thought of how her mother had risked her life to save Ricky. There had been other sides to Victoria, but that was the one she wanted to remember.

JOEY'S DIARY

Things I like about living at Hansford House:

1. Dad doesn't have to work in London.
2. The toilets have Dryflow Classic hand dryers. I think this is my favourite model.
3. I know where the deer are, so I can keep an eye on them.

ABOUT THE AUTHOR

Lorna Dounaeva has a Masters in European Studies and used to work at the Home Office before turning to crime fiction. She lives in Godalming, Surrey with her husband, three children and a crafty cat.

Did you enjoy *The Perfect Family*? Please consider leaving a review on Amazon to help other readers discover the book.

www.lornadounaeva.com

ALSO BY LORNA DOUNAEVA

The Wrong Twin

The Perfect Family

The Family Trap

Made in United States
North Haven, CT
12 January 2023

30955244R00200